D1010956

WHERE THE LOST ONES GO

PRAISE FOR *GENERATION MISFITS*

"A heartwarming story about friendship that will have readers cheering for Millie and her friends."
—**Debbi Michiko Florence, author of** *Keep It Together, Keiko Carter*

"A rhythmic, melodic story of friendship and bravery. You'll not only root for Millie and her misfits—you'll want to join them."
—**Ashley Herring Blake, author of Stonewall Honor Book** *Ivy Aberdeen's Letter to the World*

"Akemi Dawn Bowman's debut middle grade novel hits all the right notes with this authentic, vulnerable, and triumphant tale of coming into your own space with courage and grace."
—**Jessica Kim, author of** *Stand Up, Yumi Chung*

★ "This character-centered coming-of-age novel features authentic dialogue with a fully realized cast of diverse characters, and celebrates the power, importance, and value of friendship. Highly recommended for school and public library collections."
—*School Library Journal*, **STARRED REVIEW**

★ ". . . The book is uncondescending and happily celebratory about the fandom experience and what it means to the kids. Never mind cool: sincerity and enthusiasm rule here in a book that believes fervently in the value and joy of friendship."
—*Bulletin of the Center for Children's Books*, **STARRED REVIEW**

"One of the great themes of the book is how everyone is going through something . . . Bowman also gets into the good, bad, and ugly of what it means to be a friend. A great read for both misfits and insiders, this encourages readers to embrace their true selves."
—*Booklist*

"A sincere story about being true to oneself and others."
—*Kirkus Reviews*

WHERE THE LOST ONES GO

AKEMI DAWN BOWMAN

FARRAR STRAUS GIROUX
NEW YORK

Farrar Straus Giroux Books for Young Readers

An imprint of Macmillan Publishing Group, LLC

120 Broadway, New York, NY 10271 • mackids.com

Our books may be purchased in bulk for promotional, educational, or business use. Please contact your local bookseller or the Macmillan Corporate and Premium Sales Department at (800) 221-7945 ext. 5442 or by email at MacmillanSpecialMarkets@macmillan.com.

Library of Congress Cataloging-in-Publication Data is available.

First edition, 2022

Book design by Sarah Kaufman and L. Whitt

Printed in the United States of America by Lakeside Book Company, Harrisonburg, Virginia

ISBN 978-0-374-31377-7 (hardcover)

1 3 5 7 9 10 8 6 4 2

TO GRANDPA, FOR ALL THE TIMES YOU WAITED
BY THE MAILBOX AND TOLD ME
I WAS YOUR FAVORITE

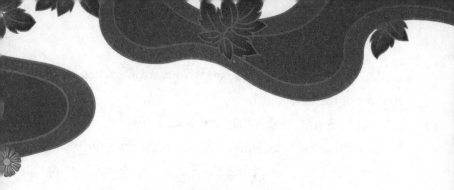

CHAPTER ONE

Our new house smells like lemons. Mom says it's because the previous owners cleaned the floors so well, but it isn't just the floors—it's *everything*.

Babung's house never reeked of scented chemicals. Most of the time her living room smelled like orchids and jasmine tea, her kitchen smelled like tonkatsu curry and dumplings, and her bedroom always, *always* smelled like peppermint.

But then my grandma died, and took all the good smells with her.

My eyes start to water, and the sharp tang of lemon hits my nostrils again, making me sneeze.

Maybe I'm allergic to this house. And not the mild kind of allergic, like Dad is around cats. The *serious* kind of allergic, like how some people can die if they eat peanuts or shellfish.

If I'm deathly allergic to this house, does that mean I won't have to live in it?

"What are you up to, Eliot?" Dad appears in the doorway and flashes one of his signature everything-is-going-to-be-great smiles. In his arms is a cardboard box marked "kitchen" with big, swooping letters.

"I can't breathe in this house. I think I'm going into ana- phylactic shock," I say with a flat tone. It takes a surprising amount of skill, considering I'm on the verge of sneezing again.

"I think you'd have to ingest part of the house to have a reaction like that." Dad hums, amused. "If you're going to test the theory, maybe start with the wallpaper? Most of it has to come down anyway. Just make sure you start at the edges, and watch for splinters."

"This isn't a joke!" I wave my hands around, motioning to—well, *everything*. "What if the house has asbestos? We could all get sick. *Really* sick."

Dad's laugh echoes through the space, and for a moment it feels like the *house* is laughing at me, too.

I glare at the walls like we're on the brink of becoming mortal enemies.

"How do you even know what that is? And anyway, this house was built in the '90s. I doubt it has any asbestos." Dad looks around, twisting his mouth thoughtfully. "Ghosts, maybe. But not any life-threatening fibers."

My heart thumps. He knows my weakness, and he's using it against me.

I can't hide the hope in my voice. "You really think there could be ghosts here?"

"You're the expert," he says with a shrug. "Why don't you get your toy out and have a look around?"

The hope evaporates. My parents never take me seriously. Not about ghosts, or allergies, or moving to this house in the first place.

Babung *always* listened to me. At least, she used to. Before everything changed.

I blink firmly, fighting the sting of frustration in my eyes. "It's not a toy. It's a scientific device that detects electromagnetic energy. It shows you when there's paranormal activity nearby."

He snorts. "For forty bucks, it had better!"

I cross my arms over my chest, but Dad is too busy admiring the wide entrance hall to notice. He made a point of talking it up when he and Mom announced we were moving. They tried to sell me on things like "crown moldings" and "exposed beams," as if it was somehow going to make leaving California easier.

For the record: It did not.

"So, what do you think?" he asks. "Pretty cool place, huh?"

I don't share his optimism. Not about this. "Everything smells like cleaning spray."

Dad tilts his head and a long strand of inky-black hair falls below his brow. In California, he wasn't the only Asian dad with shoulder-length surfer hair. But I spent the entire cross-country drive staring out the window, and there were no dads who looked like mine for at least two hundred miles. Maybe more.

Dad is unfazed. "I'm sure there are far worse things than a house smelling *clean*, kiddo. Think of the alternative."

I glance at the faded wallpaper peeling at the edges, and the water stains blotted around the ceiling. "It smells more like deception."

He shakes his head like I'm a little kid who's just said something ridiculous. Like I'm seven instead of twelve. "Try not to worry so much. This is our fresh start! Let's enjoy it."

I try to force a smile because I know it's what my parents want, but my face won't budge. Maybe when you're sad, face muscles just don't work the way they're supposed to.

I can't help it—I don't want to be here. I want our old house, and our old neighborhood, and our old memories.

Mom and Dad are desperate for a change of scenery, but did they really have to move across the country to Roseheart, Maine, to find it?

The box starts to slip from Dad's hands. He balances it awkwardly against his knee, readjusting his grip. "Why don't you start unpacking your room? The movers already unloaded your boxes. You could be all set up before dinner if you start now." He winks like we're sharing a joke, and disappears down a narrow hall that leads to the kitchen.

I wait until his footsteps fade before heading up the stairs. They creak no matter where I step. I'm pretty sure it's a sign that even the *house* wants me to leave.

"It's not like I *want* to be here," I hiss to the stairs. When I make it to the landing, they go quiet.

My new bedroom is at the end of the hall, right next to the upstairs bathroom. I recognize it from the photos Mom showed me, even though it looks a little different in person. It's bigger, for one. And I thought the walls were pink, but they're actually a pale lavender, which I guess is better. I don't really like pink anything, unless it's mochi or strawberry milkshakes.

My bed is already set up against the wall, with a brand-new rug stretched out across the floor. It's shaped like a fluffy white cloud. Hanging from the ceiling is the mobile Babung and I made together, with wooden stars and moons. It's lopsided, and the paint is chipped just about everywhere, but it's been a staple of my bedroom since I was in kindergarten.

I'm glad it didn't get left behind, or tossed out with the other mementos my parents decided we'd been "holding on to for far too long." But it feels wrong to have my stuff in this house. It feels like a betrayal.

I shove my hands into my pockets, and something soft scratches against my fingertips. Frowning, I pull the object out and hold it in my palm. A flimsy white rabbit stares back at me, ears crumpled with its body folded in half.

Babung loved to crochet little animals, but her favorites were always rabbits. She said they were lucky—that they'd make *me* lucky. That's why they were always my favorite, too.

But Babung isn't here, and I'm thousands of miles away

from the only life I've ever known. That doesn't feel lucky. It feels like a curse.

Curling my fingers over the yarn animal, I shove the rabbit back into my pocket, sit beside the nearest box, and start unpacking. Because curse or not, there's something important I still need to do.

It doesn't take me long to find the electromagnetic energy detector. It's bulky and unsophisticated, and could easily be confused with all the outdated equipment Dad thinks should be stored for an eternity "just in case." The stuff that probably should've been tossed or recycled *instead* of the old mementos.

But the detector isn't junk, and it definitely isn't a toy.

It's how I'm going to prove ghosts are real, and find a way back to Babung.

I have to—because it's the only way I'll ever be able to speak to my grandma again, and make sure she remembers all the things she forgot.

CHAPTER TWO

I hold the ghost detector in front of me, staring at the clunky device with my brows pinched. The green light doesn't waver. Not even when I shake the detector like a magic eight ball, hoping that with enough tries, it will eventually give in.

Most of the time, green is a sign that things are working correctly. No one worries when they see a green light—they just *go*. But this is the bad kind of green. Like mold, or kryptonite, or toxic potatoes.

A green light means no electromagnetic waves, which means no ghosts.

I sigh, staring up at the patches of ceiling where chunks of plaster are missing. It's been three days since we moved in. Three days of searching this new house for paranormal activity, and I haven't seen so much as an amber hiccup. And definitely no red.

Either I wasted forty dollars on something that doesn't work, or even the *ghosts* don't want to live in this house. Personally, I think it's the latter.

But I'm not going to give up on Babung—so maybe it's time for a new plan.

If there are no ghosts in this house, then I need to find a way to bring them here.

Trudging back up the squeaky stairs, I go to my room and set the ghost detector down. I kneel on the rug, peering beneath the mattress at the assortment of small boxes that still need to be unpacked, and spot the mint-green one covered in white flowers. I pull it out from under the bed and set it straight on my lap.

My heart pinches. It was Babung's before she—

Well. *Before.*

She used the box to store spools of thread and spare buttons. There were always so many different colors inside; it was like a treasure chest.

Now the box is mine.

I remove the lid and set it aside. Crocheted bears, frogs, and rabbits in different shades of the rainbow stare back at me. There's a dried four-leaf clover pressed in wax paper— "To keep the memory safe," Babung had told me on the day I'd found it.

If only it could be that simple for people.

I swallow the knot in my throat, gaze drifting to a charm shaped like a pair of geta—traditional Japanese shoes that look like wooden flip-flops—and a Totoro figurine from Babung's orchid garden. Underneath it all is a photo of me and Babung at Disneyland, standing in front of the flower beds shaped like Mickey Mouse's face.

My heart lifts a little, like a balloon caught in a breeze, and I pick up the photo and a couple of the crocheted animals, and wander back downstairs.

Most of the surfaces are still covered with moving boxes, so I find an empty corner near the unlit fireplace and set up my collection of things. I perch Babung's photo in the center and surround it with animals. After a quick trip to the kitchen, I return with several tea lights, a half-eaten pack of Hi-Chews, and a bowl of leftover rice sprinkled with furikake, and set them around the photo with care.

I step back to observe the offering, tapping my bottom lip as I think.

It needs something else. Something that doesn't just encompass Babung, but *is* Babung.

Mom appears in the doorway with yet another cardboard box. Her normally wavy brown hair is bundled into a low knot. It's almost the same dark brown as mine, except the only time my hair is wavy is when I undo my braids.

I normally have two that hang in front of my shoulders, but sometimes I keep my hair in two buns at the top of my head. Babung always said my hair reminded her of a little bunny. Sometimes she'd call me Usako when she'd hug me goodbye, like the nickname was a secret code word only the two of us knew.

Now my hairstyles are a habit I don't want to break.

"There you are! I thought maybe you'd want to help with—" Mom's voice falters when she spots the shrine in front of me. "What's all this for?"

"Babung did this every year for her parents. It's how you honor the dead." I motion to the rice, and the candles, and the candy. "I know it's not all the right stuff—we don't have lotus-shaped sweets, and there's no spirit horse because we don't have any cucumber or eggplant to carve. But the rice is okay, right?"

"Sweetheart," Mom starts, mouth hanging open in between her words. "That's for Obon. It doesn't start until the middle of August. And, well, we're not Buddhist."

"But Babung was," I argue. "And she won't care what we celebrate, or when." If Babung is a ghost, she'll be flexible. She'll visit any time of the year, just as long as I help her find the way back.

Mom's shoulders fall, and she sets the box on the floor. "I—I don't think it works like that, Eliot." She pauses like she's thinking over which words to use. "I know you're really interested in ghosts these days, but I don't want you to think that—" She clamps her mouth shut, visibly flustered.

She acts like that a lot these days. Like when she's around me, she forgets how to speak. Because Mom doesn't like talking about Babung, or what happened in California.

And she really, really doesn't like talking about ghosts.

Mom clears her throat. "Hey, what do you think about

10

giving me a hand with these last few boxes? I bet the house will be so much better once we clear out all the cardboard and bubble wrap, huh?"

I glance down at the makeshift altar. The offering for Babung isn't finished—but it's making Mom uncomfortable, and I don't understand why.

Babung was *Dad's* mom and *my* grandma, but it's Mom who gets weird whenever the topic of her death comes up. She's always quick to change the subject, and whenever I bring up spirits or the afterlife, her eyes dart around like she can't even bring herself to make eye contact with me.

But isn't talking about Babung better than pretending she never existed at all?

Besides, *I'm* the one who lost my grandma before she was even really gone.

The detector, and the shrine . . . It's not just about finding Babung again; it's about making sure she remembers who I am, and getting the chance to have a real goodbye.

I bite down on my lip to keep it from wobbling. Mom is watching me with big, round eyes, hovering over the half-open box like she's desperate for me to join in.

Unpacking isn't going to make me feel better, but I guess I can finish the shrine later, when Mom isn't looking.

"Okay," I say finally, and take a seat on the carpet.

We unpack mostly in silence, with Mom occasionally asking if I'm looking forward to starting school, and making friends, and joining some clubs. When I ask her if she thinks the school has a club for studying paranormal activity, she goes back to being silent.

Babung never made me feel like there were things I couldn't talk about. She let me ramble about Pokémon for hours, even though she didn't know what Pokémon was. She wouldn't think searching for ghosts was weird—she'd probably want to help me look for them. And she never treated me like I was too young to understand things.

I know she was my grandma, but she was also my friend.

I unroll a bundle of paper wrapping that looks like honeycomb, revealing one of Dad's collectible Star Wars coffee mugs.

Mom holds up another one shaped like Chewbacca's head and makes a face. "I really wish this box had gotten lost on the way here."

Dad shuffles around the corner carrying a wooden crate. It's filled with all the breakable stuff Mom didn't want to risk being damaged in the moving van. It sat beside me on the backseat all the way across the country, and I still have no idea what's inside.

"Oh, you found all the mugs!" Dad sets the crate in front of Mom and reaches for the Chewbacca cup. "Seems like a sign. How about we take a break and make some hot chocolate?"

Mom plucks one of the newly arrived, carefully wrapped treasures from the top of the pile. "That sounds wonderful, except we don't have hot chocolate mix. Or marshmallows. *Or* whipped cream."

"Well, that's a problem," Dad replies, then pauses. "Actually, that's *three* problems."

Mom laughs, peeling away the last of the paper. A small, milky-green animal comes into view, and she inhales so sharply that it makes my entire body stiffen.

Sitting in the curve of Mom's hand is one of Babung's jade frogs.

A lump forms in my throat, swelling to the size of a kiwi. It's hard to swallow. *Impossible*, even.

Babung's shelves used to be filled with tiny statues like this one. Frogs were nearly as lucky as rabbits, according to my grandma. But when she died, the shelves were emptied, and most of the ornaments were given to friends or sold around the same time as the house.

I didn't realize some of them were coming to Roseheart. Something that was Babung's through and through.

It would be perfect for the shrine, I think, but can't get the words out in time.

Mom stuffs the frog back into the honeycomb wrapping paper and buries it in the crate.

A moment of silence passes. Then another, and another, until it feels like the room is losing oxygen.

I read once that there's hardly any oxygen in outer space. Only about fifteen seconds' worth, unless a person is really good at holding their breath. But bodies can't decompose normally without oxygen, so it could take millions of years for a corpse to turn into dust. They'd just float through space like they were frozen in time.

Babung is already dust. She was cremated, and her ashes were scattered into the ocean. It's what she wanted—and I guess in a way, she'll get to float for millions of years, too.

But I don't want all the pieces of her to float away. I'm trying to keep them *here*.

If the jade frog is a piece of her, it shouldn't be buried in a crate with no one to look after it. It should be with me.

"I have an idea!" Mom exclaims suddenly, eyes wild with over-the-top enthusiasm. Like she *knows* we're all looking at the elephant in the room (or in this case, frog), but she's still going to pretend it's not there. "Eliot, why don't you take your bike down to the corner store and pick up some stuff for making hot chocolate? It's such a nice day outside, and you've hardly seen any of Roseheart."

Dad catches on quickly, nodding like he's a human-size bobblehead. "You could take the scenic route, through the park! I'll get some lunch ready while you're gone."

Mom looks from me to Dad and then back again. "How does that sound?" Her brown eyes are full moons—large and bewitching. It feels like she's trying to hypnotize me.

But it doesn't work. Once I get an idea in my head, it would take a meteorite landing in our front yard to make me forget about it. And even then—assuming it was a small meteorite and we survived the impact—forgetting isn't a guarantee.

"What are you going to do with Babung's frog?" I ask, and my throat already feels like sandpaper.

Mom waves a hand over the box like it's nothing. Like it doesn't *matter*. "Oh, I'll organize this stuff another time. We've barely finished setting up the furniture. There's not even a place for ornaments yet."

"I can make a place for it." I gesture toward the unfinished shrine. "The jade frog can go right in the middle, next to the candles."

Mom sucks her bottom lip in. "I'm not sure if the living room is a good place for—well . . . all of this."

"You mean the living room isn't a good place for Babung?" I ask, cheeks heating.

Mom flinches. "I didn't say that."

"We just don't want Babung's things to break," Dad jumps in, looking between Mom and me.

I open my mouth to point out that I'd take great care of the jade frog, and that I would *never* let anything bad happen to it. But I guess Dad is already in a hurry to change the subject.

"I think we need a bigger break than just hot chocolate," he says. "What about a movie afternoon? It won't take long to set up the television. And hey, with all the packing up and driving across the country, I'm sure there's something new out."

Mom nods, grateful. "That sounds like a wonderful idea."

I don't want to watch a movie. I want to get out of this

house, where I won't have to watch Mom and Dad bury Babung's things like she never existed at all.

"No." I stand abruptly. "I'd rather ride my bike than sit inside."

Mom curves her arms around herself, silent.

And because I'm terrible with long, awkward pauses, I add, "I'm just not in the mood for a movie right now. Hot chocolate sounds better."

Dad hesitates before pulling out some money from his wallet. "All right, kiddo. I know there's not a lot of traffic around here, but you pay attention to the road at all times, okay?"

I nod, take the money, and head for the coat rack near the front door, where my favorite green bag is hanging. It has a patch sewn in the corner with an image of an amethyst cluster surrounded by the words, "I have a crystal for that."

Just before I'm out of earshot, I hear Mom's lowered voice.

"You know how I feel about all this ghost stuff," she says. "I'm really worried it's getting out of control."

"She's just coping. It's normal for kids to get obsessed with things," Dad offers.

"Yes—when it's things like dinosaurs, or video games. Not someone who's passed away! If we keep encouraging this, it's only going to get worse. Eliot still thinks she's going to see Babung again. She needs to accept she's *gone*."

There's a muffled sob, and Dad's voice is too low to make out. But I already heard more than I wanted to.

I make my way outside without looking back.

CHAPTER THREE

My bike is leaning against the side wall of the garage. It's turquoise with white handlebars, and it has scratches on the paint from where there used to be a basket.

When I was little, I thought having a basket hanging from my handlebars was the *coolest*. But then in fifth grade, a boy named Greg said my bike looked like it belonged to a five-year-old.

I never used to care what Greg thought. He was always getting into trouble with the teachers, and he had the worst taste in Pokémon. But when Greg made fun of my bike, it was Cassie who laughed the hardest.

Maybe it was a sign of things to come, but I didn't realize it then.

I was just embarrassed that Cassie didn't like my bike— because she was my best friend, and I wanted her to like *everything* about me.

Now I don't have a basket, and the chipped paint is a reminder of all the things I left behind in California.

Using the tip of my foot, I flick the kickstand up and hop

on the seat, peddling down the driveway. Once I'm on the street, I pick up speed, cutting through the park like Dad suggested.

Roseheart is mostly trees, houses, and a main street that looks like it came straight from a postcard. Faded brick buildings line the road, with vintage signs hanging above the doors and shop names painted on the glass windows.

I pass a café, a hardware store, an ice cream parlor, and a post office—they're the same kinds of places that exist in California, except out here everything looks like it's at least a hundred years old. Even some of the people.

Squeezing the handbrakes in front of the corner store, I ease my bike to a stop, roll it toward the shop door, and lean it against the brick wall.

The bell dings when I step inside, and the smell of potatoes and cardboard hits me like a wave. When I glance at the counter, a man with curly gray hair is smiling down at me. His brown skin is covered in freckles, and he wears tortoiseshell glasses that are halfway down the bridge of his nose. With a pointed finger, he pushes them back into place.

I remember him from the other day, when my mom stopped to get groceries on the way to the house. Harry, or Harvey—something with an *H*.

"Hello, again." He has the kind of smile that fills his cheeks and takes over his whole face. "How are you and your parents settling in?"

I tuck my hands in my sleeves and squeeze the extra

material. I didn't expect him to remember me. Nobody at any of the stores in California would *ever* remember me. There were too many people. Too many faces.

"Oh. Um. We're all fine." My eyes drift to the chalkboard sign hanging on the wall above him. In white bubble letters are the words "Harold's Corner Store."

"That's good to hear," he says like he genuinely means it. He goes back to organizing the glass jars beside the cash register. They're filled with individually wrapped candy—saltwater taffy, lollipops, and caramels. "Just let me know if you need any help, okay?"

I take one of the shopping baskets and disappear between the shelves.

The hot chocolate mix is easy to find, and so is the whipped cream, but I wind through the aisles three more times before I spot the marshmallows. They don't have the mini ones—just jumbo size. I toss them into the basket anyway and head to the checkout.

Harold's eyes wrinkle when he sees me. "You enjoying your summer break so far?" He slides the bag of marshmallows over the counter, and the register beeps.

I shift my weight between both legs, still fiddling with my sleeves. I've never been good at talking to strangers—I either say way too much, or nothing at all.

My parents usually tell people I'm shy, but it's not that. Sometimes I just have so many thoughts in my head that it's hard to separate them into words.

Right now, I'm wondering why Harold chose caramels, saltwater taffy, and lollipops over all the other candy in the store—and why there are potatoes near the front door instead of something that smelled nice, like peaches or nectarines—and why some people get to be older than Babung and still remember every face they see, when my grandma forgot her favorite face of all?

I'm not shy—but I don't think people always like it when you say everything you're thinking all at once.

The register beeps two more times. I try to stop thinking about candy and potatoes and faces.

"We've just been unpacking so far," I say.

"In this weather? What a travesty." He clicks his teeth. "You've got to get out there and explore! Lots of the kids hang out near the old fairgrounds. You been up that way yet?"

I shake my head.

Harold hums, punching in a few buttons on the register before announcing the total. I pass him the money.

"Well, I'm sure you'll make friends soon and hear all about it." He pauses, adding with a chuckle, "I imagine they'll share all the local ghost stories, too."

The jolt that runs through me is impossible to hide. "Ghost stories? In Roseheart?"

"Oh, yeah! This town is a haven for spooky campfire stories." Harold's eyes widen, and he folds his arms over the counter and leans in closer. "The cemetery on the other side of the creek is one of the oldest around for miles. Kids swear they've seen spirits wandering around whenever there's a full moon."

I'm not surprised. Cemeteries are where bones are laid to rest. It's where ghosts are *supposed* to be.

But Babung wasn't buried. Would she still hang out in a graveyard, even if her ashes and bones no longer existed?

A small voice in the back of my head gnaws its way to the front. *Maybe Babung isn't a ghost. Maybe Mom's right—maybe she's just gone.*

I stuff the food into my bag and pull the strap over my head.

Ghosts make sense, but gone?

Gone doesn't make any sense at all.

"Have you ever seen one?" I ask.

Harold straightens, drumming his fingers against the counter. "I've lived here my whole life and never saw so much as a shadow out of place in that graveyard—but I'm not exactly what you'd call a believer." His eyes twinkle. "I probably shouldn't say that out loud though. My folks told me you should *never* announce that you don't believe in ghosts. It only makes them want to prove you wrong!"

I pause near the door. "Is the cemetery close by?"

"Sure is," he announces proudly before rattling off directions. "Just stay clear of the old railway line. I know it's a shortcut through the neighborhoods and it's not very well fenced off, but they started doing some construction over there and I'd hate for any of the kids around here to get hurt."

I nod, and return to my bike. But instead of going home, I take a detour toward the graveyard.

Babung's ghost may not be in Maine, but if there are others hanging out nearby, I need to find a way to talk to them.

Maybe they can help take a message to my grandma. Maybe they can even guide her spirit to Roseheart, so we can see each other again.

I still don't know if people who lose their memories in life get them back when they die, but if they don't, it means Babung is somewhere alone and scared and she has no idea how much she was loved.

My parents said there's no cure for dementia. That it isn't something you can "fix"—it just *happens*.

I couldn't help Babung when she was alive, but as a ghost?

I'm going to do whatever it takes to find what my grandma lost.

CHAPTER FOUR

Beyond the gates of the cemetery are bright green hills lined with gravestones. Most of them look ancient, with decorative sculptures on the fanciest graves, and smooth, rounded edges for the simplest ones. A few have carved words that are barely legible, and there isn't a single headstone that isn't covered in moss and weeds.

I'm not sure how many visitors this place gets. I've seen cemeteries in California that were always filled with flowers, and the grass was always kept short. But here there isn't a single flower in sight, and the overgrowth has ripped through most of the paving stones, making it look like some forgotten place in an apocalypse movie.

I feel bad for the ghosts who live here. I know how much it hurts to be forgotten.

I get off my bike and rest the handlebars gently on the ground, not bothering with the kickstand. Slipping through the gate, I venture up the path. Dried weeds crunch beneath my shoes, and a flock of birds fly overhead. Big, looming trees are all around me, and the hills stretch so high that I can't even see the horizon. Just a splash of light blue and clouds peeking through the branches.

I pause near one of the padlocked mausoleums, eyes scanning the cemetery. "Is anyone there?" I whisper to whoever might be listening.

There's no reply. Not even from the birds. Right now, I'm the only living person in the cemetery.

Harold told me spirits like to prove their existence to the people who don't believe they're real. Is that what the problem has been, and why I haven't seen a ghost yet? Because I believe *too much*?

My gaze sweeps over the empty graveyard, and I take a nervous breath.

It's worth a try, my mind nudges.

"I don't believe in ghosts. I don't believe in ghosts." The lie becomes a chant. It grows louder and louder until I'm practically shouting. *"I don't believe in ghosts!"*

I wait for something to happen.

I wait.

And wait.

And wait.

But if there are ghosts in Roseheart, they clearly don't want anything to do with me.

My stomach drops like a heavy stone. It isn't fair. I've tried everything: candles and crystals and electromagnetic energy detectors. So far, nothing is working.

Even in a graveyard, I feel further away from Babung than ever.

Hot tears sting my eyes, and I shut them tight.

A deep voice sounds like an echo in a cold, dark room. "You're quite early, you know."

I look up in alarm and see a man standing nearby. He's dressed in a black suit and a formal hat like someone out of an old black-and-white movie—the kind Babung used to love.

Early? I blink, processing the word and his all-black clothes.

Realizing I may have interrupted a funeral service by screaming "I don't believe in ghosts" at the top of my lungs, my gaze darts around the cemetery, frantic. But it's just the two of us.

The stranger lowers his chin, and shadows appear over his dark brown face. But his golden eyes don't darken—if anything, they glow.

Even beneath the summer sun, a chill runs up the back of my neck.

He stares at me for a few long seconds before taking a deep breath. "So many people think it's better to be early than to be late, but being on time means being *on time.*"

"I, I don't understand." I look around the empty graveyard. What does he think I'm early for?

"Nobody ever does. Time is one of the most confusing things of all, you see." He tips his hat. "I must go. Schedule to keep, and all that. But might I suggest," he pauses and raises a brow, "playing somewhere *other* than a cemetery? No need to be eager for what comes to everyone eventually." He stalks across the grass, sliding both hands into his pockets with ease. "Until next time, Eliot," he calls over his shoulder before vanishing beyond the hill.

The quiet settles back over the graveyard like an unwanted frost. There are no signs of ghosts, but that man . . .

He felt otherworldly.

I stare at the empty space he left behind, and a strange fog fills my head. It's like looking through a car window when the temperature outside doesn't match the temperature inside. Everything is cloudy, and hard to make sense of. Hard to *remember*.

I blink, staring back up at the trees and the leaves. I wanted to see if there were ghosts here, but instead I met—

For a second, I think I recall someone saying my name, but the thought keeps slipping away like water through my fingers.

I rub the side of my head.

How long have I been standing here?

I tug the strap of my green bag and remember the ingredients for hot chocolate are inside. The ingredients Mom and Dad sent me to get.

That's right—I'm supposed to be going home, I think dizzily.

After casting one last glance at the graveyard, I take a breath, return to my bike, and pedal back through town.

I guess Harold was right about never seeing a spirit in the graveyard—because I didn't see anyone either.

000

When I get home, Mom is sitting outside on the porch steps. Her brown hair is tied up in a bun, and she's wearing a sunflower-patterned dress with a hem that falls all the way to her toes. She looks lost in thought, which is how I feel most of the time.

A part of me hopes it's something we have in common. But then she spots me and waves her hand, and all her heavy thoughts appear to fade away.

I don't understand it. When I have a thought that's bothering me, it gets caught in a tornado of all my other thoughts, spinning around and around in my head until I figure out a way to fix it. But Mom didn't fix her thought—she just pushed it to the side when she saw me, like it was Future Mom's problem.

I don't have Future Eliot. I have Right Now Eliot.

I swing my leg over my bike and push it the rest of the way to the house. When I reach Mom, I grip the strap of my bag with both fists. "I got the hot chocolate mix and the whipped cream. But they only had the giant marshmallows, not the little ones."

"That's okay," she says. "We can just dip them like a cookie. It'll be a new experience." There are streaks of paint on her forearms—a sign that the project house is well underway. "What did you think of the town? Pretty cool, right?"

I take a seat beside her on the porch steps. "They don't have a boba shop. Or a Chinese bakery. And Google says the nearest Target is over an hour away."

Mom scrunches her nose. "Well, there's not much I can do about that. *But*," she says, reaching beside her for my *Animal Crossing* lunchbox, "wait until you see what your dad made for lunch."

Lifting the lid, I take one look at the massive, unsliced sushi roll, and my mouth begins to water. "Vegetable tempura wrap?"

Mom nods. "Your favorite."

It isn't exactly a *traditional* way to eat sushi. Just traditional for the Katayama family.

I lift the seaweed wrap out of the box and take a bite, chewing slowly. Babung used to make them too, but she used a special sauce that was salty and sweet and—

I stop chewing.

Mom presses her hand against my shoulder. "I'm sorry about how I reacted earlier, with the . . . well, you know. It still catches me off guard sometimes, I guess. But things are going to get better—I promise."

If *better* means moving on without Babung, then I don't want better, and I don't want new experiences.

Why are my parents in such a hurry to change every single thing about our lives?

Wasn't there enough forgetting in our family for one lifetime?

Mom continues, voice serious. "I know things were hard at

our old house, with so many reminders of Babung. And I'm sure there will be reminders here too, like with the frog. But maybe if we focus on all the exciting things ahead of us, we could—"

"I *like* the reminders," I snap. "You and Dad are the ones who moved us across the country to start over."

Mom looks taken aback. "That's not true, Eliot. Not even a little bit."

Staring at the seaweed wrap, I bounce my heels against the step, no longer hungry.

"We only stayed in California as long as we did because Babung was there. We knew her dementia was starting to get worse, and it didn't seem right to move her when she was so . . ." Mom rubs her temple like she's shaking the memory away.

All I want is to hold *on* to my memories.

I don't ever want to forget the people I love, and I don't want them to forget that they love me.

Mom sighs and folds her fingers together. "This move has been in the works for a long time. We've always loved the East Coast, and doing up a house like this is a dream come true for me and your dad." She reaches for the end of one of my braids and straightens it against my shoulder. Mom's a tidier—she always has been. "I think we'll be really happy here. We just need a moment to adjust."

"I don't want to adjust," I say to no one in particular. "I want her back."

"I know, honey." Mom wraps her arms around me and squeezes. "I know."

Except I don't think she does. Not really.

I don't think anyone does.

And maybe that's the worst part of all—that the only person who ever understood me is never coming back.

CHAPTER FIVE

The next day, Mom and Dad ask me to move Babung's shrine to somewhere safer than the living room floor. They also put a ban on leaving food out in case of an ant infestation, and lighting the candles in case the house accidentally burns down.

I suggest sprinkling the rice with cayenne pepper, since ants hate it, but Dad just goes deadpan and says, "I've seen *Ratatouille*. You can't trust pests with seasoning. They get a taste for fine dining, and the next thing you know your kitchen is overrun with all their friends and family."

I shift everything to the top of my dresser, which turns out to be an even better alternative. There's plenty of space for ornaments. I can use the wall for photos. And it's the first thing I'll see every morning when I wake up.

It takes a couple of hours to find decorations and reorganize the shrine. I want it to look perfect, and cared for—not like the old gravestones from Roseheart Cemetery.

I pick up the last of the colorful origami animals—a turtle—and hold it next to the corkboard before pushing a bright blue pin through it. Taking a step away, I stare at the paper menagerie dotted around a collection of photographs.

My favorite is the one of me and Babung from five years ago. We went on a family trip to Hawaii, where Babung and Dad grew up. All the aunties and uncles had come to greet us at the airport with fresh leis that smelled like Babung's backyard. They were purple and white, and there were so many that I almost couldn't see over the top of them.

Babung made a joke about it being a good thing I didn't have any more aunties or else I might disappear into the flowers, which made me laugh. That's when Dad snapped the photo.

I was only seven, but I still remember it. I remember the whole trip—the sweet rolls, and shave ice, and lunches at Zippy's. I remember the family karaoke nights and the potluck barbecues at the park.

It's not fair that Babung forgot all those things.

It's not fair that she forgot me.

Laughter carries through the open bedroom window, but I don't recognize the voices.

"Eliot!" Mom calls from the front yard. "Come outside— I want you to meet the neighbors!"

I rush to the window and peer through the glass. Mom holds a hand over her eyes to block out the sun. In front of her are four girls around my age, each of them perched on a bike.

My nerves immediately turn to static. I knew there were kids in Roseheart—there's a school here, after all—but I didn't expect to see any of them standing *outside my house.*

I was never very good at making friends in California. Especially after what happened with Cassie. But nobody here knows any of the embarrassing stuff that happened before.

It might be the only good thing about moving.

I hurry for the mirror and make sure there's no confetti or bits of tissue paper stuck to my twin buns. I've been digging through boxes all morning, including the one for scrapbooking, and my carpet is littered with construction paper and photograph trimmings. Something tells me first impressions are better when you don't have literal trash in your hair.

I make my way down the stairs and toward the front yard, skirting around a collection of tools and paint cans. I guess Mom is busy crafting something, too.

"These girls all go to Roseheart Middle School," Mom says, motioning to the small group. "I told them you were starting seventh grade in the fall, and they said they'd love to show you around the neighborhood!"

They stare back with blank faces. Clearly the invitation was all Mom's idea.

I lift a hand, hoping they'll understand it's both a greeting and an apology.

The tallest girl has straight blond hair tied to one side with a neon pink scrunchie. Even though it's June, she's wearing a denim jacket that looks a size too big, and bright yellow shorts. She points to her friends from left to right. "This is Madison, Betty, and Angela."

Madison waves without smiling. Betty pops her bright pink bubblegum. Angela grips her handlebars tighter.

The blond girl tilts her head. "My name's Sunny."

I rock back on my heels. "I'm Eliot."

"Maybe after your bike ride, you could all stop by for an afternoon snack?" Mom offers. "Eliot has been so excited to meet people her own age."

Don't scowl, my mind insists, but I'm pretty sure I do it anyway. Mom has never been interested in who I make friends with before. She doesn't even know the whole story about Cassie, and why we stopped talking.

Why is she being so over-the-top now?

"Sounds great." Sunny forces a smile like she's in a hurry to leave, and turns to face me. "So, uh, are you coming with us?"

Betty's face recoils slightly, still chewing her gum. Angela and Madison exchange a look and shrug.

I notice, but Mom doesn't, and by then all I really want is to get out of this situation as fast as possible. So I grab my bike and follow the girls down the street.

We turn corner after corner, zigzagging past houses with long driveways and landscaped front yards, until we stop alongside the outskirts of the park.

The sounds of kids shrieking from the playground isn't

enough to drown out what Madison whispers to her friends. "What are we doing here? We *never* come to the park."

"That's because we're not in preschool," Angela snorts.

"*Shh*," Sunny hisses, trying her best to sound inaudible. "Where else was I supposed to bring her?"

"*Home*," Betty says gruffly. "Because we shouldn't have to take her anywhere. She's a stranger. It's weird."

Angela and Madison both cover their mouths with a hand, stifling their muted laughter.

"Her mom cornered me," Sunny huffs, leaning toward them. "I didn't know how to say no!"

I wish I could teleport to the other side of the neighborhood. Or to another planet. Or to another *galaxy*. But instead, my brain goes into full-blown panic mode, and I do the absolute worst thing possible.

I start talking.

Words tumble out of my mouth like a volcanic eruption, desperate to fill the silence. "I heard the school has a marine lab. I did a report on sea otters last year—not that the marine lab will have sea otters. But otters eat sea urchins, and maybe they have those. Urchins aren't anywhere near as cute though. Not that animals without faces can't be cute. Like starfish, or jellyfish. Did you know there's a kind of jelly-fish that's immortal? It can literally reset itself to an earlier developmental stage if it gets injured. It's called turritopsis dohrnii, which sounds more like a dinosaur than a jellyfish. Except dinosaurs aren't marine animals. But horseshoe crabs are, and they actually lived before the dawn of dinosaurs and made it through five mass extinctions—which sort of makes them one of the world's greatest survivors and immortal in their own way, because they've never been forgotten in four hundred fifty million years." I take a breath, internally horrified.

My entire face feels like it's caught on fire. Why did I just say all that? And why couldn't I *stop*?

I take back what I said about trash in my hair. Talking about marine animals is *so much worse*.

Madison blinks. Betty pops another bubble. Angela side-eyes them both.

"Sounds like you're really into animals," Sunny says, scratching her shoulder uncomfortably.

"I, I like researching things," I manage to say, even though I think my throat might be closing up. "It doesn't have to be animals. I just use Google a lot."

"What kind of stuff do you research besides sea creatures?" Sunny asks, ignoring the snickers coming from her friends.

I can't think of a lie, so I tell the truth and hope it doesn't make everything worse. "Lately I've been reading a lot about paranormal activity."

"You mean like ghosts?" Sunny asks, brow pinched. "Why?"

The question hits me like a brick wall.

I'm not ready for it. Not even a little bit.

I ball my hands until my fingernails dig into my palms.

"My grandma died," I start, but the rest of the explanation doesn't come.

A small, hopeful part of me wants someone to ask what happened, and whether I want to talk about it. I think a small part of me *wants* to talk about it.

"Oh," is all Sunny says.

Betty holds up a hand like she wants to slow down the conversation, which is the complete opposite of what I want.

"Wait," she starts. "You mean you're actually trying to *talk* to a ghost?"

Madison makes a face. "That's super creepy. You should *never* mess with spirits. Don't you watch horror movies? It always ends with someone possessed or dead."

I tap my thumb against my handlebar. "There's . . . more of a science to it than that," I say slowly. "Ghosts have rules. They can't hurt the living."

"Have you talked to one before?" Angela presses.

My cheeks turn pink. I can't tell if they're genuinely curious, or making fun of me—but I hope it's the first.

"Not yet," I say. "But mediums have been doing it for years. I just need more practice."

Sunny wrinkles her nose. "There's no such thing as ghosts. If there were, someone would have video footage by now."

"What are you talking about?" Madison points a finger at her. "You *totally* believe in ghosts. You wouldn't even go through the cemetery gates last Halloween because you were so terrified!"

"That's because there were no lights in there," Sunny shoots back. "It was a safety hazard."

Angela laughs and gestures toward me. "We should've taken Eliot there instead of the park. At least it would've been less boring." She lowers her chin. "Have you ever snuck into a mausoleum before?"

"No, but I've been to the graveyard," I say, skin prickling. I don't want to sneak into a mausoleum. If I upset a ghost, they'll never want to help me.

"Forget the graveyard—if you want to visit a place that's haunted, you need to see Honeyfield Hall," Betty says matter-of-factly.

Sunny casts a warning look. "We can't take her there. Mrs. Delvaux is—"

"—an actual, real-life witch," Angela finishes.

Sunny flattens her mouth.

Madison nods. "She steals the souls of children and locks them in the house where no one can find them."

I make a face, doubtful. "Wouldn't someone just call the cops if they thought she was kidnapping children?"

"Not kidnapping," Angela corrects. "Stealing their *souls*. Nobody can see or hear them. Not unless Mrs. Delvaux marks *you* as her next victim."

"It's true," Madison agrees. "Kyle Webber saw a girl standing in the window once. He said she looked just like a ghost. And then Kyle *disappeared*."

"He didn't disappear," Sunny counters. "He died in a car accident. It was all my parents talked about for weeks. There was even a memorial, remember?"

"That's just what the parents said because it's part of the witch's curse. She makes you forget what really happened," Angela pushes. "She takes your memories."

"You're being ridiculous," Sunny argues. "That's just a silly, made-up story."

Betty shrugs. "Why don't you let Eliot see for herself?"

For a moment, I hesitate. Ghosts are one thing, but witches?

I haven't done any research on witches—I'm not even wearing my smoky quartz bracelet that's meant to help me stay calm during paranormal investigations.

But if there are ghosts in Honeyfield Hall, I don't want to miss a chance to see them.

Not when finding Babung depends on it.

I lift my shoulders. "I'd like to see the house."

Sunny grimaces but remains silent.

"Follow us," Betty says with a grin.

We ride our bikes back through the neighborhood until we reach the oldest house on the highest hill, and when Honeyfield Hall comes into view, I'm not afraid of what I'll find.

I'm hopeful.

CHAPTER SIX

Honeyfield Hall sits at the end of a long road.

Weeds sprout between the pavement and sidewalk, and a wrought iron fence separates the property from the rest of the world. Beyond it is an enormous, dark blue building shaped like it came straight out of a fairy tale. It has a pointed turret, a wraparound porch, and an ornate trim below the roof that reminds me of a gingerbread house. Ivy crawls up every wall, and thick moss has left most of the dark roof tiles uneven.

A long time ago, the yard may have been looked after, but now it's as forgotten as the house, with patches of dead grass and bare dirt stretched across the grounds, and the skeletons of a few bramble bushes near the porch.

A breeze sweeps through the rickety gate, making me think of nervous, chattering teeth. Not exactly a warning, but not really an invitation either.

I plant my feet on the ground. "Someone lives here?"

"We told you," Angela says, stopping her bike a few feet beside me. "A *witch* lives here."

"I don't like this place," Sunny says flatly. "I want to go."

Madison clicks her tongue against the roof of her mouth. "You're such a baby. It's not like Mrs. Delvaux is going to yell at us. She doesn't even come outside anymore." She motions to the front yard that's substantially more brown than green. "She might not even be *alive* anymore!"

"Careful," Betty warns, pouting. "What if she hears you and puts a curse on us?"

Sunny wraps her arms around herself protectively. "This house gives me the creeps."

"I *knew* you were scared," Angela says, and the other two laugh even when Sunny doesn't.

My gaze drifts to the upper floor windows. Every single one of them is shielded with curtains from the inside, like someone is trying to keep the rest of the world out.

Or keep someone in, my thoughts hum, remembering the story about Kyle and the girl he saw in the window before he died.

But people can't really *steal souls*.

Can they?

Something flickers from one of the windows, and when my eyes snap toward it, I realize one of the curtains is now parted down the middle, leaving a small gap.

"There's someone watching us," I say, startled.

Betty lifts a brow. "What, are you scared too?"

"No," I say, firm. "But . . . what if it's the ghost?"

Could I really be *this close* to getting a message to Babung?

Maybe it was a trick of the sunlight, or maybe it's just Mrs. Delvaux wondering who's standing outside her gate. But I really, really want to believe there are spirits in this house.

Even if the thought of a villainous witch *does* scare me a little.

Angela smirks. "I dare you to knock on the door and say hi to Mrs. Delvaux."

"What? Why would I want to do that?" I ask.

Betty shrugs. "To get closer to the ghost. That's what you *want*, isn't it?"

"Well, yeah, but—" I start.

"Unless you're too afraid," Madison interrupts, voice taunting. "It's one thing to google ghosts. It's probably another to actually *meet* one."

They're all staring at me like they don't think I'll do it. And I know I shouldn't care about their approval—and mostly I don't—but a small part of me does.

They're the first people my age I've met in this town. I'll be going to school with them in the fall. Maybe doing this will be enough to make them forget about the parts with Mom and the marine animals.

Besides, it's just a door, and an old lady, and a house that needs a coat of paint. (Or two.)

There's no real *harm* in introducing myself to Mrs. Delvaux. Even if she is a witch, she isn't going to curse me in broad daylight when there are witnesses around. I'm still not convinced curses are scientifically possible—and the kidnapping does sound far-fetched.

And if Mrs. Delvaux *isn't* a witch, I can explain that I just moved to the neighborhood. Maybe if she's nice, I could even tell her about Babung, and the research I've been doing. She might even let me come back with my detector to search the house for electromagnetic energy.

I've got nothing to lose by knocking on the door, and everything to lose if I don't.

"Fine," I say with a shrug. "I'll do it."

Sunny opens her mouth to argue, but Betty interrupts. "You have to knock on the *back* door." She narrows her eyes like the rules of the dare have to be crystal clear. "All the way on the other side of the house."

I glance at the side gardens. There's no shortcut. I'll have to walk right through Mrs. Delvaux's property. Nobody will see me from the road. Nobody but Sunny and her friends will even know I'm here.

Just a door, and an old lady, and a house, my mind repeats.

I take a step toward the gate, and Sunny's eyes widen in surprise. She opens her mouth, and for a second I think she's going to try and stop me, but then she clamps it shut.

"Oh my god, you're really going?" Angela sucks in a laugh.

I fight the hitch in my voice. "Curses aren't real, and ghosts can't hurt people. There's nothing to worry about."

The wind whistles overhead, and I remember what Harold said—about the supernatural wanting to prove you wrong.

Ignoring the sudden panic in my heart, I lean my bike against the gate. When I push the iron bars open, a horrendous creak catapults through the air. The girls' muffled laughter continues behind me, even when I slip through the opening and make my way across the yard and toward the back of Honeyfield Hall.

I turn the corner and lose sight of the girls and the road, expecting to find more dead plants and wrecked outbuildings. Instead, I find a garden.

Rose bushes surround the wide courtyard, where an empty fountain sits in the middle. A trellis full of honeysuckle leads to more overgrowth, but the area closest to the porch steps is full of bright flower beds and patches of strawberry plants.

It's beautiful, and well kept, and nothing like the rest of the property.

This garden is *loved*.

I look up at the porch. White paint is peeling from every corner, and a black screen door is fitted in front of an enormous wooden one. Even with the strawberries nearby, it looks ominous.

The skin on the back of my neck prickles.

It's just a door, I repeat to myself, again and again. *How scary can a door be?*

I walk up the stairs with my hands balled tight. There are no crocheted rabbits in my pockets today. Nothing for good luck.

It's just me—which is something I'm still getting used to.

I take a breath, reach for the handle, and pull. But it's not the back door waiting for me behind the screen. It's a *person*.

Standing in the doorway is a girl with chestnut brown hair, pale skin, and haunting blue eyes that pierce straight through me.

My fear is a shock wave, and it throws me backward. I stumble down the stairs, and the screen door clatters shut with a *bang*. I try to scream in alarm, but no sound comes out—just a breath of air that makes my lungs burn. I'm stunned by the strange girl with the strange eyes, so focused on being caught trespassing that I miss one of the porch steps. My ankle twists and I fling out a hand, desperate to grab hold of a baluster.

But it turns out I'm as bad at conquering gravity as I am at talking to strangers.

I spin and fall clumsily to the ground—face-first, right on top of the bright, well-cared-for flowers and strawberries.

My fingers sink into the soil, and there's a horrible squelch beneath my stomach. Scrambling to my feet, I look down in horror at the mess I've made. Most of the plants are flattened to oblivion, and patches of strawberry mulch are *everywhere*. Even my shirt is stained with bright red fruit juice.

Somewhere behind the screen, I know the girl is still watching me. I'm scared Mrs. Delvaux will be here soon, and I'll be in more trouble than I've ever been in my life.

How can I explain to her that this was an accident? How am I going to explain it to my *parents*?

I don't think; I flee.

When I reach the gate, my bike is still leaning against the iron bars. But there's no one else here. Just an empty cul-de-sac.

Down at the bottom of the hill, four girls are pedaling away fast, their laughter echoing through the street. Laughter that's directed at *me*.

Maybe it's good that I'm scared. It's a distraction from the hurt bubbling up in my chest.

I ride home without crying, even though I really, really want to.

CHAPTER SEVEN

All I can think about on the way home is that I may have just seen a ghost at Honeyfield Hall—but instead of making contact, I panicked and ran.

I wonder if it's the same girl Kyle saw before he died, or disappeared, or whatever it was that really happened to him.

I wonder if I'm next.

It's hard to decide what's better—the possibility that I may have seen a real ghost but will have to face the wrath of Mrs. Delvaux to see it again, or the disappointment that what I saw was just an ordinary girl in an ordinary house. Because only one of them means I'm a step closer to finding Babung.

I push my bike into the garage.

Dad notices me the second I walk into the house. "What happened?" he demands, eyes flooding with concern as he searches for obvious injuries.

"It's nothing." I feel myself shrinking by the second. "I just fell, that's all."

"That's all?" he repeats in disbelief. "Eliot, you're covered in blood!"

I look down at all the mushy, red stains on my shirt. "Oh. These are just strawberries."

Dad's brow knots in confusion, and Mom appears in an instant. She must've been cleaning because she's wearing yellow rubber gloves that are dripping with soapsuds.

"Oh my—" Her breath catches. "What on *earth*?"

Dad rubs his forehead, relieved but still confused. "She said it's strawberries."

Mom looks out the window and spots the empty driveway. "Where are your friends? I thought they were coming over for snacks."

"They're not my friends," I reply stiffly. "And you shouldn't have forced them to hang out with me."

I never used to be so angry at my parents. I think it's this house. It doesn't have a single ghost, but it has *mountains* of bad energy. And there isn't enough black tourmaline in the world to fix it.

Mom tilts her chin slightly. "I certainly didn't force anyone to do anything." She steps forward and wipes her soapy gloves on her apron before pulling them off. "Did something happen with the other girls?"

Dad offers a wry grin. "I'm more interested in where you found so many strawberries. If you share your secret stash, we could save a small fortune on our grocery bill."

Not funny, Mom mouths, but Dad is busy chuckling at his own joke. "She fell off her bike—she could've been really hurt!"

"I didn't fall off my bike," I correct, flustered. "The girls took me to an old house at the top of the hill, and I tripped in the garden."

Mom and Dad exchange a look.

"You were trespassing in someone's yard?" he asks, and all the humor he normally carries into every conversation disappears entirely. There isn't a hint of laughter in his voice now.

Dad takes private property very seriously.

"No. I mean—not *exactly*," I clarify. "I was just going to say hi."

Mom's hands immediately snap to her hips. "Since when do you go around knocking on random people's houses? That's *dangerous*, Eliot."

"They said Honeyfield Hall was haunted, and that a real ghost lived there!" My voice cracks. They won't understand—but I try to explain anyway. "I just wanted to see for myself."

Mom grimaces like I've given her the worst news imaginable. Something tells me it isn't because of the trespassing.

Dad frowns. "Wait—are you talking about that old mansion on the other side of the railway line?" When I nod, he rubs his brow and sighs. "That's someone's home. It's not a tourist attraction."

Mom shakes her head. "What were you thinking, bothering the neighbors like that?"

"I wasn't trying to do anything bad! The other girls said Mrs. Delvaux was a witch who cursed children, and that a boy named Kyle saw a ghost in the window before he vanished.

And I think I saw her—the ghost, not Mrs. Delvaux—but she caught me off guard, and I fell off the porch and into the garden and—"

"There's no such thing as ghosts," Mom interjects. The way she says it . . . It's like she's exhausted. Like *I'm* exhaus*ting*. "This has to stop, Eliot. I know you miss Babung, but this fixation on spirits and death—it isn't *healthy*."

I don't understand what she means. Searching for Babung isn't like eating too much candy, or forgetting to drink water, or never getting any fresh air. Staying busy, and looking for ghosts . . . It keeps me from being sad all the time.

So how is it *not* healthy?

"I'm not going to stop. I don't *want* to stop." I fold my arms over my chest. "I know what it feels like to be forgotten. And I'm not going to do that to Babung."

Mom and Dad exchange more silent words. I can tell by their faces they don't agree with me—but they also don't want to keep talking about it.

They want to move forward. Even if that means brushing over the only thing I care about.

Dad brings the focus back to property damage, where he's comfortable. "Well, I can see the harm the garden did to you, but how much harm did you do to the garden?"

When I think of the mess I left behind, my heart plummets. Most of the garden was a mess, but the flower bed? It was special to someone. It *meant* something. And I destroyed it.

I stare at the floor.

"That bad, huh?" Dad glances at Mom. "I'll take Eliot to the house so she can apologize in person."

Mom nods. "I don't want to start off on a bad foot with the neighbors. Let's all go together—and we'll offer to pay whatever it costs to fix the damage."

"Now?" I blurt out, alarmed.

I didn't think I'd have to go back and face Mrs. Delvaux so soon. I thought I'd have more time to process what I saw, and what I'm going to say.

Did my parents even *hear* me when I said there was a possibility of a cursed child living in that house?

Mom ushers me toward the door without missing a beat. "The sooner we smooth this over, the better."

"I'll drive," Dad says.

I follow them to the garage without another word.

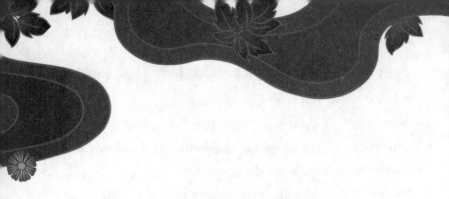

CHAPTER EIGHT

It only takes a few minutes to reach Honeyfield Hall from the main road, but it's enough time for my stomach to fill with dread.

What if Mrs. Delvaux really is a witch, and she puts a curse on me right in front of my parents? Or worse—what if she's just really, really angry, and my parents decide to ground me from ghost hunting for the rest of the summer?

I lean against the headrest as the queasiness roils through me.

When we reach the front door, Mom knocks, Dad waits, and I shrink into a shadow behind them.

After a moment, the door opens and an old woman appears, wearing a simple black dress. She has wiry gray hair spun into a braided knot, and her olive skin is covered in dark freckles. An enormous moonstone pendant hangs from her neck.

A glimmer of hope. Moonstones are all about encouraging peace and balancing emotions. Maybe she won't curse me after all.

"Hi," Mom says brightly. "I'm Margot Katayama, and this is my husband, Francis. We just moved in down the road."

"Are you selling something?" the woman asks gruffly. "I don't want anything, unless it's the cookies." She glances at me and sniffs. "I like the Thin Mints."

"We don't have any cookies, I'm afraid," Mom admits, and nobody could be more disappointed than me.

"Our daughter, Eliot, seems to have been playing in your yard earlier and caused some damage. We'd like to pay to have it fixed," Dad explains before turning to me. "And Eliot has something she'd like to say."

I shuffle forward, ears burning. "I'm really sorry about your plants," I manage to squeak. "It was an accident."

The woman peers down and huffs. Even though I'm terrified and embarrassed and I definitely do *not* want to look her in the eyes in case she puts me under a spell, she draws my gaze all the same.

That's when I see it: Mrs. Delvaux has the same haunting blue irises as the girl behind the screen door.

"My mother always insisted a decent apology is done over a cup of tea." Mrs. Delvaux steps back and holds the door open. "If you want to make it up to me, you'll come inside, eat some cake, and tell me how much better it is than that overpriced slop Bethany Thompson sells at the café."

Dad laughs, sheepish, and follows Mom inside.

I pause at the threshold.

Mrs. Delvaux watches me, unblinking. "No need to be a stranger—this house already knows you." She leans closer, eyes crinkling. "Most people who go digging around on another person's land are searching for one of two things: treasure, or bones." Her voice becomes a whisper. "Which one were you hoping to find in my strawberry patch?"

My pulse races so fast that I start to go light-headed. "I—there wasn't—I didn't mean to!"

She barks a laugh. "So, what was the dare? Were you going to steal something off my porch? Throw a rock through my window?" She tuts. "Every generation brings a new group of troublemakers, but their tricks are all the same."

"I was only going to knock!" I blurt out. "I promise I wasn't trying to destroy anything, and especially not your garden. I only fell because I saw—" My words cut short. I'm not sure bringing up the possible ghost is a good idea. Especially if she really *is* a witch.

Just because she's wearing a moonstone doesn't mean she's trustworthy. It could be a trick.

"What did you see?" Mrs. Delvaux's blue eyes gleam.

I'm too frozen to answer. Too terrified of saying the wrong thing.

"You look closer to death than I do." Her laugh borders on a cackle. "Come on inside, little one. I hope you like chocolate cake—I've been baking all morning." She disappears into the dark space along with my highly amused parents.

Peering into the enormous entrance hall, I count to five, take a breath, and step inside.

Mrs. Delvaux likes asking questions. She wants to know where we moved from, and how old I am, and whether our house was checked for "active termites," because apparently, it's a problem in the neighborhood.

She seems to know a lot about houses—especially the old ones—and if my parents were fish, talking about home renovations would be the perfect bait. By the time Mrs. Delvaux brings up roof tiles and local builders, Mom and Dad are already hooked.

I pick at a slice of cake, mostly to keep my hands busy because I don't know what to do. I thought I was in trouble— but they're all acting like friends instead of strangers. Nobody has brought up the garden incident since we sat down.

I lean back in my chair, staring down the wide hallway. I wonder if the girl is still in the house. If she really is a ghost, will my parents be able to see her too? And what are the chances that she'd take a message to Babung for me, even though I slammed a screen door in her face?

At least I didn't scream. I only *almost* screamed.

Mom's voice interrupts my thoughts. "Well, we certainly know where to come if we have questions about our house project. And thank you so much for the kind offer to put in a good word with the painters. I'll never say 'no' to a discount."

Mrs. Delvaux's gaze drifts toward me. "I imagine there's not much for you to do around the house with all the renovations taking place."

"Eliot likes to stay busy," Dad says. "She's on a mission

these days to prove ghosts are real." He grins at me like we're sharing a joke. Like searching for proof of an afterlife isn't the most important part of my existence.

Mom glances at him sideways like she would prefer it wasn't mentioned at all.

"Ah. That explains why you were in my yard," Mrs. Delvaux muses, and my face immediately heats. She nods to both my parents. "This house has a lot of history. Even *I* thought it was haunted when I was a child."

Mom clears her throat, trying to hide her discomfort. "We are really sorry about your garden. Please just let us know what we owe you."

Mrs. Delvaux waves a hand. "I don't want your money. I've been thinking of retiring my green thumb anyway. My knees aren't what they used to be—and I just don't have the energy for weeding these days." She lets out a soft chuckle. "It's only a shame my granddaughter has no interest in gardening, or she could help out. She says she's afraid of slugs, you see."

Mom and Dad exchange a look, but before they get a chance to say anything, I blurt out, "You have a granddaughter?"

Mrs. Delvaux lifts a brow. "I do, yes. Her name is Hazel. She's about your age, actually. She stays with me when her parents have to work in the city."

That's why they have the same blue eyes—she's a relative, not a ghost.

Disappointment floods my chest, and my shoulders curve inward.

I brace for Dad to make a joke about my premature assumptions, but he doesn't. Instead, he says, "Maybe Eliot could help with the garden a bit? At least until all the strawberries and things are replaced." He tilts his head toward Mom, who quickly nods with approval.

"What a great idea!" Mom looks back at me. "That seems fair, doesn't it?"

I'm pretty sure the question is rhetorical and I don't *actually* get a say in this, but I nod anyway because they're both right. I made the mess—I should be the one to fix it.

Mrs. Delvaux's eyes flicker with light. "I would appreciate the help, but I have to insist on paying you for whatever work you do. Consider it a summer job, if you like."

I frown. "You want to *pay* me to fix your garden? Even though it's my fault it's ruined?"

She waves a hand, and her face wrinkles with a smile. "I've been losing the battle to that garden for years. The help would mean far more to me than a few marigolds."

I bite the edge of my lip, trying to figure out what the catch is, and why Mom and Dad seem so enthusiastic about the idea of me gardening.

And then I see it in Mom's brown eyes: the *hope*.

They see the garden as a distraction. Something to keep me busy and focused, that has nothing to do with ghosts.

I can't exactly say "no," even if Mrs. Delvaux *is* posing it like an offer. For one, it would be wrong not to help when she literally just told me she can't do it herself. If I don't fix the garden, there won't be a garden at all. And two, if I refuse to help on the basis that I don't want Mom and Dad to get their way, I will one hundred percent be grounded instead.

I can't be grounded. I need to spend the summer searching for Babung.

Besides, a summer job at Honeyfield Hall might actually work in my favor. Hazel might not have been a real ghost, but that doesn't mean this place isn't still haunted. If any place was going to have paranormal activity in Roseheart, Maine, wouldn't it be an old house like this one?

Accidentally trampling Mrs. Delvaux's garden might be the best mistake I ever made.

"Okay," I say finally. "I'd love to help."

"Wonderful," Mrs. Delvaux announces, and she sets her teacup in its tray. "You can come by tomorrow morning, if you like."

I nod again, and listen as Mrs. Delvaux and my parents talk more about houses and Roseheart and the history behind the small town.

When the floorboards creak above me, I tilt my face up, listening.

I wonder if somewhere upstairs, someone is listening right back.

CHAPTER NINE

Mrs. Delvaux carefully inspects the damaged garden. Only a few strawberries remain, and the marigolds look as if they've been run over by an animal stampede. Most of the stems are unnaturally bent, and a collection of orange-, gold-, and rust-colored petals cover the soil.

"I know they look bad, but there's still life left in some of them," Mrs. Delvaux says, setting a bucket and a double-pronged tool beside her feet. She hands me a green apron, watching as I slip it over my head and tie the back in a knot. "Well, you may as well make a start where you can. But be careful not to damage any of the good roots," she says, and turns for the porch.

I glance between her and the tortured marigolds. "You're not staying? But I don't know what I'm doing!"

"They're just weeds, girl. Nothing to be scared of," she scolds, and disappears into the house.

I kneel in the soil, reach for the first weed, and tug. Some of the leaves fall apart in my gloved palm, but the plant hardly budges—so I lower my grip to the base and pull even harder.

I wrestle with the stems for a good few seconds before it finally comes free, and toss the leafy remains into the bucket.

I never realized taking care of a garden was such hard work. Babung had lots of plants in her backyard. There was jasmine and orange blossoms and nectarine trees. She even had a small table full of orchids that she kept on the covered patio.

But I never saw Babung battling away at the overgrowth, or covered in soil. I don't even remember her watering the flowers.

She must've done it—just not in front of me.

Does it mean anything that there was a version of Babung I'd never met? I knew Babung in the kitchen, and Babung crocheting little animals, and Babung singing along to old Japanese records. I knew *hundreds* of Babungs. But I didn't know Babung gardening.

What else did I miss? And if I had known every version of her, and she knew every version of me . . . Would that have made a difference?

Maybe I could've helped her remember more. Maybe she would've even remembered me.

I blink the salt away, and dig up weed after weed until my arms ache.

When sweat starts to pool at my brow, I wipe my forehead with the back of my hand. I've probably only been outside for thirty minutes, but it feels like hours. I stare at the bucket, wondering how much longer it will take to fill, when a voice makes me jump.

"You know you're supposed to use the weeding fork, right? If you don't, you're just leaving the roots behind."

I leap to my feet and spin around. The girl from yesterday is standing in the open doorway, staring through the screen. She's just as pale as I remember, but her eyes don't seem nearly as mysterious.

I really did let my imagination get the better of me.

I hesitate. "You must be Hazel."

She looks surprised. "You know my name?"

"Mrs. Delvaux mentioned she had a granddaughter."

"Oh." Hazel's laugh sounds like a hiccup. "What did she say about me?"

"Um. That you stay here when your parents are away. And that you don't like slugs."

She tilts her head. "You're the girl who fell in the strawberries."

"I wasn't expecting to see anyone in the doorway." My cheeks go pink. "You scared me, that's all."

"I'm sorry," she says, and she sounds like she genuinely means it. "I wasn't expecting to see you either. We hardly ever get visitors." There's a short pause. "So, are you going to tell me something about yourself?"

"Er, my name's Eliot. With one *L*."

"I don't mean your name," she scolds with a giggle. "I mean something about *you*! You already know I don't like slugs. It's only fair that I know something about you back."

There are a million things I could tell her, but right now, I can barely think of one.

"There's not really anything interesting to say about myself," I say, sheepish.

Her brow immediately crinkles. "You tripped and fell in the strawberry patch because you were scared, and still came back. That makes you the most interesting person I know."

"My parents are making me fix Mrs. Delvaux's garden," I admit. "I've got no choice but to keep coming back."

"Sounds like you're about as stuck here as I am." She sighs. "My parents are always leaving me here, but I get so bored. I never have anyone to talk to."

My fingers twitch inside the gardening gloves. "I just moved here, so I don't really have anyone to talk to either." I hesitate, mind racing. *Ask her if she wants to be friends, ask her if she likes crystals, ask her if she believes in ghosts, ask her what her favorite flavor of ice cream is, ask her . . .* "If you want, we could, uh, not talk to anyone together."

I regret it immediately.

Not talk to anyone together? What is *wrong* with me?

I open my mouth to take it all back, when Hazel's face brightens.

"I'd like that," she says. "On the condition that we can still talk to each other. Because there are plenty more things I want to know about you."

I feel like there's helium in my chest.

"What are you hanging around the door for?" Mrs. Delvaux's voice sounds from the other end of the hall.

Hazel looks over her shoulder. "We were just talking. I can't believe out of all the things you could've told her about me, you chose the *slugs*."

Mrs. Delvaux's shadow appears behind the screen, and Hazel scoots to the side to make room. The door creaks open, and Mrs. Delvaux steps onto the porch to get a better look at my progress.

"You need to dig out the roots to stop them from growing back," she says. "That's what the weeding fork is for."

Hazel mouths, *Told you*, and grins.

The edge of my mouth tugs. "Sorry. I'll fix it."

"It's warm out here already," Mrs. Delvaux says with a *humph*. "I'll get us some sweet tea and sandwiches, and we can eat on the porch." She steps back into the house but pauses in the hall near Hazel, and I hear Mrs. Delvaux add, "And you make sure to keep away from the door. I don't want you wandering around outside alone."

Hazel watches her leave, and I feel the tension like a taut rope.

It must be hard for Hazel to be stuck at Honeyfield Hall when her parents are away, with no one to hang out with except her grandmother.

Not that I'd complain. I'd give anything to hang out with Babung again. I'd be happy to sit inside for an entire year without a TV or a computer or anything, just as long as we could see each other one more time.

But Hazel isn't me, and Mrs. Delvaux isn't Babung.

"I should go," Hazel says quietly. There's a slight crack in her voice, but when she turns back to me, her smile reappears. "I don't want to distract you more than I already have. You'll be here tomorrow though, right?"

I nod. "That's right."

She takes a step back, and her figure fades like a shadow behind the dark screen. "See you tomorrow then, Eliot with one *L*."

"See you tomorrow," I say, but by the time I blink, she's already gone.

I return to the garden to pull more weeds from the soil—this time with the weeding fork—until Mrs. Delvaux appears with a tray of sandwiches and a pitcher of iced tea.

We sit on the porch swing, and she tells me all about her plans for the garden, and what kinds of flowers and vegetables she hopes to plant before the fall, but I'm only half listening.

I'm too busy thinking about Hazel, who just might be the only other person in Roseheart who needs a friend as much as I do.

CHAPTER TEN

The living room flickers with light from the television. My parents' glowing faces look even more ghostlike than Hazel did the first time we met, with the strange blue hues over their skin and their wide, open eyes.

They'd asked about the garden when I first got home. For a moment, I was even excited to talk about it. I wanted to tell them about Hazel, and how nice she was, and how Mrs. Delvaux said I could choose some of the new seeds to replace the marigolds.

I wanted to tell them I had *fun*.

Then I remembered why they wanted me to help with the garden in the first place and I didn't feel like telling them anything anymore. So I said it went fine, and that was the end of the conversation.

Dad turns his chin to where I'm standing at the side of the room. "Hey, kiddo. You all ready for bed?"

"Yeah," I say, flexing my fingers. It hadn't taken long to scrub the soil off, but I stayed in the shower for a few extra minutes to make sure the smell of grass was definitely gone.

California smelled like citrus and coconut sunscreen and barbecue grills. I'm still trying to figure out what Maine smells like—and whether or not I want it to stick.

Mom pauses the television with the remote. "Do you want to stay up and watch a movie with us?"

"I'd rather sleep. I'm going to Mrs. Delvaux's after breakfast," I say.

"That's very responsible of you," Dad notes. "I'm glad you're being so mature about this whole thing. Everyone makes mistakes, but it matters a lot more that you try to make it right."

"Mrs. Delvaux seems very kind," Mom adds. "I don't understand why the neighborhood kids give her such a hard time."

Dad shrugs like the answer is obvious. "It's the house. It's got a witch's hat turret, and fish-scale shingles, and indented coffered panels . . . And don't get me started on the bay windows. It's an ideal place for a kid's imagination!"

Mom nudges him with her knee. "That sounds more like *your* ideal place. And it's still not an excuse for the kids to be mean to her."

"Mrs. Delvaux isn't so bad," I point out slowly. "But she's kind of strict with Hazel. She doesn't let her leave the house by herself."

"Everyone has different rules," Mom says. "I think it's nice there's someone at the house your age. Maybe you two can be friends!"

I tuck my hands under my sleeves. "Maybe," I reply, even though it's what I've been thinking about all day.

Mom bites the edge of her lip. "I'm sorry if I pushed you to hang out with those girls yesterday. I wasn't trying to make things awkward—I just really want you to love Roseheart and I suppose I got carried away."

I stare at the floor. "I'm never going to love this town the way you both do."

"Never is a long time," Dad points out, running a hand through his shoulder-length hair. "You might change your mind if you tried giving this place a real chance. You might even fall in love with Victorian architecture the way we did all those years ago!"

"That's just it," I say. "You fell in love with this place *without* me. We didn't do it as a family." I shake my head. "And it's always going to be the place you brought me to after Babung died."

Mom's face splits with guilt. "But . . . maybe you could learn to *like* it one day? I know it's a big change, and I know it isn't what you wanted. But—well—I can't give you the thing you want." Her eyes start to water. "I know you don't see it now because you're still hurting, but maybe a fresh start at a new school with new friends will be something you can look forward to."

A fresh start. Something to look forward to. A big *change*.

Too fast, too soon, too much.

I tuck my arms around myself and shrug. "I don't need

anything to look forward to. I've already got plenty of things to keep me busy." And because my frustration gets the better of me, I add, "I know that's why you wanted me to work on the garden. You think it will make me stop looking for Babung."

Mom opens her mouth, stiffens, and shuts it again.

Dad takes a slow breath. "I think your mom—*we*—were hoping you could take an interest in something other than ghost hunting. At least for a little while."

I can't do that. I *won't*.

But what's the point in arguing? They'll never understand. Not when they already believe Babung is gone forever.

I know there has to be a way to reach my grandma—and if my parents won't believe me, I'll keep my search a secret.

From now on, no more talking to my parents about ghosts.

"I already have another interest, remember?" I say, firm. "I have a summer job. There's not really time for anything else."

Mom twists her mouth, unconvinced, but Dad lifts his hands like he's glad we're on the same page.

Even though we're not. We're not even reading the same *book*.

"That's right—and you could be gardening for weeks by the state of that yard." He cracks a grin. "But remember to take breaks. If you work yourself to death, you know how your mom feels about ghost hunts. We'll never see you again."

Mom looks completely horrified. "*Francis*," she hisses. "That is *not* funny."

He barks a laugh and pokes her ribs with a finger. "Come on—it was a little funny."

She swats him away and looks at me seriously. "We love you, Eliot. More than you can possibly imagine. And we only want what's best for you."

You have no idea what's best for me—and that's the problem, I want to say.

Instead, I nod once and turn back for the stairs.

CHAPTER ELEVEN

I knock on the front door of Honeyfield Hall several times, but nobody answers, so I follow the white porch to the back of the house.

Mrs. Delvaux is sitting in the garden, trying her best to remove a stubborn plant that's broken through the cracks of a paving stone. She hears the creak of my steps, which is impossible to avoid along the splintered floorboards, and motions for me to come and help.

I hop down the last porch stair, reach for the spare set of gardening gloves, and pull them over my hands. Kneeling beside Mrs. Delvaux, I grab the plant while she digs out the roots with a trowel. Eventually, it comes free.

Mrs. Delvaux tosses it into the nearby bucket. The bright red flowers are tilted upward, making them stand out in the pile of uprooted plants.

"Why did you dig that one up?" I ask, feeling a little sorry for it. "It's pretty."

"It's a weed."

"It doesn't look like a weed."

"My mother used to say the only difference between a weed and a flower was judgment." She waves her trowel at the air. "But I say you can call it whatever you like—I still don't want it in my garden."

I watch her work through the soil, plucking at bits of unwanted vegetation. I do the same and toss my findings into the bucket along with the rest of the weeds.

I'm so focused on the garden that I don't realize how warm it's gotten until sweat trickles above my brow. When I squint up at the sky, there isn't a cloud in sight. Just a bright, unforgiving sun.

"Why don't you run to the greenhouse and grab one of my spare gardening hats?" Mrs. Delvaux says without looking up. "I don't want you getting sunburned."

"The greenhouse?" I repeat.

She hums and points farther into the garden, where I spot the edge of some outbuildings. "Follow the pavement past the old rose gardens. You can't miss it."

I leave the gloves beside the bucket and follow her directions, avoiding the stinging nettle and overgrown hedges that have taken over the path. Even though the rose garden looks as if it's gone into hibernation without a flower in sight, Mrs. Delvaux was right—the greenhouse is unmissable.

The building is covered in panels of glass, and it's as wide as it is tall, with a faded duck-egg blue frame. The roof is curved and covered in cathedral-like spires, and cobwebs trail beneath the overhang. Some of the lower glass windows are broken, and several hardy weeds have spread through the opening and into the greenhouse.

Even in the daylight, it looks nearly as haunted as Honeyfield Hall.

But today I'm prepared. I press my fingertips to my bracelet, feeling the row of smooth, round beads. There's smoky quartz for open communication with the paranormal. Labradorite for specifically finding ancestral spirits. Jet for protection from curses—*just* in case. And a crocheted rabbit in my pocket for luck.

"If you're out there, I'd like to talk to you," I whisper to whoever might be listening. To any spirits that might be wandering the grounds. "I need your help."

I wait for a response—for a gust of wind, or a flutter of leaves—but there's nothing but quiet stillness all around me.

With a sigh, I reach for the greenhouse door and pry it open with a forceful tug.

A bag of soil is tipped on its side, and there's a layer of dirt spread across the entire floor, with flecks of broken glass flickering up at me. I don't see any gardening hats, but there's a stack of boxes at the back of the room that look like they're full of gardening equipment.

I make my way down an aisle of long-dead plants, forgotten tools, and empty ceramic pots. Pushing a rusted lawn chair out of the way, I lift the lid on one of the boxes and peek inside. It's full of random things—old newspapers, glass bottles, broken lawn ornaments—things that look like they should've been recycled or thrown out years ago.

I look in the next box, and the next, but there's no hat to be found. I'm nearly ready to give up my search when something moves in the shadows, making goose bumps appear all over my arms.

My heart thumps. I focus on the space between the boxes where the light can't reach, unable to shake the feeling that someone—or something—is watching me.

"Hello?" I call out to the darkness. "Is someone there?"

I know I shouldn't expect Babung to answer, but I do. I wait for her raspy voice, and soft, freckled face to appear. I wait for her ghost to step out of the shadows, for her laugh to fill the room, and for her arms to wrap around me with the warmth of home that I've missed so much.

But it isn't Babung.

A pair of yellow eyes flash open, brimming with life.

Before I can even process what it is that I'm seeing, the creature leaps. I yelp in alarm and stumble backward until my back hits the edge of a wooden shelf. It happens quickly—one by one, a series of pots topple over, knocking one another down like dominos. The pot closest to the edge stills, teetering, and then it shatters against the floor with a horrendous *crack*.

Pieces of ceramic explode in every direction—and a few inches away stands a black cat with its teeth bared and its back arched. It looks more terrified than I am.

It hisses, yellow eyes latched on to mine, before jumping onto the next shelf and escaping through one of the broken window panes.

It was just a cat, my mind reels. I blink several times and fight to control my breathing.

When I look down at the mess I've made, an anxious tremor runs through me. A dozen jagged pieces are strewn across the floor. Pieces of the flowerpot that I broke.

I really hope it wasn't one of Mrs. Delvaux's favorites.

I can't find a broom, so I do my best to carefully pick up the shards and set them back on the shelf.

I broke a vase at Babung's house once. I was trying to get a board game out of the garage and accidentally knocked the vase off a shelf—almost the same way I did today.

Babung wasn't angry. She told me that repairing pottery is an art form called kintsugi. She said that by embracing flaws and imperfections, we can become even stronger.

I know she was talking about the vase, but I think she was talking about people, too. Babung always spoke like that—with double meanings, and explanations that sounded like poetry.

We fixed the vase together.

But Mrs. Delvaux isn't Babung. *No one* is like Babung.

I'll miss her for the rest of my life.

I reach for the last broken shard, when I notice something flicker beneath the layer of soil. Frowning, I brush some of the dirt away.

Lying on the ground is a shiny gold key.

I pinch it between my fingers and hold it up to the sunlight. The head is shaped like a flower and a star mixed together, with big swooping edges. Most keys I've seen have lots of jagged teeth, but this one has hardly any at all.

I run my thumb over the curved metal. I wonder how long it's been here? I wonder what it's for?

I should ask Mrs. Delvaux. I'm sure she'd know.

I tuck the key into my pocket and return to the garden. Mrs. Delvaux is still pawing at the earth, picking out bits of leftover weeds.

She frowns when she sees me, hand perched at her brow to block out the sun. "No luck finding the hat?"

"No," I say, already reaching for the key. "But there was a cat in the greenhouse, and I accidentally bumped a shelf—"

"Dorothy got outside?" Mrs. Delvaux interrupts, voice inching quickly toward concern. "Where is she now?"

"I-I'm not sure. She jumped out the window." I close my fingers over the grooves of the gold key. "But one of your flowerpots broke, and I saw this on the floor and—"

"I can't believe she escaped again." Mrs. Delvaux rises from the garden patch with a tired groan and dusts her apron with soil-stained hands. "I was *sure* I closed all the windows," she murmurs before marching toward the greenhouse.

I guess she wasn't bothered about the pot—but I still need to tell her about the key.

I know it doesn't belong to me and that I need to return it.

But the key feels like a secret begging to be uncovered. One I'm too curious to let go of, the same way I can never let go of my thoughts. I want to know how old it is, and why it was left in the greenhouse. I want to know what it *opens*.

I look up at the old manor, squinting against the sunlight, hoping Hazel might appear in the doorway so I can show her what I found. But she doesn't appear, and Mrs. Delvaux is too busy searching for Dorothy to entertain my questions.

I leave the key in my pocket and go back to digging through the soil, wondering if there really could be secrets in this garden, and how far I'd have to go to dig them up.

CHAPTER TWELVE

That looks like a skeleton key to me." Dad lowers his chin so he can see over the top of his reading glasses. He's halfway up a ladder with his hair in a half-knot and a measuring tape in one hand.

"What's the difference between a skeleton key and a regular key?" I ask.

"A skeleton key is a lock-picking tool. It can open multiple locks rather than just one," Dad explains, climbing to the top of the ladder and stretching out the tape measure.

I feel the weight of the key building in my palm. "You mean it could open anything? Even our front door?"

"I think most modern locks have wards that prevent that kind of thing." He removes the pencil resting over his ear and marks the wall with a barely there dot. "But with old-fashioned locks, it would probably work just fine."

Old-fashioned locks. Like the ones in Mrs. Delvaux's house.

Which means there's a good chance I'm holding a key that opens every door in Honeyfield Hall.

I bite down on my growing intrigue. "Why would someone *need* a skeleton key?"

"Locksmiths use them. Or it could be someone's old master key." Dad lowers his voice. "But my guess is that the key belonged to a bandit."

I roll my eyes. "I'm being serious."

He lifts his free hand innocently, and the measuring tape snaps back together with a *click*. "So am I. Have you ever read a mystery book? Skeleton keys are *always* used for nefarious reasons." He motions toward the floor. "Could you pass me one of those nails and the blue hammer?"

I send the tools up the ladder and step back. "You think whoever owns this was doing something *bad*?"

Dad tilts his head back and holds the nail to one of the practically invisible pencil markings. "Who knows? But I've never read a story about a *hero* with a skeleton key, is all I'm saying." He hammers a nail into the wall, hangs a picture frame, and tips the edges back and forth until it's perfectly level. After a long pause, he glances down at me. "Where did you say you found it again?"

"I . . . um . . . found it on the ground. In the dirt." It's *almost* the whole truth.

"Well, you should keep it safe," he says. "I don't think they make them like that anymore—and I've never seen an old key in such good condition."

Except for the scratches, my mind notes.

I rub my thumb over the tarnished head, wondering what

it looked like when it was brand-new, but when I turn the key under the light, it isn't scratches or scuff marks I'm looking at. It's *writing*.

I hold the key closer and try to make out what it says. But I don't recognize the letters, or the language. A long row of symbols follows the key's design, etched in black.

It doesn't just look old. It looks *ancient*.

Guilt swirls through me. I didn't take the key on purpose. Mrs. Delvaux was distracted with the cat—I didn't even remember I still *had* the key until I got home.

I never meant to steal anything. Certainly not anything valuable.

Gardening with Mrs. Delvaux was meant to be a punishment, but meeting Hazel has been the best part of moving to Roseheart. I don't want to mess that up. Especially over something as silly as an old key.

I have to return it before anyone realizes it's missing.

"What's wrong?" Dad asks from the top of the ladder.

I clear my throat and stuff the key back into my pocket. "Is it okay if I go out on my bike?"

Dad glances out the window and then at his watch, checking to make sure they add up. "It's getting pretty late for a bike ride. Dinner will be ready soon."

"I won't be long," I say, rocking back on my heels. "I just . . . need to talk to Mrs. Delvaux about something."

"Can it wait until tomorrow?"

I shake my head. "It's important." When he's still staring

like he's waiting for a better explanation, I add, "It's about gardening stuff."

"Oh, well if it's *gardening* stuff . . ." He chuckles, amused. "All right, kiddo. But hurry back, okay? I think your mom is making lasagna."

It doesn't take long to throw on my hoodie and shoes, and then I'm out the door, on my bike, and racing toward Mrs. Delvaux's house.

Honeyfield Hall appears through the looming front gates. Apart from a softly lit window glowing in one of the downstairs rooms, the rest of the house is cast in shadows.

I make my way up the path, set my bike near the porch, and wonder whether I should knock on the front door and explain myself.

Just put the key back where you found it, my mind hisses. *No one will even know it was missing.*

I follow the wraparound porch toward the garden, but when I reach the stairs, the creak of the back door makes me freeze.

I turn, frowning beneath the dimming sky, and see that the door is halfway open.

"Hello?" The sharp squeak in my voice makes my heart race even faster.

No one replies.

"Mrs. Delvaux?" I try again.

The door opens wider in response, but I can't see anyone. Just a dark, empty hallway.

Someone wants me to come inside.

My throat catches, and a cold shudder runs through me. *Babung?* I mouth, curving my fingers over my beaded bracelet.

Is she here? Could a ghost really be *here*?

I can't help myself—not when doors are opening by themselves and the only explanation that makes sense to me is that Honeyfield Hall really is a hub of paranormal activity.

I step into the house and close the door behind me.

There are no lights in the hall, apart from a sliver of amber beneath one of the faraway doors, where I can hear the faint laughter of a sitcom. Maybe that's where Mrs. Delvaux is— maybe the television is why she couldn't hear me calling.

I shouldn't be here. I shouldn't be sneaking inside her house without her knowing.

I'm sure the house senses my hesitation, because the stairs creak up ahead, drawing my attention. I'm chasing after the sound without thinking, following the wide staircase until I reach the second-floor landing.

Fading sunlight pours through the upstairs windows, creating a trail of shimmering dust that leads down the corridor. The stained, ancient carpet softens my footsteps, but the house still groans beneath my weight. A reminder that I'm still a stranger here. A *trespasser*.

The house is trying to tell you something, my mind insists. *This is what you've been searching for—your* proof.

A cold draft escapes through the uneven floorboards,

making me shudder. I fold my arms around myself and tuck my hands into my sleeves for extra warmth.

Moving down the hallway, I peer curiously into every open doorway I can find. Other than my padded footsteps and my thumping heartbeat, the house is completely silent.

At the end of the next corridor, I find a room with high ceilings and fancy carvings embedded in the plaster. They look like patterned flowers, beautiful even in the darkness. Bulky pieces of furniture sit all around the room, covered in dust sheets like they've been in a decades-long slumber.

It's a room designed for parties and dancing—but it looks as if it hasn't been used in years.

I stare at the peeling wallpaper and the cracks in the window frames, wondering if there's a spirit here, trying to get my attention.

But this room is as empty as all the others.

The house isn't speaking to me; it's just my imagination again, seeing things that aren't really there. Because I'm hopeful and desperate and I want to see Babung again so badly that sometimes I can barely breathe.

I ball my fists and turn from the room, blinking away the tears in my eyes.

I'm sorry, Babung, I mouth to the emptiness. *I'm sorry I don't know how to bring you back.*

I wipe my cheeks with my sleeve and take four steps down the hallway, when the door slams shut behind me.

I spin around quickly, expecting to see Mrs. Delvaux, or

Hazel, or even Dorothy, but there's no one there. My eyes fall to the room I just left—the room that had been empty—and I realize whoever closed the door must've done it from the inside.

Heart hammering wildly, I try to turn the handle but it's locked. I press my hands against the door, wondering if someone is listening from the other side.

Do they know I'm here? Are they trying to keep me out?

Or do they want me to come *in*?

I reach into my pocket for the gold skeleton key, certain it's a sign. With a shaky hand, I pause in front of the lock and stare in wonder as the shape of the keyhole starts to *change*.

The metal twists and morphs until it's no longer a flat panel—it's curved into the mouth of a monster.

I should be terrified. Any rational person would be. But I've never been this close before, and I can't turn back now.

I shove the key through the lock and turn it until I hear a thunderous *click*, twist the handle, and step into the room.

Moments ago, the room was cold, dark, and filled with layers of dust.

Now it's a different room entirely.

An elaborate chandelier made of thick branches glitters with candlelight. Emerald green leaves trail around the edge of the coving, like the ceiling itself is part of an enchanted forest. Polished oak gleams beneath my feet, and there isn't a dust sheet in sight.

Instead, I see *faces*.

A woman dressed in a lavish ballgown sits on a green chaise longue, with her gray hair spun into tight ringlets and a string of pearls around her neck. Another woman sits in front of a grand piano, lips painted a dark plum and her eyes shut tight like she's lost in a daydream. A child with shaggy hair and suspenders slipping from one of his shoulders runs around the room, eyes puffy from crying, and a man with a thick mustache and plaid coat waves a finger like he's in the middle of berating him.

They look like four mismatched parts of a riddle. A set that doesn't quite belong together. But they all have one thing in common: an unmistakable white glow to their skin.

I stumble backward until I hit the wall with a *thud*.

Ghosts. They are *ghosts*.

"You're still too early, Eliot Katayama," a voice drawls, other-worldly and smooth.

My eyes dart around the room, searching for its owner, and I find a man with golden, glowing eyes staring back at me.

He flashes his teeth—and I'm too terrified to remember to scream.

CHAPTER THIRTEEN

My mouth hangs open. I blink once. Twice.

The man with golden eyes watches me carefully. He's dressed in black and is wearing a hat I know I've seen before.

"Y-you're a ghost," I manage to sputter.

He lifts a brow. "Fortunately, no." He looks to the side and nods toward the small crowd of semi-translucent humans emitting their eerie glows. "But the rest of these souls certainly are."

The man in front of me isn't glowing. He looks . . . normal. Like any other living, breathing human I've ever seen—with the exception of his golden eyes.

"If you're not a ghost," I start, unable to hide my bewilderment, "what are you?"

The corners of his mouth twitch upward. "I'm merely passing the time until I have somewhere else to be."

I check my own skin for a glow, reality dawning on me. "Wait. Am I *dead*?"

"Hardly," the man declares. "You've just stepped through

the veil. Something only a person with a *closeness* to death can do."

I immediately think of Babung. After she died, all I wanted was to see her again. To help her remember all the things that were important. It didn't matter that she was dead—I had to find her.

Maybe all the electromagnetic detectors and Obon offerings and trips to cemeteries have finally paid off. Because I wanted a connection to the spirit world—and now I have one.

Is that what he means about having a closeness to death? Because I searched for the afterlife instead of running from it?

A memory rushes back to me. One I didn't even realize I'd forgotten until now.

"I've seen you before," I say, stunned. "You were in the graveyard. You knew my name."

"Yes." The man tips his hat. "Mine is Graham, by the way."

"Graham," I repeat, like maybe this time I can stop the memory from slipping away.

"Exactly like that." He lowers his chin. "You can't imagine how many people have been mispronouncing it over the years."

But his name is the least of my worries. Because up until this moment, I forgot I'd ever met him. I didn't remember his face or the fact that we'd had a conversation.

It's like someone erased him from my mind completely.

How is that possible?

Graham senses my confusion. "You will only know me when you're in front of me," he explains gently. "It's easier that way. For everyone."

Before I can ask what exactly he means, the ghost child releases a horrible wail.

"Get out of my way, Hatter!" he shouts to the man with the mustache.

"I'm sick and tired of you running around this house ranting about secrets and keys and—oh for goodness' sake, will you stay *still*?" The man's hands are firmly at his hips. "And stop calling me Hatter!"

"Why should I? You're nothing more than an oversized hat stand," the child snaps, wagging his finger and glaring up at the man and his arguably tall top hat. "You do nothing to help. I'm beginning to think you actually *like* being trapped here!"

The man throws his hands up, exasperated. "You're giving me a headache. And not having migraines is supposed to be one of the very *few* benefits of being dead!"

The boy lets out a bloodcurdling shout. "You can't tell me what to do. You're not my father!" With supernatural speed, he runs straight toward the far wall—and disappears right through it.

The man pinches the bridge of his nose and sighs.

The woman at the piano sways, eyes half-lidded. "You should go after him, Hatter. You know how he gets when he's left alone."

"Why do you think I was trying to keep him *here*?" he growls. "And why does everyone insist on calling me that awful name?"

"You are Hatter for the same reason I am Trill—because none of us can remember our old names," she replies sleepily, slender fingers dancing across the keys.

The man—Hatter—flattens his mouth. "There are plenty of other names that would've been less insulting."

"But none that you could remember," Trill sings back.

Hatter glowers. "You just insist on making excuses for him."

The woman from the couch waves a hand dismissively. "Oh, let Lock have his fun. What's the harm in letting him rummage through the cupboards?"

"The harm?" Hatter scoffs. "Haven't you noticed that the more he *rummages*, the worse he gets?"

"We're *all* getting worse," the woman corrects. "But at least he's keeping himself busy."

Hatter shakes his head and straightens the edges of his collar. "I may not be ripping the house apart for clues that don't exist, but I am doing everything I can to ensure we keep the few memories we have left. So forgive me, my dear, for not being in a hurry to forget who I am completely." He takes several forceful strides toward the opposite wall and vanishes.

"They're . . . losing their memories?" I look at Graham, and my throat knots.

This is what happened to Babung. This is how I lost her before she even died.

Graham lifts his shoulders matter-of-factly. "All ghosts in the Hollow forget who they are eventually."

"What's the Hollow?"

"It's neither here nor there, really. Sometimes when a soul begins to cross over to the afterlife, it gets stuck on the way through the veil. Think of it like a stalled train on its way to the next station." Graham waves a hand around, fingers flicking delicately through the air. "It tends to happen to the heavier souls—the ones weighed down with *unfinished business*."

"How long are they stuck here for?" I ask.

"Until they let go of whatever it is that's weighing them down. And of course, they'll need their memories too. They cannot cross over without them," he explains. "It's the way of the dead—they need to know who they are, to know where they're meant to go."

"But," I say, flustered, "if they can't cross over without their memories, and this place makes them *lose* their memories, then how are they supposed to move on? Who's going to help them remember who they are?"

Graham doesn't answer at first. Maybe that's answer enough.

"The Hollow is not a place where things are found," he finally says. "It's a place where they are lost."

"That isn't fair," I argue.

"Death is rarely fair. It is only inevitable," Graham replies.

I stare at the two ghosts still left in the room. They have no idea who they were. They don't remember their names or their families or their past lives. They don't remember the people who loved them—who they might've loved back.

Is Babung trapped somewhere like this too?

I bite the inside of my cheek. "Can they . . . Can they see us?"

"We most certainly *can*," the old woman barks from the couch. "And didn't anyone ever teach you it's rude to gossip?"

My back stiffens. "I, I'm sorry! I didn't mean to—"

"Don't mind her," Trill says with a delicate sigh. "Pearl just likes to feel important."

The woman scoffs. "For all you know, I was a *queen* in my past life!"

"For all you know, you might've been a criminal," Trill replies.

Pearl smooths her skirts and purses her lips. "In this dress? Be serious."

I tug at my sleeve, running a thumb over the smoky quartz out of habit. Graham notices.

"That day in the graveyard," he says, serious. "You were looking for someone." A newfound understanding flashes behind his eyes. "Someone who is no longer alive."

"My grandma," I say, and the admission makes the sadness flare in my chest. "I need to talk to her."

"The living cannot commune with the dead." Graham motions to my bracelet like he knows what it's for, but it still won't be enough. "It isn't allowed."

I motion to Trill and Pearl. "I can talk to them. Why can't I talk to Babung?"

"You shouldn't even be here," Graham points out. "I don't know how you stepped through the veil, but it is breaking an entire *host* of rules. Not to mention, even if your grandmother *were* in the Hollow, she has no connection to this house. You won't find her here, no matter how hard you look."

My heart falters. "You mean she might still be in California?" How am I supposed to help her if there's three thousand miles between us?

"I cannot tell you what happened to her soul," Graham says. "But try not to worry—most ghosts move on quite easily. The ones who stay only do so because they have something left to do."

"Babung had plenty of things left to do. I didn't even get a chance to say goodbye." I twist my mouth. "She had dementia and forgot almost everything—even me. How is she going to cross over if she doesn't even know who she is?" My voice splinters. "Can you at least get a message to her, so she knows I'm looking for her?"

If she remembers me, she'll come and find me. And if she doesn't . . .

I'll just have to find another way.

Graham is silent for a long time. "I'm sorry," he says. "I cannot interfere."

Pearl rolls her eyes. "Don't waste your time—Graham's about as helpful as a snowman in July. You'd have better luck asking one of *us* to take your grandmother a message." The moment I open my mouth, she holds up a hand. "I didn't say we *could* help you—I was just pointing out that Graham *won't*." She shrugs like it's pointless to even try. "Leaving this house has repercussions. We've already lost all our memories from before we died, but going outside makes us forget all our memories from *after* we died, too. When Lock tried to leave, he could barely remember the way back—and he was only a few steps from the porch!"

"Poor Lock," Trill says softly, eyes still half-closed. "He was never the same after that."

Lifting my shoulders, I meet Graham's gaze. "If I left the house . . . Would I lose my memories, too?"

"My knowledge on what happens to a living child in the Hollow is limited—but even if you could safely step foot outside this house, there'd be nowhere for you to go." Graham points toward the window. "See for yourself."

I walk across the room to look outside and find . . . nothing.

No moon, or gardens, or streetlights. All I can see is an expanse of gray nothingness, stretching into the distance like a heavy fog.

"Where you are now is merely an imprint. It exists because

it makes sense to the ghosts who are stuck here. But it does not lead anywhere." Graham tucks his hands behind himself and lifts his chin. "And it will not last forever. Not without their memories to hold it together, which as you can see, are destined to fade with time."

For the ghosts of Honeyfield Hall, this house really is their prison.

It's also their end.

I ball my hands. "That's not good enough. Someone has to help them."

"No one helps the lost souls in the Hollow." Trill looks up from the piano, eyes a dull gray. "We are the forgotten ones. And someday we will forget even that."

I turn away from Graham and face the ghosts. *"I'll* help you. I'll help you remember who you are so you can move on to the afterlife."

It's the right thing to do. It's what I hope someone would do for Babung, if they found her trapped in the Hollow.

"You would do all that, just to get a message to your grand-mother?" Pearl asks softly.

"I would do it anyway," I say, and I mean it. "It's not right that you're forgetting and nobody is doing anything to stop it." I meet her gaze and try not to cry. "But after I help you leave this place, if you could find my grandma, and give her a message for me . . ."

Pearl bows her head. "Consider it a promise—if you free us

from the Hollow, we will take any message to your grandma that you like."

The chandelier above us trembles in response, and a groan builds beneath the room like the house is coming to life.

From somewhere deep in the mist, a monster roars.

Trill stops playing abruptly, fingers striking a wrong chord. "It's awake," she says softly. "After all this time."

Pearl stands and presses a hand to her chest. "It's never been able to come inside before. But . . . perhaps you should come away from the window, just in case."

I shouldn't look—every alarm bell in my brain is screaming at me *not to look*—but I turn around to face the gray nothingness outside.

A shadow slams against the glass, rattling the frame and making the lights in the room flicker. It howls, menacing, but it's moving too fast for me to see clearly.

Despite the fear taking over my body, Graham looks relatively calm. "How did you do that?" he asks, lifting an eyebrow. "How did you call the lost one?"

"I-I didn't do anything." I look from the shadow, to Graham, to the door behind me that's still ajar.

Where the skeleton key still sits inside the lock.

Graham's voice turns breathy. "So *that's* how you got here."

I don't get a chance to reply, because the shadow smashes into the window again, this time making the ceiling shudder.

There's a loud *snap* overhead, and the chandelier falls like a felled tree and shatters against the floor.

In an instant, the branches become leaves, exploding in every direction. They scatter, colors shifting from emerald green to a rotted brown, until they shrivel at my feet and turn to ash.

Pearl screams. Trill vanishes into the next wall.

"A word of advice?" Graham says, tipping his hat in farewell. "Never leave a key in a door. You don't know who might try to lock it behind you." He fades away like a cloud of smoke. One second he's there, and the next he's—

I blink, staring at the window and wondering who it was I was just speaking to, when the shadow pounds at the glass once more, like it's trying desperately to get inside.

It wants something. Something it's only just realized I have.

The key, my thoughts growl. *You left the key in the door.*

The last of the candlelight flickers into darkness, and suddenly I'm racing across the room like my life depends on it. And maybe it does. Maybe without the skeleton key, I'd be nothing more than a lost soul, too.

I'm nearly to the door when the monster lets out a ferocious, guttural snarl. It's like thunder and sorrow and *pain*. It doesn't sound human. It doesn't sound like anything I've ever heard before.

If it makes it through the window while I'm still here . . .

I throw myself over the threshold and yank the door shut. The doorknob rattles violently as I twist the key free.

The light below the door vanishes, and the lock shrinks from the mouth of a monster to an ordinary keyhole, but I don't wait to make sure I'm safe.

I run without looking back.

CHAPTER FOURTEEN

I'm racing down the hallway with a burning throat and aching ribs, when I realize I'm about to collide headfirst into a dark figure. I manage to skirt around them just before impact, and stumble against the wall with a loud *thud*.

Hazel's blue eyes widen. "Eliot!" She blinks, watching the way my breaths heave in and out of me. "What happened? Are you okay?"

I should be relieved it's Hazel and not the shadow monster, but I'm too panic-stricken to form any coherent thoughts. "I—the door—and I locked—" I try to hold on to my words, but they sift around my head like sand, too hard to grasp.

Ghosts are real.

Monsters are real.

And I just found a doorway to the Hollow.

Hazel attempts to translate. "You . . . locked a door?"

"No. I mean, yes—but that's not important," I say, flustered. Maybe I'm silly for trusting someone I barely know, but I can't keep this secret to myself. I need to tell someone what I *saw*. "I think I just stepped through some kind of portal world. A place where *ghosts* exist."

Hazel scrunches her face. "I'm not following."

I hold out the skeleton key in my palm, but it's practically a shadow in the dimly lit hall. "It's this key—it changed the shape of the lock on the door, and when I walked through it, I met a bunch of ghosts who are losing their memories. And a *smoke monster* was trying to steal the key!"

"They need a key to get through the door?" She giggles, and it would be completely infectious if my heart wasn't about to beat its way to oblivion. "Seems like kind of a sad excuse for a ghost. Aren't they supposed to walk through walls?"

My expression falters, and I fold my fingers back over the key protectively.

Hazel clasps her hands to her chest and says, "Oh—you're serious. As in, this isn't some kind of game."

"I know how it sounds." My shoulders are still trembling. "But I'm not making it up. The Hollow is *real*."

I wait for Hazel to tell me that I sound ridiculous, and that I'm weird, and that she doesn't want to be my friend after all.

But instead, Hazel says, "You trusted me with something important, and I just reacted like a jerk." She shakes her head. "I'm so sorry—can we try this again?" She holds up her hands and clears her throat. "Okay. Tell me about this portal world."

So I do. I tell her about the ghosts, and how they're trapped in between the veil. I know there are pieces I'm forgetting, because when I try to remember how I know so much about the ghosts, it feels like there are gaps in my memory. Like something—or someone—is missing entirely.

But I tell her everything I know, and I hope it's enough.

When I'm finished, Hazel pauses for emphasis. "Holy Hole in a Doughnut!"

I lift a brow, surprised at how quickly the tension is easing in my chest. "Um. What?"

Hazel smirks. "I heard it on TV. I always wanted to say it out loud."

The corner of my mouth twitches, but my eyes are still watching the hall, waiting for a monster to tear through the door.

I stare at my open palm and the gold key resting against my skin. "I found this in your grandma's greenhouse. My dad said it's called a skeleton key, but I don't think normal skeleton keys are meant to unlock ghost doors." I look at Hazel seriously. "Do you know why your grandma had it?"

Hazel shakes her head. "I have no idea. I've never seen it before. Are you sure it's definitely hers?"

"I mean, it's got to belong to this house, right? So if it isn't Mrs. Delvaux's, whose is it?"

And why was it just sitting on the floor of the greenhouse?

"Previous owner maybe?" Hazel offers.

"Maybe," I say.

"Will you show me the room?"

"I just told you there was a *monster* in there. It's dangerous!"

"Didn't the ghosts say it couldn't get inside? Maybe the house is protected." Hazel makes a face like she isn't afraid. "If there's a monster living in my house, I want to know what it looks like."

Mrs. Delvaux said Hazel was terrified of slugs, but here she is, fully prepared to face a smoke monster and go on a ghost-hunting mission with me.

Hazel might be the coolest person I've ever met.

"I guess we could have another look. It would be good to know if the monster really can't get in—especially since I'm planning on going back to help them," I say. "But I'll keep hold of the handle, and if there's any danger at all, we can pull it shut right away."

"This is the closest thing to an adventure I've ever had." She beams. "We're just like Batman and Robin."

I lead her down the corridor, and when we reach the door, I hold the key outside the lock. But this time, it doesn't shift or morph into anything else.

Frowning, I twist the key inside and shove the door open, making the hinges screech in response.

There's no monster waiting for us. There are no ghosts, either.

The room looks exactly the way it did the first time I saw it. The piano and couch are covered in white dust sheets. The wallpaper is peeling from the edges. There's no broken chandelier on the floor.

This isn't the Hollow at all.

Hazel hums and taps her chin. "Maybe the key only works when you're alone. Or maybe it only works for *you*."

I remove the key from the lock and stare at the curved edges. *The reason I can see ghosts is because I have a closeness to death.*

Didn't someone tell me that once?

No matter how hard I try to remember, the thought won't stick in my head, so I shake it away and trade it for another one.

"I think I need to do some research on Honeyfield Hall," I say, tucking the skeleton key back in my pocket. It doesn't matter where I found it—what matters is that I have to protect it. "If I can figure out who used to live in this house before Mrs. Delvaux, I might be able to find out who the ghosts are."

"Honeyfield Hall has been in the family for a long time," Hazel says. "But I could ask my grandma."

"No!" I say, a little too quickly. "It's just—if Mrs. Delvaux knew we were going through a portal world, she might not be happy about it. She would probably tell my parents too, and they're sort of under the impression that I'm on a break from anything ghost-related." If they knew what I was doing, and what I found, they might never let me come back.

Hazel lowers her voice. "So what you're saying is no grown-ups?"

I nod. "No grown-ups."

Before she can respond, a door opens downstairs. Hazel and I exchange a nervous glance and lean over the railing to get a better look. Light floods the downstairs hallway, and we watch Mrs. Delvaux's shadow move across the floorboards, each footstep creaking louder than the one before.

I hold my breath until the sounds fade and the shadow disappears.

"You should go while the coast is clear." Hazel glances at me. "If she sees you, she might find out you have the key."

I tilt my face toward her. "It means a lot that you want to help."

"I may not be able to see your ghost world, but I can totally provide moral support. Not to mention I know this house like the back of my hand." She twists her mouth, turning her hand over. "Which, now that I've said it out loud, is a weird thing to say. Who actually studies what the back of their hand looks like? Do you think if you saw a thousand hands, you'd be able to pick yours out from all the rest? Eyes, maybe. But not hands."

I stifle a laugh. "Is it weird that I've wondered that before too?"

Hazel grins, and I'm sure my heart beats a little faster.

"Thanks," I say. "And not just for helping—but for believing me about the ghosts, even though you have no proof."

"You told me it's true," she says easily. "That's more than enough for me."

I make my way back to my bike and realize that out of all the things I've experienced tonight, it isn't the monster that scares me most.

It's the thought of finally finding someone I can talk to the way I talked to Babung—and being terrified that someday they might disappear, too.

CHAPTER FIFTEEN

D oes Roseheart have a library?"

Mom and Dad look up from the table as if I'm an alien standing in the middle of the dining room and not their twelve-year-old daughter.

"There's one across from the hardware store." Mom sets her coffee mug down like she's finding her bearings. "Are you going to apply for a library card?"

Dad holds up his hands, impressed. "Look at you, integrating with the local community. I'm so proud!"

"That's not what I'm doing," I say dryly. "But Google isn't giving me the information I need, and I'm trying to research something." Mom looks nervous, so I add, "It's not about ghosts." Which is sort of true, since I'm researching a *house.*

Ghosts just happen to live there.

Mom relaxes. "You know, I was planning on picking up paint today. Maybe we could head into town together?"

"I can just take my bike," I say. "I have to go straight to Mrs. Delvaux's afterward anyway."

Mom takes another sip of coffee and waves her hand. "I

can call her and let her know you'll be a little late. It's not a problem."

I frown. "You have Mrs. Delvaux's phone number?"

Dad snorts. "Of course we do. We aren't going to let our daughter hang out at someone's house without exchanging contact information."

"You know, if you let me have a phone, we could exchange contact information ourselves and it would be way easier than having to go through a third party," I try. It would be so much better if I could text Hazel about my plans. If Mrs. Delvaux would ease up on her rules, Hazel could even meet me at the library and we could do research together.

"Not a chance," Dad says, holding up his mug like he's saying "But nice try."

"You can have a phone when you start high school," Mom says, and steps around the kitchen island to set her mug in the sink. "I'll grab my keys."

We get in the car and drive toward the main street. Mom points out some landmarks along the way—a local statue of a beloved dog, and a plaque that claims to be an exact point where lightning struck twice.

When we arrive at the hardware store, Mom parks the car out front and tells me she'll come and find me when she's done picking out paint. I head for the old brick building wedged between a locksmith and a hair salon, where a sign out front reads "Roseheart Library."

Inside, the building smells like worn pages and new carpet.

There's a big circular desk where a man with curly brown hair is typing at a computer. A woman stands beside him, organizing books onto a metal cart. Neither of them looks up when I walk in.

I follow the signs around the library until I find the history section, but there are so many books that it would take hours to go through them all. I find a computer instead and do a search for Honeyfield Hall.

Nothing comes up. But when I search for Roseheart, Maine, there are two results. The first is a book about gardens featuring several small towns across the East Coast. The second is a book called *Roseheart: A Local History*.

I wonder if it's intentional to use "local history" instead of just "history."

Babung and Dad are from Hawaii, and so are Babung's parents and grandparents. They've always called themselves "locals." Babung said it's the word for people who've lived on the islands for generations—people like my family, who came over from Japan and China in the late 1800s and early 1900s—who *aren't* Hawaiian.

"'Hawaiian' is for the Indigenous people of Hawaii—kānaka maoli," Babung would say. "We call ourselves locals—kamaʻāina—because we are people of the land who do not have Hawaiian ancestry. Language is something that changes over time, but no matter what word we use to describe ourselves, we must always respect the people and cultures whose land we are on."

I guess that technically makes everyone in Roseheart a "local" too, since Indigenous people lived here first. But I've never heard that word used the same way outside Hawaii.

I track down *Roseheart: A Local History* on one of the high shelves. It has a dark red spine and it's a lot thinner than I thought it would be, but it's full of old photographs and tidbits about the area. There's even a paragraph dedicated to the dog statue that Mom pointed out.

I don't see anything useful at first, but when I reach the page with a black-and-white photo of Honeyfield Hall, my heart quickens.

It's a photo of a little girl standing with her parents. There's a stone well behind them, and a row of massive hydrangea bushes that makes it appear as if the photo was taken in a secret garden. Written underneath the picture are the names Sarah Delvaux, George Delvaux, and Cora Delvaux.

The little girl . . . *Cora*.

Could that be Mrs. Delvaux?

The paragraph doesn't say a lot—just that the Delvauxs inherited the house from Mr. Charles Honeyfield, a reclusive war vet who was the last surviving member of the Honeyfield family. It also mentions that Mr. George Delvaux passed away shortly after moving into the house, which many believed was a result of the "Honeyfield Curse" that's plagued the house since the original family lived there.

A curse. My shoulders tense. Is this about the ghosts?

Did someone else see them too?

I turn the page, hoping to find out more, but the next section is about a vineyard that burned down years ago. There's nothing else about the Delvauxs *or* the Honeyfields.

I frown, flipping the page back and forth to see if I've somehow missed something, when Mom's voice makes me jump.

"This isn't the section I thought I'd find you in," she says in a hushed voice.

I snap the book shut like I'm hiding a secret. And I guess I am.

Mom eyes the cover, but she doesn't ask why I'm reading a book about Roseheart. She's probably too worried she'll jinx it.

"Did you find the paint you wanted?" I ask, hoping to change the subject.

Mom holds up a collection of color swatches. "I'm thinking 'buttermilk' or 'vanilla ripple.' I know you prefer the ones with food names."

It's true—I'd much rather paint my wall "orange creamsicle" than plain old "orange."

When Babung was alive, she let me pick out the paint for her bedroom. We settled on "mint macaron," even though "sea blue" was probably a nicer shade of blue-green.

I miss that color.

I miss everything about that house.

"We should paint the bathroom mint macaron," I say suddenly.

Mom hesitates, lining up the paint swatches in her hand

like she's getting ready to shuffle a deck of cards. She remembers the color—I can tell by the way she pushes out her bottom lip.

To my surprise, Mom nods. "Mint macaron sounds lovely."

She goes with me to the desk and helps me fill in all the information to register for a library card. When it comes out of the printer, it has my name on it and a place for my signature, along with a fancy Roseheart emblem in the corner.

It's . . . kind of cool.

I tuck it into my bag along with the book, and try not to pay attention to how proud Mom looks of me.

CHAPTER SIXTEEN

Mom drops me off at Mrs. Delvaux's front gate. I'm barely to the porch steps when I hear music blasting from one of the upstairs windows.

I've never heard music that loud coming from Honeyfield Hall before. In fact, I've never heard music coming from the house at *all*.

I look up, trying to make out which room it's coming from, when Mrs. Delvaux appears at the front door and waves me inside.

"Hazel is upstairs," she says with a sigh. "I've told her several times to turn the music down, but I'm certain it's only getting louder."

I frown. "Is she okay? Did something happen?"

Mrs. Delvaux glances toward the second-story balustrade. "I don't know. She frequently gets in these moods. I suppose if something *was* wrong, she wouldn't actually tell me."

I press a hand to my bag, where the library book is tucked away. "Could I go up and see her? There's something I wanted to talk to her about."

Mrs. Delvaux looks surprised. "I didn't know you two were getting along so well." She motions toward the stairs. "You're welcome to try. Maybe you'll have better luck than me."

I nod and take the steps two at a time, following the sound of blaring music until I reach a freshly carpeted hall. It's cleaner than some of the other places, and the white door I stop in front of is the only one I've seen with a new coat of paint.

I knock. "Hazel? It's Eliot."

I'm not sure if she can hear me over the music, so I knock again, louder this time.

"I said *go away!*" she shouts from the other side of the door.

I flinch, tugging the bag at my hip. I thought she'd want to know what I found. I thought she'd be *excited*.

I retreat back down the stairs and find Mrs. Delvaux waiting at the bottom.

I shrug, sheepish. "She didn't want to talk, I guess." I think the hurt must be written all over my face, because Mrs. Delvaux looks at me like I'm a wounded animal.

She folds her hands together. "I'll get us some cake and tea. Maybe she'll come down for food." She ushers me toward the sitting room and whispers over my shoulder, "Don't take it personally. If you let everyone's bad days ruin yours, you'll never be happy."

I take a seat on one of the couches while Mrs. Delvaux heads for the kitchen. The weight of the bag sits in my lap.

The plan was to tell Hazel about the book, and look for

answers together. But if she isn't in the mood to talk today, I'll just have to do this next part on my own.

It's not like she can go to the Hollow with you, I think. *You can tell her everything the next time you see her.*

I dig the skeleton key out of my bag, turn my head, and listen for the sound of Mrs. Delvaux in the other room. When I'm certain the coast is clear, I jump up and grab the handle of the nearest door, shutting myself into the sitting room.

I lift the key to the lock and take a breath.

The keyhole morphs into the jaws of a monster. I turn the lock until it clicks, and slowly push the door open.

The hallway looks similar to Mrs. Delvaux's house in shape, but the decor in the Hollow is drastically different. The makeshift stairs are roots of a tree, sanded on top but rough on the sides. Vines trail from the ceiling where the light fixtures used to be, and some of the plaster seems to be breaking off the walls.

But all the doors are where they should be, and I don't see or hear any evidence of the shadow monster, so . . . so far so good?

I remove the skeleton key, tuck it safely in my bag, and make my way upstairs. Maybe one of the ghosts here can tell me more about the photo in *Roseheart: A Local History*.

And the curse, my mind adds, solemn.

There's no bass drum beating through the walls. Hazel's music doesn't exist in this place—neither does she, I suppose. Normally houses are filled with the kinds of sounds nobody really pays attention to, like cars rolling in the distance, or the groan of an air conditioner. But on this side of the veil, it's like there's an *absence* of sound.

Which is why the moment I hear whispering coming from one of the rooms, my ears perk up like a rabbit in the woods.

No—not whispering. *Reciting.*

"*I hold life without a heartbeat, I have a face but cannot see, I am a tree that's cold*—no, no, no, that's not it at all!" the voice growls, exasperated.

I peek into the room and see a study with tall bookshelves that stretch the whole way around the room. Random branches seem to have broken through some of the shelves, but the wooden floors have the same polished gleam as the piano room. Apart from the branches, the only thing that looks oddly out of place is the position of the books. Instead of the spines facing outward, the pages do.

A man I've never seen before sits at a desk with his head resting in his palms. A hint of ivy has sprouted near his feet and is winding quietly around his ankles. Not that he seems to have noticed—he's too busy repeating the same lines, again and again, trying to remember how they end.

"*I am a tree at night*—no—*the cold stars I cannot see*—no, no, no. Why can't I remember?" He drags his fingers against his glowing skin.

I shift near the doorway, and one of the floorboards buckles in response. The sound is enough to draw the ghost's attention, and his eyes snap to mine.

"Do I know you?" he asks, puzzled.

I press a hand to the doorframe, unsure whether it's safe—or stable enough—to step inside. "I was here yesterday. But I don't think I remember seeing you."

I assumed there were only four ghosts in this house. But what if there are more? What if there are hundreds?

I promised to help, and I will. But maybe this job is too big for a single summer. Maybe this job will take a *lifetime*.

He drops his hands to the table. "Yesterday . . ."

I pause. "I told Trill and Pearl I'd help the ghosts remember who they are."

His brow twitches. "Help?" A laugh bursts out of him like a horn, and in a single flash, he shrinks into the size of a boy.

I lean back in alarm.

Lock grins wildly. "Those two won't help you!" he squeaks. "None of the others ever do. They don't understand. They won't help me *find it*."

"That's why I came back. I brought a book—"

Lock stands abruptly, and the ivy at his ankles snaps before turning to ash. He stomps toward the shelves and reaches for one of the books. The pages fly from the shelf—and they don't stop. Paper is flung in every direction, sheets exploding from the book like they're infinite.

The dozens of pages all over the floor . . . They're *blank*.

"The books don't help," Lock cries, scratching his hair with curled fingers. "I can't read them. I've *forgotten*." He plants his face back in his palms, shoulders sinking, and stretches into a man again. "I need to find something important. Something lost."

Beneath his sobs, his body shudders, and the bookshelf stops spraying paper into the room. On the floor, the pieces of paper curl up from the ends like they're caught on fire, fizzling into more ash.

I reach into my bag for the book on Roseheart, turn the page to the Delvaux family photo, and walk carefully to where Lock is standing.

He peeks through his glowing fingers. "Your book—it's different from mine."

"It's a library book. From the living world."

"I miss reading. There's so much life in a good story."

I hold the book up, trying to focus his attention. "Do you recognize any of the people in this photo?"

"She took them all," he says, voice hollow. "All the things we need to find."

I follow his gaze to the photograph. "Which one? Cora or Sarah?"

He points to the girl. "I saw her once. I wasn't meant to—I wandered too far from the house and got lost. But I know what she did." Lock paces across the room, half floating, half stumbling through the desk with each turn. "She hid everything away—it's impossible to find them all without the map. And I couldn't get it open without the key."

"Key?" I blink, and reach into my bag for the skeleton key. "Are you talking about this?"

Lock plants his feet in front of me, eyes wide, but I clutch the key to my chest on instinct, too afraid of his hungry eyes. He hisses, sharp as a blade, and turns his back to me. He shrinks, smaller and smaller, until he's the size of a child again. Even though I can't see his face, I hear him sniffling.

"I'm sorry," I say, gripping the key. "But if I lose this, I might never be able to get home."

"Home?" His voice turns into an echo. "I had a home once. A big, beautiful house on a hill."

"Are you talking about Honeyfield Hall?"

He looks delighted. "Yes, that's right! It was a beautiful house. Right at the top of a hill."

"This *is* Honeyfield Hall." I motion around the room. "We're standing inside it." Or at least, a distorted version of it.

Lock stares at the ceiling and gasps. "That's right. It's *here*." He races for the wall, and I hurry after him.

I trail Lock as he darts in and out of the corridor, and follow him up another set of stairs. At the end of the next hallway is an oak tree. Its trunk bursts from the floor, curving upward into a narrow incline. Its highest branches have punctured right through the attic, and beside the jagged hole, a hatch remains.

Lock's feet barely touch the ground as he scrambles up the tree and vanishes through the ceiling.

I wedge my foot against the bark, searching for places to grab hold of, and climb. A few branches stick out from the sides, and I use them to lift myself farther up the tree, until eventually I reach the attic hatch. I grab the handle and throw the door open, listening as it cracks against the floor.

Light pours through a glass window in the roof, making the dust ripple around us like microscopic fireflies. I haul myself over the ledge and find Lock hovering above a small wooden chest.

He points at me with a small finger. "You should try your key."

I stare at the latch. "What's inside?"

Lock blinks, then shakes his head like he doesn't know.

Or doesn't remember.

I hold out the skeleton key, but the hole doesn't shift like the doors downstairs. As far as I can tell, this is an ordinary lock.

The key fits, the same way it did when I tried to show Hazel the piano room, and I unlock the trunk. Lifting the lid, I peek over the edge to see what's inside, and find a single piece of folded parchment. I pick it up, offering it to Lock, but he thumps his head with his knuckles.

"No, no, no. I left something here," he cries, and he stretches once more into the height of a full-grown man. "She took it. I saw her. She *took it away*."

I start to unfold the paper, eyes trailing over the swooping cursive. It's the poem Lock was reciting.

But it's incomplete.

There are words scattered across the page—*tree, face, stolen, heartbeat*—but they disappear and reappear all over the page, glinting with wet ink like the words aren't permanent. Like they *can't* be permanent.

"I don't understand what it says." I tilt the parchment toward Lock. "The words keep changing."

But he doesn't seem to hear me. "It should've been here. They all should've been here." He drifts back through the walls, dragging his feet in the air behind him.

I turn back to the letter, when I hear the sound of metal talons scraping along the roof. They make the tiles rattle and click, like a giant bird is out there hunting for its prey.

I stare at the small window that looks out into the gray mist.

The monster—it's out there.

I think it's looking for me.

I need to get back to the living world—before the monster sees me, and before Mrs. Delvaux realizes I'm missing.

I shove the parchment in my bag, hurry for the hatch, and leave the attic behind.

CHAPTER SEVENTEEN

When I'm back in the sitting room, I lock the door to the Hollow and give the handle a sharp turn. The door creaks open, and where I expect to see an empty hallway, I find Hazel.

She's wearing a thin cardigan with blue and white stripes that's baggy around the arms. Her chestnut hair frames her face in loose waves, and there's a dark reddishness to it I hadn't noticed before. She has more freckles than I remember too—I think it's because I've only ever seen Hazel in the dark or behind a screen door.

I'm so busy staring at her that it takes me a minute to remember where I am, and where I just came from.

Eyes wide, she hurries into the room and looks me up and down like she can't believe I'm really here. I think I might be looking at her the same way.

When we speak, our voices collide together, words tumbling out at the exact same time.

"I just came back from the Hollow!"

"I had no idea you were here!"

We exchange looks of puzzlement.

"I knocked on your bedroom door earlier," I tell her.

"Really?" Hazel drops her hands. "I didn't hear you."

One of my twin buns is starting to come loose, and I tuck a fallen strand of hair behind my ear. "You, uh, told me to go away."

"I'm sorry," she says in earnest. "The music was so loud—I didn't know it was you."

I glance up at the ceiling, and realize it's gone quiet. Quiet enough to hear the whistle of the teapot next door.

I guess it was Mrs. Delvaux she was yelling at all along, and not me.

I shrug, face curving into an awkward grin. "That's a relief. Because I have a bunch of things to tell you. Starting with—"

Mrs. Delvaux appears with a tray of cake and a teapot painted with blue flowers. "Thank goodness the music has stopped. I can finally hear myself think," she huffs just as Hazel and I scoot out of the way. She sets the tray on the low table and frowns. "Ah. I forgot the teacups."

Mrs. Delvaux shuffles back out of the room, and Hazel takes a seat beside me on one of the patterned sofas.

I whip out the book as fast as I can and skip to the page with the photograph. I point to the girl. "Is this your grandma?"

Hazel stares, forehead crumpling. "I think so. Why?"

"I went back," I whisper in a low voice. "I spoke to one of the ghosts—Lock—and he says this girl took something of his. Something from the attic. And then I found—"

Mrs. Delvaux reappears with a pair of teacups and sets them down on the tray, and I tuck the book back into my bag before she notices.

"Help yourself," Mrs. Delvaux urges, and sits gracefully in the opposite chair. "There's walnuts in the ginger cake. You don't have any food allergies, do you?"

"Not to walnuts," I say, fighting to appear normal. "Kiwi makes my mouth feel tingly though."

"What's kiwi?" Hazel asks, peering curiously at the cake.

"You've never had kiwi before?" I look between Hazel and Mrs. Delvaux. "It's the green fruit that's fuzzy and brown on the outside. My dad says you can eat the skin, but I don't know anyone besides him who does."

"I've never tried it," Hazel says.

Mrs. Delvaux peers down her nose. "You think I'd have a house this size and not know my way around a luncheon? Of *course* I know what kiwi is."

"She hasn't hosted a party in years," Hazel mutters under her breath. "All she does is watch movies, sleep, and tell me I have terrible taste in music."

I start to laugh, but Mrs. Delvaux lifts a brow in warning and I clamp my mouth shut.

Hazel giggles beside me.

"You know, there was a time when people actually *liked* coming to this house." Mrs. Delvaux glares out the window for an extra second. "But people treat you different when you get older. You get more wrinkles, and your hair turns gray, and suddenly young people start looking at you like you're a piece of furniture rather than a person with feelings."

Babung never spoke like that. She always said she loved her wrinkles, and that they were signs that she got to live a long and happy life with the people she loved most.

Maybe that's the difference though. Babung had people who loved her, and Mrs. Delvaux has . . .

I glance at Hazel, who looks as guilty as I feel.

"I don't think you're a piece of furniture," I say quietly. "And I *do* like coming here."

Mrs. Delvaux looks at me like she's only just remembered I'm here. "That's kind of you to say. Please don't mind me—I can be a little grumpy now and then, that's all. It has nothing to do with you." She folds her hands in her lap and motions to the table. "Go on. Don't let the cake go to waste, hmm?"

Dorothy appears on the windowsill and lets out a tired mew.

Mrs. Delvaux turns, distracted, and the cadence in her voice turns into a song. "Why, Miss Dottie, I don't think I've seen you since breakfast!"

Hazel reaches for the teapot. I don't know if she moves too fast or doesn't grip the handle tight enough, but all I hear is the collision of porcelain, and by the time I look down to see what happened, the walnut cake is drowning in steaming hot tea.

I jump to my feet.

Hazel is frozen. "I'm sorry—it was an accident."

Mrs. Delvaux turns quickly, assessing the damage. When it's clear no one is burned or hurt, she seems to relax. "Don't worry. It's nothing we can't clean up." She scoops up Dorothy from the windowsill and sets her on the couch before grabbing the tray of soggy cake remains. "You may as well head outside while I tidy up. I'll bring some new snacks to the porch, and then we can get started on replanting the marigolds," she says before disappearing around the corner.

"I'm sorry," Hazel repeats. "I don't know what happened."

"It's not a big deal," I say gently. "It's just a spill."

But Hazel still looks like she's in a trance. "I'm always disappointing her. It's never on purpose, but I can't seem to help it."

"You didn't do anything wrong. And Mrs. Delvaux didn't care at all about the tea."

"She doesn't show it when people are around. But I can tell. I can always tell."

I bite my lip. I don't know why she's so upset—it didn't seem like a big deal to me. But I guess she knows her grandma way better than I do, and if I was upset about my parents, the last thing I'd want is for someone to tell me I was imagining it.

I just wish there was something I could say that would cheer Hazel up.

I pause. "Do you want to see what I found in the attic?" I reach into my bag for the folded parchment, but Hazel stands abruptly, ignoring the letter in my outstretched hand, and hurries out of the room without saying a word.

"Wait!" I call after her, just as Mrs. Delvaux reenters the room with a rag and some cleaning spray. I tuck the letter behind my back.

"Not in the mood for gardening today, hmm?" Her eyes flicker with humor. "Are you making a run for it?"

"It's not that," I correct, stumbling over my words. "It's just—I was talking to Hazel, and she got upset and ran off."

Mrs. Delvaux moves for the table. "She does that. I can't remember the last time I *didn't* upset her. It was like that with her father, too. Talking to him always felt more difficult than it needed to be."

Sometimes I think I have that problem with Mom and Dad.

I tell Mrs. Delvaux what I'd tell them, if they ever bothered to ask. "Relationships are usually hard when you're trying to make someone be something they're not." I lift my shoulders. "Most people just want you to get to know them, and love them even if you think their hobbies are weird."

She looks up, fingers tightening around the rag. She opens her mouth like she wants to say something but thinks better of it. "Go on," she says, ushering me toward the door. "Let me get this cleaned up and I'll meet you outside."

I take three steps backward out of the room and hurry for the back door. The grandfather clock chimes as I pass. I ignore my reflection in the glass and the way it makes *me* look like a ghost, and I make my way down the porch steps toward the disheveled flower bed.

When I'm certain I'm alone, I look down at my fist—at where the letter had been—and gasp in disbelief as the parchment becomes dust in my palm, vanishing into thin air.

I stare at my empty hand, turning my fingers over just to make sure I'm not imagining things.

"You can't steal from the Hollow," Graham's voice sounds from the porch.

I reel, only to find him sitting quite contentedly on the rickety swing. His hat is tipped low, but it isn't enough of a shadow to hide the vibrant gold hue of his irises.

He rocks back and forth. "Whatever you're searching for, you'll need to find on this side of the veil."

I lower my hands. "I don't think they sell magic parchment in Roseheart."

His mouth curves. "Perhaps there are other things to be found."

"You talk in riddles. I never understand what you mean."

Graham merely smiles, watching me with that strange shine in his eyes.

My brows knot. "You seem to know everything about everything. I'm guessing you even know what the ghosts need in order to move on to the other side. So why won't you help them?"

"I told you before—it's against the rules for me to interfere with the Hollow."

I stare at the garden and imagine the gray mist stretching into infinity. "But it's not against the rules for *me* to interfere . . ." My mind turns and turns like it's studying every corner of a puzzle. "Is it breaking the rules to answer my questions?"

"That depends on the question. But be quick—I have somewhere else to be."

"Why can I remember some of the things you tell me, but I can never remember *you*?"

"It's easy to forget someone you never wanted to see in the first place," he says, chuckling darkly.

I cross my arms. "Do you know where the skeleton key came from?"

"Yes."

"Did you leave it for me to find?"

"I most certainly did not," he clarifies, the disapproval on his face clear.

"Okay. Well, what about the monster?"

"That's not a full question."

"Do you know what it wants?"

He sighs. "I always liked this house, and its ghosts. There was something . . . sentimental about them." Graham stands, straightening his waistcoat and checking his pocket watch. "I mustn't be late," he says, and makes his way around the porch.

"Wait!" I call after him, the urgency burning in my throat. "Can't you at least give me a clue?"

"I thought that's what I was doing," he notes, voice already fading around the corner.

The moment Graham leaves, I feel a shift in the breeze. The absence of something magical.

I blink a few times, wondering why I'm standing near the porch steps when I still need to find Hazel and tell her about the letter—

I glance at my empty palm.

That's right. The parchment—it vanished. Because . . . because . . .

Whatever I'm looking for, I need to find on this side of the veil.

I rub my temple, trying to ease the dull ache growing behind my skull, and wait for Mrs. Delvaux near the basket of marigold seeds. She returns with sandwiches and lemonade, and after we eat, she teaches me how to rake the soil into a fine, crumbly texture, and shows me the perfect distance to sow the seeds.

I don't get a chance to tell Hazel about the letter, because she doesn't come back downstairs.

CHAPTER EIGHTEEN

I'm standing inside Honeyfield Hall, shuddering against the cold. Every window is layered with frost, and my breath is visible in the air in front of me. I tuck my arms around myself and walk farther through the hallway, quickening my steps because I know I'm not alone.

Even though I can't see it, I feel its presence. The shadow monster trails behind me. *Hunting* me.

I reach for the closest door, but the handle won't budge. I try the next door, and the next door, and the next, but it's no use. They're all locked.

Frowning, my hand drifts into my pocket, searching for the familiar edges of the skeleton key. But it isn't there.

"Looking for this?" says a dark voice.

I spin around, terrified, and see the black mist approaching, crackling like wildfire, with eyes that glow a terrible, familiar gold.

I try to scream, but no sound comes out. So instead, I run.

It feels like moving through peanut butter. I'm slower than I've ever been—like there's an invisible force pushing against me, fighting my every step. I barely make it to the stairs when I hear the figure turn the corner and call my name.

"Eliot."

I freeze, and my entire body goes hollow.

That voice . . .

It can't be.

I turn toward the sound. "Babung?" I call to the mist, too hopeful to hide my longing.

The shadowy figure begins to shift, and the darkness clears away like a fading fog. In the center is a woman with glowing white skin and tired, dark eyes. Her lips press together, but she doesn't look at me. She looks *past* me.

She doesn't recognize me. She doesn't realize who I am.

My grandmother turns, calling my name again and again to the walls and the ceiling and everything around her. *Eliot. Eliot. Eliot.*

"Babung—it's me!" I shout. "I'm right here!"

But Babung's ghost only reels back in alarm and retreats into the shadows of the corridor.

"Don't go!" I plead. "I've been looking everywhere for you."

Babung's ghost doesn't stop, and I chase her back down the hallway, tears flooding my eyes.

"*Please*," I beg. "Please remember me."

Babung vanishes into the room at the end of the hall. When I reach the doorway, the ghosts of Honeyfield Hall are already there, blocking the way. All four of them, standing like a barely corporeal gate. One with gray curls. One with slender hands. One with a mustache. And one with the face of a child.

"You can't come in," Pearl says. "This is no place for the living."

"But I need to talk to Babung!" I sob in ugly, desperate breaths. "I need to tell her who I am. I need to make her *remember*."

"You can't talk to her," Trill says. "You'll never be able to talk to her again."

"Why not?" I demand.

"Because," Lock replies, crossing his small arms. "You broke your promise. You didn't save us. And now it's too late."

Hatter slams the door shut. Before I have time to reach for the handle, I hear the lock click into place, shutting me out forever.

My eyes flash open in the darkness of my bedroom and I bolt upright, breaths wild and uncontrolled. My fingers scramble across my quilt, trying to remember where I am.

Moonlight peeks through the gap in the curtains, making Babung's Obon offering glimmer, and I sink with understanding.

It was just a dream.

There are no ghosts in my room.

The low rumble of voices is barely audible, but it's still hard to ignore. My bedside clock says it's nearly midnight. It's not unusual for Mom and Dad to be up late. Ever since they started the house project, it seems like they do everything they can not to sleep at all.

I push the covers off and tiptoe into the corridor. Maybe they can't sleep either. Maybe they have nightmares about Babung, too.

I don't know what I'm expecting to find—comfort? Understanding? Someone to talk to?

But instead, I find my parents sitting on a white sheet in the partially renovated office, surrounded by half-painted walls, eating fried egg sandwiches and drinking fruit cider like they're having a late-night picnic.

And they're *giggling*.

Dad's always been a joker, but Mom hasn't seemed to find anything funny in over a year. She looks relaxed. *Happy.* And more like her old self than she ever is with me.

I don't get it. I don't get any of it.

Babung has been gone for six months, but it still feels like six days. Like she was here one moment and gone the next, and I don't know how my parents find it so easy to just act like it never happened. Like something awful and horrible didn't rip apart the fabric of our family.

I back away, jaw clenched, and bury myself under my covers until I'm a part of the darkness.

It's not fair to be mad at Mom and Dad for moving on, but I guess I always thought that if our family lost someone, we'd miss that person together. But my parents . . .

My parents got us a brand-new life.

I squeeze my pillow tight, hating how helpless I feel when it comes to my grandma. She was supposed to be somewhere I could find her—but instead, I found the ghosts of Honeyfield Hall. Pearl. Trill. Hatter. Lock.

The only way to get a message to Babung is to set them free—but I have absolutely no idea where to start. And if I don't uncover whatever it is they've forgotten, they'll be stuck between the veil forever.

I'll never see my grandma again, and they'll never be able to remember who they are.

I can't let that happen to them.

I can't let that happen to anyone ever again.

CHAPTER NINETEEN

The next day after breakfast, I grab my bike and head to Mrs. Delvaux's house. I turn down the first street, and then the second, when I spot Sunny and her friends at the opposite end of the road.

My chest tightens. I haven't seen them since the day they left me at Honeyfield Hall, like I was the punchline of a cruel joke. I knew it was inevitable that I'd run into them eventually—it's a small town, after all—but I guess I'm not as prepared as I thought I'd be.

They don't notice me. I'm still too far away, and I doubt I made the same impression on them as they did on me. So I veer up the nearest off-road path and try to put as much distance between us as possible.

In some twisted way, I suppose they did me a favor. If they hadn't dared me to knock on Mrs. Delvaux's door, I never would've gotten in trouble. I wouldn't have met Hazel, or had a summer job, or found a key to the Hollow.

But it doesn't feel nice to be laughed at. Being laughed at is how I lost my best friend in California. Over a *candy* gram, of all things.

Cassie had been desperate for one. "Brittany Greene already got *three!*" she'd complained one day at school. "*Everyone* has a crush on Brittany because she has nice hair and the best clothes. I wish someone had a crush on me."

"You have much nicer hair than Brittany," I'd told her. It was true, but I also really, really wanted to cheer her up.

"You are my favorite person in the whole school," Cassie had said, and she was beaming on the outside.

I was beaming on the inside.

The next day, I bought a candy gram for Cassie. It arrived in the middle of science class. Cassie had perked up when she heard her name; she looked like she'd won a contest. Like a candy gram was a sign of success.

I didn't care about winning contests, but I wanted Cassie to be happy. When she read my note, her smile got bigger and bigger—until she got to the bottom where my name was, and then her smile disappeared altogether.

"Oh," was all she'd said, and she started to fold the card back up.

Lucas Garcia was sitting behind her. He'd leaned over just in time to read the name.

"Eliot?" He'd snorted, staring at me with muffled laughter. "You sent your friend a candy gram? You know that's supposed to be for Valentine's Day crushes, right?"

My cheeks started to turn pink. I didn't know what to say.

Cassie hadn't noticed—she was too busy arguing with Lucas. "They don't *have* to be for crushes. Friends can send candy grams too. It doesn't mean anything." And then she looked straight at me. "Right, Eliot?"

She wanted me to agree. To clarify that it was just a friendly note. *That it didn't mean anything.*

But for some reason, when Cassie asked me to say the words out loud, I just . . . couldn't.

Everyone started laughing after that. They sang songs, and made jokes, and pointed their fingers.

"Eliot just confessed her love!"

"Cassie's got a date to the Valentine's Day dance!"

"Eliot and Cassie sitting in a tree . . ."

Our teacher told everyone to put their candy grams away and return to their work. But it was too late. I shared a secret I didn't even know I was keeping, and I didn't even have to say a word.

After that, Cassie acted different. She got quieter and quieter, and eventually one day I walked into the cafeteria and found Cassie sitting at a new table, with different friends, and no empty chairs.

I told Babung what happened, and she had nodded like she understood more than I did. She said I didn't do anything wrong; that sometimes kids just get embarrassed and don't know how to explain it in words. She said Cassie was probably acting that way because of something *she* was going through—and that it had nothing to do with me.

Except it felt like it had everything to do with me.

Babung always seemed to know everything, even the unspoken things, and she told me, "If there's ever anything you want to talk to me about, I'll always be here for you, Eliot-Chan."

But for all Babung knew about life and the world and all the unspoken things, she still couldn't keep a promise that big. And I never got the chance to tell her the truth that is still bubbling its way up inside me, bursting to get out.

There are so many things I still need to tell her.

So many things I want her to remember.

I pedal faster, leaving Sunny and her friends and the memory of my old school behind.

A chain-link fence is partially blocking the road. There's a fallen construction sign lying on its side, but I can't see what it says. I consider turning around and going back the other way, when I notice the gate isn't locked, so I slip through the opening and race down the dirt track.

Enormous trees line both sides of the path, arching overhead like an oak tunnel. It winds all the way around the massive hillside. When I break through the clearing, I see Honeyfield Hall at the top of the hill.

I found a shortcut, I think to myself, pleased. *Maybe if I keep using it, I can avoid Sunny and her friends for the rest of the summer.*

I make my way toward the iron gates and park my bike next to the porch.

"You came a different way," Mrs. Delvaux remarks from the doorway.

I point over the road. "There's a trail that cuts right through the neighborhood."

"That's the old railway line. The grocer used to come through there when I was a little girl. I still remember the sound of his station wagon, like it had run twenty miles up a hill in the snow." She frowns. "Isn't that a construction site now? They've been talking about flattening the whole lot for ages and filling it with apartments."

"The fence wasn't locked," I say with a shrug. "It didn't look like there was any work going on."

"I'm sure they'll get around to it one day. Just be careful riding your bike there. I don't want you to get hurt if they've got machinery and things lying around." She shuts the door behind her and ushers me around the corner. "It's supposed to be a hot afternoon—but I bet we can get some cabbage planted before the sun starts to blaze."

We only manage thirty minutes before Mrs. Delvaux takes one look at the sun and gives in.

"Tell you what—I've got some indoor plants that need repotting. Let's spend today in the shade." She leaves her gloves beside the gardening tools, climbs the steps, and I follow her inside.

I've never repotted a houseplant before, and I make a bigger mess than Mrs. Delvaux expected. But she's patient—nearly as patient as Babung—and doesn't seem to mind that there's soil all over her conservatory floor.

"There's a broom in the hall cupboard," she says, snipping a few of the leaves that look out of place. "Would you mind bringing it here?"

I head back through the house, struggling to figure out which hall cupboard she means, when I run into Hazel near the stairs.

The second she spots me, her cheeks dimple. I don't know why she always looks so surprised to see me, but it's nice to think she looks forward to seeing me as much as I look forward to seeing her.

If it had been Hazel with the candy gram instead of Cassie . . . would she have acted differently?

I motion behind me, even though I've sort of lost track of which direction the sunroom is. "Your grandma is repotting some kind of plant that smells like lemon sherbet. And, super random fact, but I learned today that some people say sher-but, some people say sher-bert, and some people say sore-bay, even though, technically, sorbet is a totally different thing."

Hazel steps closer, grinning. "That's a lot of confusion over a palette cleanser."

"Yeah." I hold out my arms like I'm checking my sleeves. "I think it's all over me now, too."

She leans in without warning to smell my wrist and I stiffen, cheeks turning carnation pink.

When she straightens, she tilts her head. "I can't smell anything."

"Oh . . . er . . ." I tangle my fingers together, hoping I don't look as nervous as I feel. "I can show you the plant if you want. Your grandma has, like, three of them."

"I'm more interested in what you were trying to tell me yesterday." She runs a hand against her neck, blushing slightly. "You know—before I got so upset."

I shuffle my feet. "If you don't mind me asking, why *did* you get so upset?"

She twists her mouth like she's untangling a thought. "My relationship with my grandma, and my parents . . . It's complicated. My mom and dad have this idea in their head of who I'm supposed to grow into, and how I'm supposed to behave. All I really want is for them to listen to me sometimes, you know? But instead, they leave me here in this house, where my grandma listens to me even less." She folds the sleeves of her cardigan over her fingers, the way I do when I'm nervous. "I hate being here. Usually, I hate it so much that all I want to do is run away, but I can't because, well, family ties and all that. But I never hate this house when you're around."

At first, I don't know what to say. She poured her heart out about her family, which probably means she's sad. But then she said something nice at the end, which means . . .

Well . . .

What *does* it mean?

I try to fight my way through the static of my thoughts. "I'm sorry things are weird between you and your family. I don't always know what to say to make you feel better." I fiddle with the end of my braid. "But I'm glad you like being around me. Because I like being around you, too."

Hazel smiles, and I think maybe I said the right thing for once.

"Now, are you going to tell me what happened yesterday," she starts, "or am I going to have to fight my way into the Hollow myself and demand answers?"

Laughing, I wrap my fingers around the strap of my green bag, where the book and the key are tucked inside. I can't risk setting my bag down and losing the skeleton key, so I keep it with me at all times. Even when I'm gardening. "I was in the attic yesterday. In the Hollow," I explain. "And I found a letter."

"Wait, seriously? To who? What did it say?"

"That's the thing," I say, checking over my shoulder to make sure Mrs. Delvaux isn't in earshot. "It didn't really say anything. It was just a bunch of words that kept moving around. I brought it back with me because I wanted to show you, but it vanished right out of my hand."

Hazel's blue eyes are wide. "Holy Disappearing Act!"

I bite my lip, trying to stay focused instead of laughing. "I think—I think I need to find it in the living world. The ghosts don't remember everything in the Hollow, right? So maybe if the letter exists here, it'll be whole."

She peers around me, keeping an eye out for her grandma. "I can take you to the attic. How long until she notices you're gone?"

"I can get some extra time—hang on," I say, and I retrace my steps to the conservatory, where I mumble something to Mrs. Delvaux about the bathroom and needing to talk to Hazel about something. She waves me away, busy with her lemon plant, and I hurry up the stairs to the third floor.

There are no vines or trees like there were in the Hollow. Instead, a narrow set of ladders leads to the attic hatch. Once we're both inside, we make a beeline for the old boxes.

"What does it look like?" Hazel asks, gazing around at the cobwebs.

"It's a wooden chest with a latch on it," I explain, ducking below the rafters and checking behind a stack of dusty suitcases and a giant, framed poster of the 1960s *Batman* movie.

Before I get a chance to show Hazel, I hear her voice.

"Wooden chest with a latch . . . You mean like that one?" she asks.

I follow her pointed finger to a box perched on top of an old shelf. It looks as if it hasn't been touched in a century, with enough layers of dust to rival frosting on a birthday cake.

I use some of the boxes to boost myself up, reach for the chest, and slide it carefully toward me. It isn't heavy, but the layers of cobwebs make me sneeze, sending a cloud of dust scattering away from me.

When I'm back on the floor, I set the box down and run a finger over the latch. It wiggles back and forth, loose.

"The latch is broken," I note. "It looks like someone forced it open a long time ago."

We exchange a look, and I open the lid.

Hazel leans over my shoulder, and she's so close I can almost feel her hair tickling my cheek. "Is that the letter?"

I don't answer; I'm busy trying not to breathe too loud.

I pick up the lone piece of parchment, unfold the creases, and hold it up so we can read it together. It's written in swooping cursive, but there are no words missing this time—just a poem.

> I hold life without a heartbeat,
> I have a face but cannot see,
> I give hope on the coldest nights,
> I have roots but am not a tree.
> I carry the stars but cannot fly,
> and will always answer your call,
> I am the keeper of all that was stolen,
> and the master of Honeyfield Hall.

Hazel mouths every word beside me, concentrating on each line.

"*The keeper of all that was stolen*," I read out loud. "Lock—one of the ghosts—seemed to think something else should've been in this box." I take *Roseheart: A Local History* out of my bag and find the photograph of the Delvaux family. "I showed him this picture. He said the girl took something—something that belonged to him." I tap the name. "Cora Delvaux."

Hazel leans back. "You think my grandma took something from the ghosts?"

"Maybe." I chew the inside of my mouth. What does it mean if Mrs. Delvaux is the reason the ghosts can't move on?

Sunny and her friends said she trapped souls in this house.

Is it possible they were right? That Mrs. Delvaux is keeping the ghosts here on *purpose*?

I don't know. I've been around Mrs. Delvaux all week, and she really doesn't seem like the "trapping innocent souls" type. Maybe Lock made a mistake. It's not like his memory is one hundred percent reliable.

But the fact is, *someone* wrote this poem.

If not Mrs. Delvaux, then who?

I read it again, trying to make sense of it. "If your grandma really knows about the ghosts, and has been keeping them a secret all this time . . ." I glance at Hazel. "What is it she stole? And *why*?"

Hazel stares at the words, expressionless. "We can't ask her. Not until we know for sure she didn't do this on purpose."

I nod. "Agreed."

We read the poem at least half a dozen more times, and when Hazel speaks again, her voice is strained. "What do you think it means?"

"Lock said something about a map." The more my thoughts

click together, the faster my heart starts to race. "Maybe this isn't just a poem. Maybe it's a *riddle*."

Why does it feel like someone tried to tell me that before?

I shake away the thought and stand, using the light from the window to study the words. "*Life without a heartbeat . . . I have a face but cannot see . . .* Sounds kind of like the monster, doesn't it?"

Hazel hums. "Possibly. But aren't we looking for something that was stolen? A monster is more likely to *guard* treasure, not *be* the treasure." She lifts her brow. "Unless it *is* guarding the treasure, in which case you might have to slay the monster yourself!"

My face pales. "Are you serious? I can't slay a monster. I'm twelve years old."

Hazel isn't listening—she's too busy forming a plan. "We just need to figure out its weakness. Or get you a really good weapon, like a batarang, or a sonic charge . . . Ooh, or a *dagger*!"

"I don't think that's a good idea," I say warily. "If your grandma catches me with a weapon, I could be arrested. I can't help the ghosts from a jail cell."

"That's fair," Hazel sighs. "But I wish I could visit the Hollow. I'd love to have a dagger."

"If it makes you feel better, I don't think what we're looking for is in the Hollow anyway," I point out. "The paper I brought back vanished right out of my hand. So I think whatever Mrs. Delvaux took from the ghosts, she took from the living world." With any luck, she hid it here, too.

A door closes downstairs, loud enough to make the echo rise through the floorboards.

I fold the paper at the creases and tuck it into my bag for safekeeping. "I should go back downstairs before she wonders where I am."

"I'll search the house and see if I can find anything helpful," Hazel offers.

"Okay. But be careful," I say. "I don't want you to get in trouble." Or worse, put in any danger.

We don't know what Mrs. Delvaux did, or what she's capable of.

For now, we have to treat her like a suspect. And we absolutely *cannot* let her find out.

"Don't worry," Hazel assures me. "I can keep a secret."

I'm halfway down the stairs when I think about how lucky I am that I don't have to do this alone. After Babung died, it felt like I was going to be alone forever. But now . . .

I wonder if it's possible that Babung sent Hazel to me, knowing how much I needed a friend?

CHAPTER TWENTY

The next day, to my great disappointment, Mom calls Mrs. Delvaux and tells her I can't come over to help with the garden. We're going *antique shopping*.

"Come on, kiddo," Dad says when we're in the car. "What twelve-year-old doesn't love antiques?" When I don't crack so much as a smile, he adds, "Some of them could be haunted, you know."

Mom glares at him and mouths, *We talked about this*, but I don't really care.

I'm not going to find ghosts at the antique store.

They're waiting for me in Honeyfield Hall.

We drive to the coast, and Dad parks the car near the harbor and says we can get ice cream first. I know he's trying—they both are—so I tell them I'd like two scoops of butter pecan and try to seem happy when they tell me about the plans for the living room.

"We'll gain so much room with that wall knocked down," Mom says. "And do you remember that artist you loved with the rabbits and the doughnuts? I thought we could get one of their prints and hang it up near the bathroom."

"Sounds cool," I say.

Mom smiles, pleased, and goes back to talking about wallpaper and color swatches with Dad.

After we finish our ice cream, we walk up the main street. I can see the ocean for miles, but it looks nothing like it did in California. And I finally figured out what Maine smells like—seafood, pine, and smoke.

It's less crowded too, and quieter. There isn't the same music blaring from the boardwalk. But the thing I notice the most is how happy my parents seem.

Like living in Maine really does feel like home to them.

Mom grew up on the East Coast. She even went to college a few states away from here. It's where she met Dad.

But Mom didn't have a lot of family around. She wasn't close to her parents the way Dad was to Babung. So when my parents graduated and decided they wanted a family of their own, they moved to California to be closer to Dad's family.

I don't have history on the East Coast like they do. Not yet.

But maybe there's room for that to change.

Maybe.

When we step into the antique shop, a collection of chimes ring above us. Someone comes over to greet Mom and Dad, and when they're busy discussing "heirloom pieces," I wander around the store.

It's cooler than I thought it would be. There are a lot of fancy desks with designs painted on the tops, and there's even a shelf full of creepy clown dolls that definitely look haunted. Babung used to organize her treasures the same way, in compact rows along her shelves.

I wonder where my parents put Babung's jade frog after they wrapped it back up that day in the living room.

I wonder if I'll ever see it again.

An ancient-looking baby doll stares back at me with unblinking glass eyes. It's more unsettling than any of the ghosts in Honeyfield Hall.

Hazel would probably think it was funny. Maybe next time, I could invite her to come with me.

I start to make my way back toward my parents when the chime of an old clock sounds behind me. I jump, startled, and search for the sound. An enormous grandfather clock is perched several feet away, tucked behind a shelf littered with teacups and brass soldiers.

The pendulum swings from side to side, and the hypnotic ticking draws me in like a spell. Mrs. Delvaux has a clock in her hallway that's nearly identical to this one. I remember because I catch my reflection in it every time I leave through the back door—

My throat knots. I blink, staring at my face in the glass while the sound of the clock chimes pummel through my memories, blaring like an alarm.

I have a face but cannot see.

I can feel it in my bones—this is the answer to one of the clues. A clock with a face that cannot see. The grandfather clock in Mrs. Delvaux's hallway.

When Mom places her hand on my shoulder, I practically leap out of my own skin.

"Sorry," Mom says quickly. "I called your name a couple of times, but you were lost in a daydream." She offers an apologetic smile. "I didn't mean to scare you."

"You didn't," I say breathily. Because I'm not afraid—I'm *excited*.

I just need to get back to Hazel as quickly as possible, so I can tell her my hunch and find out if I'm right.

Mom motions behind her. "We saw a sideboard that would be perfect for the dining room. I wanted to see what you thought."

"You don't need my opinion," I say with a shrug. "It's your house."

"It's *our* house," Mom corrects. "And we're a team. If you hate the sideboard, we can pick something else." She hesitates, chewing the edge of her lip. "You know, I think maybe we didn't have enough conversations about moving before we left California. I think—I *wish*—that we'd made you feel more included in the decision. And I know furniture won't make up for that, but from now on, I want us to make decisions together. As a family."

I roll my wrist in front of me and shift my weight. I'm so used to my parents not listening to me, I don't really know how to react when they actually do.

Mom raises her eyebrows, hopeful. "So? What do you think?"

"I'll look at the sideboard," I say, and her reaction is so full of unfiltered joy that I feel guilty for not being more enthusiastic.

But then I think about how Mom would react if I told her about the riddles and the ghosts and the clues. She'd feel the *opposite* of enthusiasm.

Mom listened to some things, but not everything. I'm not the one who should feel guilty. Not when it comes to furniture, and definitely not when it comes to Babung.

Still, I follow Mom to the other side of the store, tell her the sideboard looks great, and wait while she and Dad talk to the man at the desk about delivery.

On the drive home, Mom and Dad ask if I'm excited about getting my class schedule in the mail, and I feign enthusiasm like a perfect, happy, well-adjusted child, even though all I can think about is searching for clues in Honeyfield Hall.

They don't notice I'm keeping a secret. They never notice, because they never ask.

For the first time in my life, I'm happy they don't.

CHAPTER TWENTY-ONE

The moment we pull into the driveway, I ask my parents if I can go and visit Hazel. They say it's fine, as long as I'm back in time for dinner, so I grab my bike and take the shortcut along the old railway line.

When Mrs. Delvaux answers the door, she looks surprised to see me.

"Is Hazel home?" I ask, bouncing on my toes. "I wanted to talk to her about something."

She waves me inside and wrinkles her nose. "I haven't had much luck getting her out of her room today, but maybe she'll come downstairs for you. Let me have a word with her."

I wait in the hallway and listen to her footsteps fade down the second-story corridor. The grandfather clock isn't far away—and I'm too impatient to wait for Hazel.

With a few quick steps, I place myself in front of the glass, staring at my smudged reflection. It's the answer to one of the riddles. It *has* to be.

I run a hand along the side of the clock, searching for a handle or a door—anything to pry the glass open. My fingers find the edge of a small latch, and I lift it up and slowly open the panel.

Aside from the pendulum swinging inside, it's empty.

I frown, ducking my head low to inspect all the hidden corners, but all I find is deep mahogany wood and a thin layer of dust.

There aren't any clues here.

Flustered, I close the glass door and stare up at the face of the clock, wondering if there's a hidden compartment somewhere. *Something* to point me in the right direction.

Maybe this is the wrong clock, my mind hums.

I can't remember seeing another grandfather clock in the house, but I've been in less than half the rooms here.

Voices sound from upstairs, too low for me to hear through the floorboards. But I turn toward the noise instinctively, and my eyes land on the cupboard beneath the stairs, and the small keyhole below the handle.

I don't know what's taking Hazel so long, or why she doesn't seem in a hurry to come downstairs, but maybe there's someone else I can ask about the clocks in this house. Maybe I can even ask them about the clues.

I slip into the cupboard and quietly pull the door shut before twisting the skeleton key into the lock. A gray light floods through the crack above the floorboards, and I step through the veil.

It's snowing in the Hollow.

At least, I think it's snow. There's a strange mist in the air, and tiny flecks of white that float down from the ceiling.

I hold up my palm, catching some of it, and I realize it's flakes of the *house*. I think . . . I think it's starting to fall apart, and turn to ash.

I look up, terrified this is the start of something really, really bad.

I grimace, dust my hands, and make my way up the stairs. Ivy has found its way through the walls, splitting the plaster at the corners like it had to fight its way through. I look for Lock in his study first, but he isn't there. I follow the corridor to the piano room next, hoping one of the other Honeyfield ghosts will be nearby.

But the piano room is nothing like I remember. Parts of the wall have transformed into stone and moss. Tree roots weave through the floor. And there's a giant hole where the piano once sat, where vines have curled their way into the darkness.

My first instinct is to try another room, but the echo of a song makes me pause.

Someone is singing.

I make my way across the roots, balancing carefully with every step. When I reach the hole, I peer over the edge. It's a long way down. And it doesn't look like it leads to the floor below at all, but into the *earth*.

I ignore the smell of fresh soil and grass and call down into the pit. "Hello? Is anyone there?"

I can still hear it—the faraway hum.

The vines are thick and tangled, and I test a foot in one of the loops and realize it's nearly as sturdy as a ladder. Carefully, I make the climb down, gripping as firmly as I can, and enter the dark space.

The singing grows louder, and when I reach the bottom of the pit, I know whoever is singing must be nearby.

Except I don't see anyone. Just a dark, hollow space surrounded by dirt-packed walls and prickly tree roots, with a grand piano in the center. My ears perk up when the hum continues, and I move around the space like I'm hunting for the voice.

That's when I see her face in the wall. Trill. Eyes half-lidded, her gray skin is textured like tree bark. Like she's more a part of the earth than the ghost world.

I tilt my head, afraid to lean too close. "What happened to you?"

Trill's eyes flutter open, but she doesn't see me right away. I'm not sure she can see me at all—not when her eyes are pitch-black, like the empty hollows of a tree.

"Who's there?" she calls, voice brittle.

"It's Eliot," I say.

"I'm sure I've never met an Eliot."

"You have. I met you and your friends upstairs once. You were playing the piano."

"Piano?" She frowns, and her lips crack like dried clay. "I can play the piano?"

"Yes." I motion behind me, toward the enormous instrument in the center of the room. "You're really good. And I don't just mean for a ghost."

"A ghost?" she repeats.

My stomach drops. She's forgetting already. Forgetting who she is, and *where* she is.

Just like Babung did.

I swallow the knot in my throat. "Your name is Trill. At least, that's the name you have here, in the Hollow. You . . . um . . . you died, you see. A long time ago. And you're stuck here until you figure out your unfinished business."

She blinks several times, and the blackness disappears, replaced with two silver irises. "Yes. Yes, that's right." She tries to look down at the rest of her body that's trapped within the tree-bark wall. "I don't remember how I got here."

"I think that's the problem. The more you forget, the more this house seems to fall apart." I look around nervously. "But I'm working on it. I think I even figured out the first clue."

Trill blinks again, and I watch as the darkness stains her eyes like ink.

She's struggling to hold on to her memories, even now.

I lift out a hand. "Maybe I could help you to your piano? It might help you remember."

She struggles to pry her arm from the earth, and when she does, flecks of wood and dried sap shudder free. But when her fingers brush against mine, they go straight through me.

I stiffen and curl my fingers into a ball. "Sorry. I, I forgot there might be rules about that."

Trill's arm falls, and I watch the bark mold back to her skin.

"No!" I say quickly. "Keep trying. All you have to do is make it to your piano."

"I don't think I can do it on my own," she whispers softly.

I glance between her and the piano, terrified I'm running out of time. Terrified of what I'll find the next time I come to visit.

With Babung, it was slow at first, and then—then everything went faster than what I was ready for.

I look at the empty piano stool. At the place where Trill has been for more years than I can imagine, playing a melody that reminds her of who she once was.

I take a breath and sit at the piano. I can't play the way Trill does, but Babung taught me a few songs when I was younger. I can only remember the melody on one hand, but I lift my fingers to the keys and play it anyway. The notes are clumsy. I fumble from one key to the next, trying to remember the song from when I was little.

For a moment, I hear Babung's voice in my head. The memory of what she used to say. "You're rushing again, Eliot-Chan. You're always in such a hurry. You have to slow down, and take your time."

I'm trying, I mouth. *But I don't like this part. I want it to be over.*

Now when I hear her, she isn't a memory. Just my

imagination. "If you rush over the bad parts just to reach the good, you'll miss the things that make the good matter. It will be okay—you'll see. Just breathe. Don't rush. I'm not going anywhere."

My eyes water, and my fingers tremble, but I keep playing. For Babung, for me, and for Trill.

It isn't perfect. But I guess it doesn't have to be, because it works.

Trill hesitates before breaking free of the wall, her footsteps heavy and lacking the grace she usually has. She makes it to the piano, and I scoot over a few inches to make room for her. Trill sits, places her fingers to the keys, and plays a lullaby.

She closes her eyes dreamily. "Yes. I do remember this."

"Good," I say, wiping beneath my eyes. Maybe it will be enough to stop whatever was happening to her. At least for a little while longer.

She doesn't turn, but her voice is aimed straight at me. "Thank you, little one. I fear this house would've devoured me whole if you hadn't turned up."

"Is there anything you can remember from before?" I ask.

"I can't even remember my name."

"But you remember your music."

"That is true." She stills above the keys, before continuing on. "I remember a girl once. I think she might have been about your age. She was here one moment, and gone the next. And . . . and for some reason, of all the things I've tried to remember, that seems to be the only one that's stuck."

I frown, and pull out the book from my bag, turning to the page with the Delvaux family. "This little girl's name was Cora. Do you think it might've been her?"

Trill glances at the image and widens her eyes. "I've seen that house before. I know that garden." Above us, the ceiling rattles, and ash crumbles to the ground.

The monster. It's lurking nearby, somewhere outside the house.

How does it always seem to know I'm here?

"This is Honeyfield Hall," I explain quickly. "It's where we are now. But the girl . . ." I tap the black-and-white page. "Have you ever seen her before?"

I need proof Mrs. Delvaux really did lock up their souls. I need someone who *remembers*.

"I don't know," Trill says softly. "Should I have seen her?"

I sigh. "She owns the house now. I found a poem in the attic that talked about the master of Honeyfield Hall. I think she had something to do with why you and your friends are stuck here. I just need to solve the riddles to figure it all out."

Trill sways to the music. "You're mistaken. I don't have any friends. I've been down here on my own for a very long time."

I open my mouth to tell her about Lock and the others, but I think better of it. Babung used to get upset if I kept reminding her of all the things she'd forgotten. I didn't realize it then—I was just so desperate for her to recognize me and remember what we were to each other.

But now I think sometimes I pushed too hard.

I wish I could tell her I'm sorry about that part.

I wish I could have another chance to do a better job.

I watch Trill's fingers dance across the piano. "You really do play beautifully."

She shuts her eyes. "I think . . . I think I'd like to see the garden again."

I swallow the knot in my throat, and do what I should've done with Babung. I play along. "It's going to be beautiful this year. There's marigolds and lettuce and lavender and tickseed—which sounds like a bug but it's a pretty yellow flower."

"And the tree? Has it grown tall?"

"So tall," I say. "With enough shade to sit under in the summer."

She smiles. "Yes. Yes, I remember the garden."

The ceiling rumbles once more, and I know it's time to go. I close the book and tuck it into my bag. Trill closes her eyes again and resumes her song.

"I'll be back as soon as I can," I promise, and stand up.

"The hydrangeas were beautiful in the summer," Trill says like she's caught in a dream.

I climb the vines, return to the cupboard under the stairs, and make my way back to the living world.

My head is buzzing with so many thoughts: about Babung, and Trill, and memories, and mistakes. My heart is aching and my throat feels like sandpaper, and I don't think people are meant to hold on to so much sadness on their own. I think people are supposed to be there to help you carry it, so the weight of grief doesn't crush you whole.

I need to talk to someone.

I need my friend.

I step back in the hallway, searching for comfort, when I hear Mrs. Delvaux and Hazel arguing upstairs. Quiet at first, but then loud enough that Hazel's voice reverberates straight toward me.

"I don't care about making friends in this town! Stop trying to force me to hang out with people I don't even know!"

Her words spin around in my head, and each time I hear them on repeat it feels like being hit by a thousand paper cuts.

I don't wait for Mrs. Delvaux to come downstairs and give me the news. I hurry home without looking back.

CHAPTER TWENTY-TWO

E very time I reach for a memory of Hazel, it feels like I'm chasing a thread to a mess of tangled thoughts. I thought we were friends. I thought she liked being around me.

But maybe I got it all wrong.

I think back to each time we've met. She seemed happy—she even said she didn't hate being in the house when I was with her. But if that were really true, then why would she say those things to her grandma?

It doesn't make sense.

Unless . . .

Unless . . .

My thoughts twist and turn around themselves, trying to understand. Trying to think of a scenario where this could all just be a misunderstanding.

But I can't shake the memory of Mom trying to push Sunny and her friends to hang out with me, even though they didn't want to. Was Mrs. Delvaux doing the same thing with me and Hazel?

I sit in bed all night worrying about the things I have so

little control over. I wonder why, even though it's hard to make friends, holding on to them seems even harder.

What's so wrong with me that I can't make anyone stay?

000

I spend the morning gardening with Mrs. Delvaux. I don't bring up Hazel, and neither does she. I guess we both know it's easier to pretend yesterday never happened.

When I step inside to use the bathroom, I pass the living room and spot Hazel sitting at the windowsill, staring into the side garden.

I hesitate, shuffling my feet to decide whether I should head straight for the bathroom or say hello, when I realize Hazel doesn't look angry—she looks sad.

I step over the threshold.

Hazel turns sharply, eyes wide like she's struggling to register where the sound came from. When she sees me, her face softens. "Eliot?"

I lift my shoulders awkwardly. "Yeah. Me again."

She stands up but doesn't move toward me. Her eyes seem more red than usual, and her skin is pale. It looks like she might have been crying.

"Um. Is everything okay?" I ask.

Hazel folds her arms around herself. She doesn't answer, but her face looks like it's holding back a floodgate. Like inside her head are a thousand thoughts she hasn't untangled.

I understand the feeling.

"If you need to talk to someone, I'm here," I say. "I know we're still kind of strangers, but—"

"Strangers?" She hiccups a laugh of disbelief. "You're my best friend. We're hardly strangers."

My cheeks darken. I debate whether to tell her the truth or not. But I think if we *are* best friends, the truth is better.

"I heard you talking to Mrs. Delvaux yesterday. You said she was forcing you to hang out with me. And . . . I know what that feels like, to have your family push things on you. I don't want someone to be my friend just because they feel like they have to, or because I'm the only person around. So if you need an easy out . . . It's okay. I understand."

This time, Hazel *does* take a step closer. "That's not what I want at all." She looks flustered. "I say a lot of things to my grandma that I don't always mean. I don't know why I do it. Usually, I'm upset about it afterward, when I'm in my room by myself. But I don't know . . ." Hazel shakes her head. "Sometimes I get so angry, and I feel so trapped, and it's like—it's like I'm not even *me* anymore."

I've been angry at my parents before, but never like that.

Whatever Hazel is going through is bigger than what I can see.

"The only time I feel like myself is when you're here, which makes it extra bad that I said those things," she says quietly. "It doesn't matter how angry I was—I shouldn't have taken my feelings out on you. That wasn't fair. I'm sorry, Eliot. Really, *really* sorry."

I pluck at the smoky quartz bracelet with my fingers. I should've worn amazonite today—it's good for misunderstandings and communication.

But then again, maybe I'm doing okay without it.

"It's all right—I forgive you," I say simply.

Hazel relaxes.

"You should really talk to your grandma about how you feel," I add, staring toward the window. "It's not good to be so angry. It causes all kinds of problems, like headaches and high blood pressure. Whenever my mom had a backache, Babung always said it was from stress. She said people carry their feelings in their bodies, and when the feelings get to be too much, the body starts to hurt."

"Is that true?"

"Babung was never angry, and she was the healthiest person in the world. I mean. Up until . . ."

Hazel waits while I find my words.

I twist my fingers together and shift from foot to foot. "I know it might be weird that I'm going through so much trouble to get a message to my grandma, but she loved her life." *She loved me.* "I want to make sure she remembers."

"It's not weird at all," Hazel says. "I can tell you miss her."

The first memory that pops into my head is a happy one, and it makes me grin. "I remember this one time she found a bunch of stones and painted them to look like dogs. My parents never let me have pets, but I was desperate for a puppy. Babung put the stones all over the house, and sometimes we'd just be sitting around doing something else, and she'd randomly start talking to them—like they really were pets. She even gave them all names."

Hazel laughs. "She sounds nice."

"She was the *nicest*," I say. "You would've liked her." I bite the edge of my lip. "I know you feel lost sometimes in this house without your parents, but I think Mrs. Delvaux really does want to be around you. She's nice too."

"Unless she turns out to be the reason the ghosts can't find their memories," Hazel notes.

"Yeah. But we don't have proof of that yet, and she *is* your grandma . . . You should give her another chance."

"Sometimes she acts like I'm not here at all. Like she's just waiting for me to *leave*." Hazel's eyes soften. "But . . . I suppose we both could make more of an effort. Maybe someone has to make the first move." She glances at my bag and frowns. "Wait—if you were here yesterday, does that mean you figured out the riddle?"

"A part of it, I think." I quickly explain about the clock and the antique store and what happened in the Hollow with Trill. When I finish, I lower my voice. "Do you know if there are any other clocks in this house?"

"I'm sure there are plenty, but not anything as fancy as the one in the hall." She scrunches her nose. "But—did you check all the panels?"

I frown. "I thought only the glass door opened."

Hazel motions for me to follow her, and we hurry back to

the grandfather clock. She stands on her tiptoes and studies the wooden edges. "There are hidden panels around here. I've seen my grandma open them before, when she's been cleaning."

I follow her gaze, trailing the edges of the clock in search of any hinges, when I find one just to the right of the clock's face.

My eyes widen. "You're right—there's a door here." I pry the panel open with my fingers to reveal a small opening. I'm hit with a wave of old, stale air, but it's the glint of silver that catches my eye.

Hazel spots it too. "There's something there!" She points to the small object wedged in the hiding place.

I reach up, careful not to nudge the clock in any way, and clutch the silver item carefully. When it's snug in my hand, I press the panel door shut and hold the treasure in my palms for Hazel and me to inspect. Despite the tarnished surface, I recognize what it is immediately, but Hazel doesn't.

"Holy Mysterious Clock Object," she says, face blank. "Er . . . what is it?"

"It's a trinket box," I explain. "Babung used to have something similar that was made of wood. She said it was called a snuffbox." I lift my shoulders. "I remember because when I asked her why it was called that, she told me it was because I 'ask su-nuff questions,' and then she laughed really hard. I didn't get the joke back then, but I do now."

Hazel stifles a giggle. "You're right—I definitely would've liked her."

I focus on the box in my hand. The metal is a dark silver, and there are small carvings along the edges. On the top are two letters: *EH*.

"Is it supposed to do something?" Hazel asks.

I push the lid with my thumb and it pops up easily, but there's nothing inside. Just more tarnished silver.

My brow crumples. "I'm not sure. I think it's just a box. But maybe the *EH* is part of another clue?"

"The *H* has to be for Honeyfield, right?" She rolls her tongue over her teeth, thinking. "Did your library book mention anyone with a name that starts with *E*?"

I shake my head. "There was a Charles Honeyfield and the Delvaux family. But no names with an *E*."

"Maybe you should ask one of the ghosts," Hazel offers. "I know they aren't very good at remembering things, but you said the piano helped Trill. Maybe the trinket box could help them, too?"

I nod, stuffing the ornament box into my green bag with the rest of my things. "Can you keep an eye on Mrs. Delvaux? I'll go back through the closet door."

"Of course," Hazel says.

I make my way to the space under the stairs, locking eyes with Hazel one last time before pulling the door shut in front of me. I take out the key, and make my way back to the Hollow.

CHAPTER TWENTY-THREE

The state of the house makes me jerk back in alarm.

Every wall has turned to bark, just like the room where I found Trill. Except it doesn't look old and dry—it looks like it's started to rot. Black mushrooms sprout from the corners of the hall, and heavy branches sweep through the room like cobwebs.

I clamber through a narrow gap, trying to make it to the stairs, when I hear a wail from across the hallway. "Come back! Please—*please*, come back!"

I follow the sound to the front hall, where Lock, Pearl, and Hatter are staring out into the open gray nothingness. The front door is wide open.

"What happened?" I ask, immediately concerned. They aren't supposed to go outside. Not to mention there's a *monster* out there.

The three ghosts turn to look at me, eyes wide with a mix of shock and terror.

Pearl presses a hand to her chest. "Oh good heavens, it's a living girl!"

Lock tuts. He's the size of an adult today. "This is no place for a child—certainly not one that's still breathing."

Hatter motions me away from the door. "Whoever you are, you should leave at once. We don't need anyone else wandering through the wrong door today."

I count their faces and dig my heels into the ground. "Is *Trill* out there?"

"You know Trill?" Pearl asks, surprised.

"I know all of you," I correct, but decide there isn't time to explain. "Why did she go outside? I thought you said it was dangerous?"

Hatter waves a hand at Lock. "Ask *him*."

"Do not blame me for this," Lock snarls. "I never told anyone to go outside. In fact, I distinctly remember saying *not* to."

Hatter shifts his jaw, and the corners of his mustache twitch. "Trill has been going on and on about seeing the garden again, and you just *had* to bring up the fact that we've never searched outside before. You planted the idea!"

My stomach sinks. *Oh no.*

I showed Trill the picture from the book. *I'm* the one who reminded her about the garden, and the hydrangeas.

If Trill is out there with the monster, it's my fault.

Pearl's voice shifts. "All this bickering isn't helping. Someone needs to go out and fetch her before it's too late."

They told me before that the farther they get from the house, the more of their old selves they lose.

Is that what's going to happen to Trill?

And what will happen if the monster finds her first?

I push past a branch that seems to be stretching closer by the second. "You can't go out there. You'll lose more of your memories, and this house is already getting worse."

Hatter rubs the back of his neck, anxious. "We can't leave her alone. We made a promise to stick together."

"A promise she broke by leaving," Lock offers quietly. "Perhaps we should consider that Trill is not coming back."

"How can you be so cold?" Pearl hisses, clutching her necklace. "Trill is our *friend*."

"She could barely remember who we were," Lock argues. "How much longer until the same happens to you, or Hatter, or even me?" He runs a hand through his disheveled hair. "If we follow her into the gray, we are lost. And if by some miracle Trill *does* make it back, then perhaps we can learn something about the nothingness. Maybe she'll even bring back a clue."

"She is not one of your experiments!" Hatter growls, angrier than I've ever seen him.

They start talking, one on top of the other, and all I can hear is noise and words and yelling when I decide to make my voice louder than all of them.

"I'LL GO!" I shout.

The others stiffen, blinking at me like they've only just remembered I'm here.

"I'll look for Trill." I put myself between the ghosts and the front door. "It's my fault she's out there anyway. I tried to make her feel better by telling her about the garden. So I'll be the one to go and bring her back."

"But," Pearl says, lip wobbling, "you don't know what's out there. What will *happen* to you."

"I know what will happen to Trill if I don't try," I say. "I promised to help you all—and I keep my promises."

I hold on to the strap of my bag, squeezing tight, and step out onto the misty porch.

The nothingness is quiet. Empty. It feels a little like being asleep, while knowing you're in a dream. Like I'm teetering on the edge of the Hollow.

There's no crunch beneath my shoes, even though in the living world I'd be trampling over Mrs. Delvaux's flower beds right about now. My eyes scan the pale gray mist, unable to make out any shapes at all.

"Trill?" I call out.

Maybe she'll hear me. Maybe it will be enough to remind her who she is.

I follow the path I've memorized toward where the overgrown garden should be. But there's nothing here. Just an empty fog that feels like it's pulling me farther and farther from the house.

When I look back at Honeyfield Hall, I can still see the faint outline of the roof, but most of it is shrouded in mist.

I need to hurry.

I push through the strange cloud, calling Trill's name, when I see a figure standing a few feet away. The ghost has the same translucent glow as the others, but her hair is long and matted, and there's a boniness to her shoulders that doesn't look human at all. She hasn't just aged—she's started to decay.

"Trill?" I say again, more timidly than before.

The ghost turns, cheeks gaunt. Her lips are cracked, like the very essence of life was sucked from her skin. She blinks, seeing me but not *really* seeing me.

"We're supposed to meet by the tree," she says softly.

"Trill." My voice becomes urgent. "You'll forget everything if you stay out here. Please come back to the house with me. Your friends are waiting for you."

Trill looks around, eyes scanning the mist. "Perhaps I'm early. Or maybe I'm late."

I reach out a hand, and my fingers go straight through her skin. I hover my hand nearby anyway, hoping the comfort will help a little. "Let me take you home. Maybe the others will know what you're talking about. You could even play the piano, like you did before."

"But . . . the garden . . ." Trill stills, confused. "We made a promise."

I think quickly. "It's too cold to be out in the garden today," I say, and coax her toward me, out of the mist. "But if you come back inside, I'll tell you all about it. I could even show you the picture again—the one with the hydrangeas." I hesitate, desperate. "I can try to help you remember whatever it is you've forgotten."

I'll do what I never could for Babung, my mind cries, making my heart ache and ache.

"All right," she says finally, lifting her tired eyes.

Her feet shuffle, trailing my footsteps as I lead her to the porch.

"We're almost there," I say. "Just a little farther."

Honeyfield Hall comes into view like a dark shadow, and my chest floods with relief. I turn back to face Trill—to tell her it's just up the steps—when I trip over my own feet and fall hard against the unforgiving ground.

Wincing, I start to push myself to my knees, when I realize the trinket box has rolled from my bag, tumbling several yards back into the empty space.

And it's *glowing*.

Trill pauses near the porch door, face blank, and says without any emotion at all, "Oh, look. You've found a memory."

From deep in the mist, a monster roars to life.

The earth vibrates, and the sound is like thunder tearing its way toward me. Toward the silver box that Trill called a memory.

I scramble to my feet, but the monster appears like a black cloud of ribbons and smoke. Its body is more beast than human, with strange alien-like limbs and a face that's distinguished only by a pair of hollow, empty eyes. When the monster shudders, I feel my bones turn to ice.

It launches itself for the trinket box, but so do I. I have to protect it—the promise to the ghosts, and to Babung. I have to keep it safe.

I'm running as fast as I can, but the monster is too quick. It's after the memory, face stretched apart like it wants to devour the object whole. It rears back, preparing to pounce on top of the ornament box.

I need a distraction—something to send the monster looking in a different direction, long enough for us to get into the house.

But I'm just a kid. How can I possibly stop a monster? All I have is a bag and a key and a library book, and it doesn't want any of those things. It wants—

I skid to a halt, mind racing quickly.

The monster is after a memory. Maybe that's exactly what I need to give it.

I slip my fingers into my pocket, hoping it's still there, and find the crocheted rabbit from Babung. The soft yarn scratches at my fingertips, and I cup my hand around it.

I think of Babung. The way her glasses always slid down her nose when she was knitting. The way she'd keep all her unfinished projects in a recycled cookie tin. The way she'd watch me play solitaire on the carpet in front of her, telling me which cards to put where because solitaire was one of the few things Babung had no self-control over.

She loved card games. She loved knitting. But she loved me most of all.

I can't give all of my memories of Babung to the monster,

but could I sacrifice one? Just one, to trade for the ornament box?

There isn't enough time to think about how much it will hurt to lose a piece of Babung. When I remember the memory of the crocheted rabbit, it's because I know I don't have a choice.

Babung gave it to me on my first day of sixth grade. She was forgetting a lot of things by then, but she still knew me. Even though her knitting was loose and not quite what it used to be, I loved it anyway.

"It's for good luck," she'd said, tucking the rabbit into my backpack. Fifth grade had already been humiliating enough, but at least Cassie was going to a different school. Junior high could be different. I could start over—make new friends.

I wasn't even sure I needed luck when I was full of so much hope.

I didn't know a lot of things back then. I didn't know how much more Babung would forget, and how fast things would start to change. And I didn't know that when the doctor said there'd be good days and bad days, that Babung would have a heart attack before the good days ever came back around.

But on that day, I hugged Babung tight.

"Just remember, Eliot-Chan," she said into my ear. "You don't have to be anyone but yourself." A little quieter, she added, "You're my favorite. Don't tell your dad."

I look into my palms and watch the crocheted rabbit start to glow.

Holding the memory up in the air, I shout toward the beast. "Hey!"

It freezes in front of the ornament box, twisting its head back and forth, snarling when it realizes what I'm holding.

With every bit of force I have, I throw the rabbit across the empty landscape and into the mist. The monster charges after it.

I snatch the box from the ground as fast as I can, but the moment my fingertips graze the edge, the entire world spins. The mist evaporates, dripping with streaks of bright paint like I'm trapped inside a watercolor, and then shapes take form, stacking one on top of the other like building blocks.

I blink, and I'm no longer in the mist.

I'm in a memory.

CHAPTER TWENTY-FOUR

A young girl sits at a piano, hair bound in tight ringlets. She tries not to appear nervous, even though playing the piano in front of so many neighbors makes her stomach spin.

When she finishes the song, she gives a short curtsy. Her mother waves her over, face lit up with the kind of joy that doesn't feel warm at all. Even though the girl's eyes are searching the doorways and windows for a familiar face, she joins her parents and proceeds to be shuffled around the room like one of their favorite ornaments.

The girl is miserable, but she smiles because she's supposed to.

She does *everything* she's supposed to.

When the party ends, the girl sits in her room to re-pin her curls before bed, when a pebble cracks against the glass windowpane. The girl hurries to look outside and finds a young boy standing in the grass, a lopsided grin on his face.

The girl opens the window and folds both arms over the windowsill. "What are you doing? Someone might see you!" she whispers.

The boy grabs hold of the wall and climbs anyway, and when he reaches the window, the girl takes a step back to give him space. There are bits of straw stuck to his hair and clothes, and even though he's made an effort to scrub his hands, there is dried mud caked to his knees.

But she doesn't mind. She plucks one of the pieces of hay from his shoulder and stifles a laugh. "I wondered where you'd been all day."

"I did try to get here sooner," he admits, rummaging through his bag for a small silver object. He holds it out to her. "Happy birthday."

The girl's eyes widen. She hadn't expected a gift from him at all. It isn't fancy—not like the things her parents had shipped all the way from France—but somehow that made it all the more perfect.

Her heart flutters, and she takes the small ornament box, running her fingers over the edge.

"It's not *real* silver, but it's the birthday wish that's the important part," he says, and when she frowns, he motions toward the lid and cups his hands in front of him like he's showing her what to do. "You have to whisper your wish into the box—whatever it is you want most. And then close the lid as quick as you can." He smiles. "That way you can keep hold of it until I can make sure it comes true."

She presses her lips together, eyes crinkling as she shakes her head. "You're silly."

He keeps smiling with half of his face. "Silly or not, you still have to make a wish. And make sure it's a good one."

The girl tilts the lid open and holds the box up to her mouth. She could wish for anything—a new piano or a dress like Marianne's from across the park—but she didn't want just anything.

With a quiet breath, she whispers, "I wish to someday have a family that's genuinely happy instead of just pretending to be." She snaps the lid shut quickly, swallowing the knot in her throat.

The boy doesn't reply at first. She's worried she was too sentimental, or personal. That maybe she should pay more attention to her mother's rules about seeming "proper."

But then he smiles, and she isn't worried anymore. "That's easy," he says. "I was planning on asking you to marry me one day anyway; we're always happy when we're around each other."

The girl scrunches her nose, still too caught up in the silliness to consider he might be serious. "My father would never allow it. We'd have to travel across an ocean in the dead of night."

But the boy just shrugs and says, "That's easy, too. I'd cross a thousand oceans for you, Emma."

In that moment, the girl is certain her heart begins to glow.

The memory vanishes, and I blink several times, trying to process where I am. The mist is everywhere, and I see the monster panicking several yards away, angry that the memory of the rabbit isn't the one it wanted. It isn't *enough*.

I don't wait for the monster to see me; I run back into the house with the ornament box tucked in my hands, and slam the door behind me, drowning out the monster's call.

The ghosts of Honeyfield Hall are standing in a circle around Trill, who kneels on the floor with her frail, skeletal arms wrapped around herself.

"Trill, dear," Pearl says.

"Trill? Who is that?" she replies, eyes turning silver. Her skin is no longer glowing like the others; it's as dull as stone.

She's starting to fade away.

Pearl chirps one cry after the other. Hatter adjusts the collar of his shirt, nervous. And Lock's gaze is ever fixed on Trill's trembling bones.

"You see?" Lock says, voice hardened. "No matter what I do, I can't stop it. I can't figure out what we're *missing*."

Pearl casts a look of admonishment, eyes glazed. "Trill is our friend. And she may not remember she loves us, but we know what's real, and we'll just have to keep on loving her twice as much to make up for it."

The trinket box is still glowing in my hands. It makes the initials stand out even more—*EH*.

E for . . . Emma. The girl from the memory, who played the piano.

Could that have been . . . ?

My heart hammers, and I step between the ghosts, pausing

in front of Trill. "You recognized this outside, didn't you?" I hold up the ornament box. "Did it . . . Did it used to be yours?"

Trill lifts her head, silken hair falling over her shoulders. There's a long pause, and I wonder if maybe she didn't hear me, but then she reaches out a hand and takes the object, cradling it to her chest.

Her face morphs rapidly. She is a little girl and then a young woman and then an older woman. It's as if she's racing through time. Reliving her very life through a single memory.

Finally Trill sighs, face settling into wrinkles and tidy, gray hair, and smiles. She hands back the trinket, making sure it's firmly in my hands. "I remember now," she says. "Please. Put it with the others."

I open my mouth to ask what she means, but Trill— *Emma*—glances around at the other three ghosts, eyes overflowing with contentment, and vanishes from the Hollow.

CHAPTER TWENTY-FIVE

What just happened?" Lock asks, staring at the empty space Emma left behind.

The silver box is no longer glowing. Whatever memory it held is gone.

"I, I think she found her lost memory," I say.

"A memory about what?" Hatter shakes his head, flustered. "Did it show her what her unfinished business was? The reason we're all stuck here?"

I explain what I saw in as much detail as I can remember. When I finish, I realize the three remaining ghosts only look more upset.

"I don't understand," Pearl says, voice cracking. "That isn't any help at all."

"It was a help to Trill," Hatter notes, solemn.

Pearl's eyes look puffy. I think as much as she's worried, she also misses her friend.

Lock paces, kicking at the mulch on the rotted floorboards. "I thought remembering our past would remind us what to do. But Trill's memory was just that—a memory." He stiffens, fists clenched, and glances at me. "How did you know what to look for?"

"I don't think you remember, but you took me to the attic and showed me a locked box. This was inside." I take the parchment from my bag, exchanging it for the trinket box. "I think it's a list of riddles—riddles leading to the memories you've lost."

Lock reads it over my shoulder several times, brow crumpling in severe lines the more his eyes dart back and forth. "I've seen this before . . . When I—" His eyes widen, and he starts to shrink. When he's the size of a small boy, his voice becomes a screech. "It needed a key! It's upstairs—I'll show you!"

Lock bolts from the room, racing straight through the twisted branches, and makes a run for the stairs.

I start to call after him—to tell him he's already shown me the attic—when the entire roof gives a shudder.

Plaster falls all around us, raining ash and soot. I yelp in alarm, jumping out of the way of a gnarled branch that swoops low to the ground. It splits at the end, stretching into two sharp points.

Outside, the monster's howl turns ferocious.

"That doesn't sound good," Pearl says softly.

Hatter doesn't move.

"The monster," I start. "It's after your memories, isn't it?" They both turn to look at me, and I motion toward the door. "It was after the trinket box first, but I threw one of my own memories to distract it. Is that why it's trying to get inside the house?"

"It doesn't want to come inside, dear," Pearl explains. "The monster only seems to react when—well—"

Hatter tilts his head like he's only just realizing something important. "It reacts when *you're* here."

"Me?" I blink. "But—that's not true." Is it?

Hatter steps forward. "What were you doing the last time you were here?"

"I went to see Trill. She was trapped in the wall, so I reminded her about her piano, and the garden."

"And before that?" he presses.

I think back to the attic. "It was when I found the poem upstairs. When Lock remembered the box." My brows pinch. "And before that was when I met you all in the piano room. When I promised to help you find your memories."

Pearl and Hatter exchange a glance.

The shadow monster reacts when the ghosts start to remember things. Maybe it doesn't *want* them to remember.

My stomach turns and turns. "Is the monster trying to stop us?"

"That I cannot say," Hatter muses. "But you ought to be careful all the same. Perhaps the more you help us, the more danger you put yourself in."

I don't need to be careful—I need to be *faster*.

The ghosts here are running out of time.

Pearl's expression softens. "I do hope you solve your riddles, dear. Things are changing quickly here. The next time you visit, you may not recognize it at all."

"I'll be back," I promise. "Just—don't go outside, okay?"

It doesn't feel right to leave them here, but there's nothing more I can do to help right now. The rest of the clues have to be found in the living world.

I retreat to the closet, where I use the skeleton key to travel back to the other side of the veil.

Hazel isn't there, so I check the living room and the sitting room. When I turn the corner that leads to the hallway, I nearly run into Mrs. Delvaux.

"There you are," she says, folding one gardening glove neatly over the other.

"I was looking for Hazel," I say, twisting my bag slightly so it's hidden at the back of my hip.

Mrs. Delvaux frowns. "Didn't I tell you? Hazel's parents came back from the city. They took her home."

"What?" I shake my head like I don't understand, because I don't. Hazel was just with me, and she didn't say anything about leaving today. She didn't say anything about leaving, *period*. "When will she be back?"

"It's hard to say, but I think Hazel was quite desperate to leave," Mrs. Delvaux notes. "I'd be surprised if she was back before the end of the summer."

The realization that Hazel left without saying goodbye hits me like a sucker punch. I knew she didn't live here permanently, but to just *go*?

Maybe after Babung I should be used to people leaving without saying goodbye. But I'm not. If anything, not saying goodbye hurts *more*.

Maybe that's why Hazel looked so sad, my mind thumps. *Maybe she didn't know how to tell you.*

"Come on," Mrs. Delvaux says. "Why don't we have a look at the seeds I've got? We've still got plenty of marigolds and cosmos. If we plant them now, we'll get some nice blooms in about a month or so."

We walk back outside together and find a space near the freshly turned soil. Mrs. Delvaux scatters seeds while I tend to the plants that are mostly grown, using the green watering can to keep them hydrated.

"Watch the leaves," Mrs. Delvaux warns, hands scooping up dark soil. "If you get too much water on them, they'll burn in the summer. You've got to keep the water close to the roots."

I lower the watering can and watch the soil darken.

Mrs. Delvaux hums with approval. "Yes—that's just right."

I stare back at the plants, and the roots that are too far buried to see. They remind me of the Hollow, where the trees seem to be taking over the very foundations of Honeyfield Hall.

Roots, my mind repeats, and something flutters to life in my rib cage.

I have roots but am not a tree.

Frowning, I look around the garden. Between the weeds,

the overgrowth, and the fresh flower bed, there has to be at least a thousand plants out here. A thousand things with roots that are *not trees*.

Could one of them be the answer to the riddle? Could it be buried somewhere in the garden?

And maybe more important, would it still be here, after all these years?

"Not too much," Mrs. Delvaux warns, patting the dirt with a flat hand. "If you overwater—especially around the seedlings—they'll rot."

"How long do plants live for?" I ask, the urgency in my voice too powerful to hide.

She dusts her hands against her apron, studying me. "If you care for them properly? Depends on the plant. Flowers are mostly seasonal, but the shrubs and trees have been around for years." She casts a wary eye around the garden. "Maybe some of the weeds, too."

"Are there any shrubs that have been around for—I don't know—since before you were born?"

She barks a laugh. "There are a great many things in and around this house older than me."

I debate whether to tell her I only care about the things with roots but think better of it. I'm still not a hundred percent sure who wrote the riddles in the first place. It's better if Mrs. Delvaux doesn't know what I'm up to.

"What about your indoor plants?" I try. "Do any of them live a long time?"

She presses her lips into a line. "You've got a lot of questions today. Are you planning a garden of your own? Because I can take some cuttings off of something hardy. A jade plant might be a good starter."

I stop watering and grip the handle tightly. "My grandma used to keep jade plants in her house." She had at least a dozen of them. I don't know where any of them went after she died.

Mrs. Delvaux looks up and shifts her jaw. "It's a good plant. Maybe it could be good for you, too."

My cheeks turn pink. "I . . . um . . . don't know anything about taking care of plants."

Mrs. Delvaux motions to the soil. "What do you think you've been doing all this time?"

"Yeah, but not on my own. I'd be too worried I'd mess something up and wouldn't be able to fix it." I stare at the droplets falling from the leaves. "I don't want to be the reason a jade plant dies."

"Ah. I see." She shifts to get a better look at me, eyes glassy, and waves a gloved finger. "Everything dies one day, whether we want them to or not. But if we try our best to care for them, and put love into the world while they're still around? Well, at least we gave them a good life. And the life part matters more than the death, I think."

I don't say anything. I just nod.

Mrs. Delvaux goes back to planting seeds, and I go back to watering plants, and all the while, I think of Babung, and what Pearl said about loving someone twice as much.

If I love Babung *fifty* times as much, will she feel it somewhere in the afterlife?

I hope so. I hope she knows how sorry I am that she died before I could keep my promise—but that I haven't given up.

I have a chance to help Babung remember her life, and this time, I won't be too late.

CHAPTER TWENTY-SIX

I use the computer to research roots, and it turns out there aren't just plant roots, but edible roots too. There's yams, radishes, turnips, carrots—but if the clue was buried in a vegetable garden years ago, I don't know how I'm ever going to dig it up.

The grounds at Honeyfield Hall are huge. There are countless places that could've been used for gardening, and most of it is such a mess that I'd need an industrial digger to search the soil.

Or a metal detector, I think.

Dad finds me rummaging in one of the downstairs closets. He's wearing navy coveralls and his hair is more disheveled than usual. "What are you looking for, kiddo?"

I let the heavy coats fall back over the collection of ski boots and winter gear, and I look over my shoulder. "Didn't you used to have a metal detector?"

"That old thing?" Dad laughs. "I threw that out years ago. Partly because it never worked properly, and partly because your mom wouldn't stop calling me Inspector Gadget." His mouth curves. "Why? Are you searching for something?"

I stand, heart sinking with disappointment. "Sort of." When Dad lifts a brow like he wants to hear more, I say, "Something got lost in Mrs. Delvaux's garden. I wanted to help find it."

He leans back, amused. "I thought it might have something to do with that skeleton key you found. I thought maybe you'd found a treasure chest to go with it!"

I roll my eyes like he's being silly, even though he's not *that* far from the truth. There was a box. And the treasure does have something to do with the skeleton key.

"I'm really glad you're having so much fun helping with the garden," he says. "I can tell you're doing a lot better these days. I'm proud of you."

I flinch. *Better* is code for "no longer talking about ghosts." They think that because I don't mention Babung to them as much, I'm not as sad as I used to be.

They have it all wrong, except for the part about how much I like going to Mrs. Delvaux's. Not just because of the ghosts, and the mystery, but because it's the only place in the world where it feels okay to talk about Babung.

Hazel and Mrs. Delvaux . . . They listen to me. They listen to my memories.

I start to move for the stairs, but pause a few feet away. "Do you miss her?"

Dad's quiet. He doesn't ask who I'm talking about, because he already knows. When he speaks again, his voice is full of rough edges. "All the time."

I blink, and turn to face him. "Then why do you never want to talk about her?"

"She wouldn't have wanted us to be sad," he says seriously. "Especially not you."

"I'm trying to *remember* her. It's different."

"You're trying to find a way to bring her back," Dad corrects. "And your mom and I—we don't think that's a good idea. We don't want you to get false hope, and have to lose her all over again. That day we sat you down, and told you about the heart attack . . ." The muscles in his jaw tense. "It was one of the worst days of our lives. Not just losing Babung, but seeing what it did to you."

"But I'm okay now," I argue. "I barely cry anymore. Looking for Babung was *helping*."

"Is it?" Dad lowers his chin. "Because I worry it's making things harder. One day you're going to realize you'll never see her again, and it's going to hurt. Bad. Maybe even worse than it did the first time."

He's wrong. I can see her again. I can *reach* her again.

"I can handle more than you think," I say stiffly. "I'm not a little kid. I know how death works." *I know about the Hollow.*

Dad's expression doesn't change. "That's the thing—I'm not sure anyone in the world really knows how death works. It's why it's so scary."

"I'm not scared of death," I say. "I'm scared of forgetting Babung the way she forgot me."

He doesn't hesitate. "That will never happen."

"It will if no one talks about her," I argue. "I only have *some* of her memories. You and Mom have even more."

Something in Dad's eyes cracks like lines splintering across frozen water. "It's complicated, Eliot. We're just trying to do what we think is best."

"Yeah, well, it would be nice if you asked me what I thought was best sometimes. I'm part of this family too, you know. And I deserve more than an opinion on sideboards and paint."

Dad opens his mouth, but no sound comes out. He just stares and stares, because for all he talks about knowing what's best, he still doesn't know what to say.

I turn for the stairs and make my way to my bedroom.

My parents work in the house, and I work in the garden— and maybe that says a lot about our family. It doesn't matter that we all love each other. I'm always going to be on the outside.

CHAPTER TWENTY-SEVEN

It's been a week since Hazel left. I can't figure out any more of the riddles, and every time I visit Mrs. Delvaux's garden, I get more and more overwhelmed by how much searching there still is. It could take *months*. And I'm not sure the ghosts have that much time left.

I miss having a friend to help.

I miss having a friend, period.

Mrs. Delvaux spends the morning telling me about how some flowers and vegetables grow well together. She's in the middle of explaining why cucumbers and lettuce are good planting companions for marigolds, when I decide I'm not really helping anyone by sitting outside—I need to take another look around the house for clues.

"I have to go to the bathroom," I announce suddenly.

Mrs. Delvaux bites down on a laugh. "You have been coming here long enough that you don't need to ask permission. And neither am I all that interested in hearing about it."

I make my way inside, pausing near the threshold to make sure Mrs. Delvaux isn't following me, and turn down the first corridor. I scan the walls, the decor, and the shelves—anything that might relate to the riddles in the poem.

Taking the first flight of stairs up to the wide landing, I turn down the hallway and realize I've been here before. It was the day Hazel had her music too loud, and I'd tried to talk to her through the door.

I forgot how new and clean everything was on this side of the house.

Hazel's door is slightly ajar. I start to walk past it, searching instead for a room with old furniture and potential clues, when I see Hazel sitting on her bed. She's wearing her favorite striped cardigan, with her wavy hair draped over her shoulders.

The moment she sees me, her eyebrows shoot up.

I take a step into her room. "Mrs. Delvaux didn't tell me you were back!"

"I-I wasn't sure when I'd see you again. I was starting to worry." There's a scratch in her voice, as if it's been a while since she used it. It's the way I sound when I first wake up in the morning.

I don't know if she means she was worried about not seeing me again, or if she's talking about the ghosts. Personally, I've been worried about both.

"I'm so glad you're here," I say. "Something major happened in the Hollow. There are so many things I've been wanting to tell you. It feels like you've been gone for *months*."

A hint of light returns to her eyes, and the lines in her

brow disappear. "I'm sorry I haven't been around to help. Being away has been *awful*—I keep having nightmares about being trapped in this house, and no one is around—not you or my grandma—and it felt like it was going to be like that for the rest of my life."

"Whoa," I say. "That sounds really creepy."

She offers a weak smile. "It was the lonely part that bothered me the most."

I lift my shoulders. "Well, if it's any consolation, I've been useless without my partner in crime."

Hazel laughs. "I thought I was the sidekick?"

"You're invaluable," I say easily. "Partner feels more . . . *right*."

Hazel beams, grinning with all her teeth, when I notice how bare her walls are. There aren't any photos, or posters, or signs that this room is really lived in. Just clean carpet, a shiny doorknob, a small bookshelf, and an immaculate wardrobe.

It's even less decorated than my room, and I've only lived in this town for part of a summer.

Hazel tangles her fingers together like she knows what I'm thinking. "This place has always felt so temporary to me. I guess I was never bothered about making it feel like my home."

That's how I used to feel about Roseheart. But then I met Hazel and the Honeyfield ghosts, and now I'm not so sure I want it to be temporary.

It wasn't posters and curtains that changed my feelings though. It was the people.

"You don't have to decorate to make it feel like home," I say. "I don't think home is a place—I think it's more of a feeling."

She lifts her shoulders. "What is a home supposed to feel like?"

I think for a moment. "When I was really little, I fell off my bike and scraped my knee. Babung brought me inside, and when I wouldn't stop crying, she got some ice cream to cheer me up. But the ice cream was way too frozen to eat. So Babung kept scraping it with a spoon, over and over again, until it got so soft that she could pack it down again. When she gave me the bowl, she said it wasn't ice cream—it was 'mush'—and that I'd enjoy it way more because it was made with love.

"After that, anytime I was sad, Babung would make us mush, and we'd eat together. I don't know how to explain it, but it always made me feel safe. Like it didn't matter anymore how sad or hurt I got—because I knew where I could go to feel better again. Where I could go to feel loved." I shrug. "I think that's what home is supposed to feel like."

"I'm not sure if I've ever had that," Hazel admits. "But it sounds wonderful."

I hesitate, staring at the walls. "You should get the Batman poster from the attic," I offer. "It would look good in here—and it may not be mush, but it could at least remind you of something that makes you happy."

She smiles. "You have good ideas."

I fiddle with the end of one of my braids, embarrassed. "I wish I had better ones. I haven't solved any more riddles since you've been gone."

I tell her about the memory, and the monster, and how Trill's name was really Emma—and how, after she touched the trinket box, she disappeared.

"I can't believe you went out there on your own," Hazel says. "What if you had lost your memories, too?"

"I hadn't really been thinking about that. I just wanted to save Trill." I frown. "I guess it works different for living people."

"Yeah, well, just don't test your luck with the monster," she warns. "Who knows what could've happened if it got hold of you?"

I think back to the mess of black smoke. "It didn't want me—just the memory."

"I know I said I was up for monster hunting earlier, but after that story, I'm not so sure I'm brave enough." She shudders. "I saw a badger in the attic once, and it was horrible. I screamed so loud, I'm sure it almost broke the windows."

"Wait—there was a *badger* in your attic?" I try not to laugh. "How did it get there?"

"Holy Creepy Taxidermy is how it got there!" She makes a face of disgust. "It has these giant claws and snarling teeth. And some of the old skin is so worn down, you can see the roots of the teeth and—"

We both freeze.

A rush of static spreads all over my skin. "Did you just say . . . ?"

". . . teeth have *roots* . . ."

". . . and are definitely not trees," I finish.

Our eyes meet.

"It's a clue!" we shout in unison.

We don't waste any more time talking—we run up to the attic, not bothering to mask our footsteps or the sound of our hurried breaths.

Hazel weaves around a collection of boxes, and I duck to avoid one of the low beams laced with cobwebs. There in the back, sitting on an old coffee table and covered in heaps of dust, is a stuffed badger.

"Why would anyone do that to an animal?" My stomach coils. "It's literally dead. And it's just . . . staring at us."

"I feel like it's going to come back to life and attack me." Hazel lowers her voice. "I don't want to touch it."

"Neither do I," I whisper back. "But how else are we going to check for clues?"

"I'll look for a stick or something. We can poke it and see if there's something hidden underneath."

Hazel moves around the attic, searching for something long and pointy, when a glint of silver catches my eye.

I inhale sharply. "Hang on—I see something!"

Hazel hurries back to my side. I point to the badger's lower jaw, where a small object is covering one of the canines.

"Still not touching it," Hazel hisses.

Even though my skin feels like it's crawling with bugs, I step forward, reach into the badger's jaws, and remove the piece of silver.

Hazel and I both scurry backward, just in case the animal isn't *completely* dead. I've seen ghosts in this house. Who knows what else is possible?

I hold up the piece of metal to the light. It's a thimble. A really, really tiny thimble.

"Who do you think it belongs to?" Hazel asks.

"I don't know," I say. "But I know where to go to find out."

Hazel hurries downstairs to keep an eye on Mrs. Delvaux, and I use the skeleton key on the attic door.

When I emerge in the Hollow, the glowing thimble is stuffed in my fist, and in an instant, a flash of a memory races through my mind, taking over all my senses.

CHAPTER TWENTY-EIGHT

A little boy sits on the floor, surrounded by toy soldiers and a wooden horse. He's trying to ignore the sound of arguing in the next room; it's too loud, and he doesn't like the fighting.

"Why must you be so difficult?" one of the voices says, exasperated.

"I wouldn't have to be if you'd just *listen* to me!" the other replies.

"These are just the way things are done."

"Just because it's done doesn't make it right!"

"All the other young ladies understand that—"

"I don't want to be like *all the young ladies*. I want to be *me*. And I want that to be good enough."

The shouting gets louder and louder, and the boy lowers his head to the floor and focuses on the pretend battle instead.

Beneath the couch, a piece of metal draws his eye. Belly-crawling across the floor like his toy soldiers, he reaches a hand into the shadows and pulls out a small thimble.

The perfect hat, he declares to himself proudly, and sticks it on top of his horse's head.

A woman marches back into the room and sits on the couch with an overwhelming sigh. She picks up a partially embroidered handkerchief and frowns. "All this fuss over a bit of sewing. Imagine being a woman and not being able to mend a shirt!"

The boy settles his chin over his folded arms. He didn't think mending a shirt sounded like much fun either, but he thought it was better not to say anything. His mother always seemed to think boys and girls had different rules, and she'd get upset if anyone tried to argue about them.

But sometimes the rules didn't seem fair. Girls had to mend shirts and make sure their words were polite and talk to people even if they didn't want to. Boys had to be strong and brave and never cry.

Except the boy doesn't always feel strong, and sometimes he's scared, and there are plenty of times he wants to cry. Hiding it all just makes everything feel worse, like he's been made to carry a secret he never wanted in the first place.

He stares at the horse wearing a thimble for a hat. Maybe it's better to be a horse. They can win races and pull carriages and play in the fields, and nobody tells them those things are only for boys or girls. They're just things for any horse.

Not that the boy *wants* to be a horse. The stables always smell funny, and he'd hate to have a metal bit in his mouth all day, and he'd rather not eat hay.

The woman looks around, patting at the couch cushion. "Where did I put—" She stops, eyes falling on the wooden horse. A smile spreads across her face. "Is Sir Duncan hoping to do a bit of sewing?"

The boy looks up. "No. Sir Duncan has to be a soldier. He's not allowed to sew—which is a shame, because he's actually very good at it, deep down."

The woman's face falls, but she says nothing. Not at first. And then, "When you say it like that, it doesn't sound very fair, does it?" She plucks at her skirt. "But a parent's job is to prepare their children for the world. And the world is never fair."

The boy taps a finger against the horse's back. "No wonder grown-ups are so unhappy."

She pauses. "Why do you say that?"

He looks up. "Because they have to fit in a world that doesn't like them as they are. And everyone knows it's not fair, but they do it anyway because it's how things have always been done."

The woman's eyes glisten. "You sound the way your father used to, a long time ago."

The boy plucks the thimble and holds it up to his mother.

She shakes her head. "Keep it. Sir Duncan needs it more than I do." She leans forward and brushes the boy's hair from his eyes. "And thank you for reminding me about my wish, Charlie."

"You made a wish?" the boys asks.

"A long time ago." The woman smiles. "I wished for a family that was genuinely happy instead of just pretending to be. And I think I forgot how much parents are responsible for that."

The boy puts the piece of metal back on the wooden horse's head, and makes a *clip-clop* sound with his tongue as he bounces the horse across the floor. His horse is a soldier today—but maybe when the war is over, he can be the tailor he always dreamed of.

The rest of the world may not be welcoming, but he'll just have to make sure his own world is.

My eyelids flutter and I suck in a breath, realizing I know the woman from the memory. *Emma.* Which means the boy, Charlie . . .

He looked too much like the child version of Lock for it to be a coincidence.

I clamber down the tree branches connecting the attic to the rest of the house. There's no carpet in the hall—just a layer of soil and leaves strewn in every direction. Everything looks grayer than before, and the flecks of ash floating through the air are *everywhere*.

It's almost like Honeyfield Hall is disintegrating.

I flatten my mouth, not wanting to think about what that means.

When I turn the next corridor, I hear pacing in the room

that looked a bit like a library the last time I was here, with the strange, backward books and Lock sitting at his desk.

Now it looks like something out of a nightmare.

Enormous mushrooms have sprouted from the furniture. All the books are barricaded with thorn-covered branches that claw at the room like a harrowing creature. Wisps of gray nothingness seep into the room from above, where the ceiling has been partially torn away.

Lock is on his hands and knees, scraping through the mulch like he's digging for something. Something he's desperate to find. He crawls toward me without realizing it, and when he spots the tips of my shoes, his gaze trails to my face.

Lock pushes himself up and stands, immediately shrinking to the size of a child. Nearly identical to the boy in the memory.

Except this boy's hair drips with sap. Even his skin shines like glass, and his movements are stilted. *Hardened.*

"Where did you hide it?" he demands, voice shrill. "I know it's here somewhere. I saw you with a, with a—" His lips clamp shut, and then he grows to the height of a man again, eyebrows knotted with confusion.

The sap pinches his mouth together. He can't speak.

I don't know how to stop the panic in his eyes.

"Lock," I say quickly, holding the glowing thimble in my palm. "I think this memory belongs to you."

The lines in his face soften, and he plucks it from my hand

with care, holding it between two fingers. The thimble continues to glow, but the man's face doesn't change at all.

He passes it back, and shakes his head. I can read his eyes—the memory isn't his.

"But," I start, frowning. "The boy with Emma . . . He looked just like you."

The sap spreads, coating Lock like it's flowing right from his skin.

My heart thunders, frantic. "I know it isn't your memory, but if Emma and the boy are connected, maybe you are too." I shake my head again and again, watching in horror as the sap builds like honey over his entire body. "His name was Charlie. He had a toy horse. He was playing in the living room. And—and Emma was arguing with someone. Someone I couldn't see."

Lock stops blinking. He gleams beneath the sap from his head to his toes. I'm not even sure if he can hear me anymore.

But I don't stop. I can't. "She said she made a wish to have a family who was always happy instead of just pretending. It's the same wish she made to the trinket box when she was little."

Lock remains stoic. I take a step closer, throat tightening.

Am I really too late?

"You have to remember something. I promised I'd help you," I say, voice hushed. "And you promised each other you'd stick together."

But the sap has taken control. Lock doesn't move at all.

I drop my arm, and turn for the door. The sting in my eyes makes me sniff.

I'm almost past the threshold when I hear a cracked voice breaking free of its slumber.

"Wait."

I spin quickly. Lock's mouth is parted, and the sap is cracked in a dozen places all over his face. He strains, and the brittle sap shatters, giving his limbs movement once more.

"Lock!" I cry out.

He wobbles slightly before taking three heavy steps forward. "I think I know whose memory that is." He turns to his left as if he's staring through the mushroom-ridden shelves. "Come with me," he says, and vanishes through the bookcase into the next room.

I can't follow him through walls, so I step back into the hallway, peering through room after room until I find Lock in the old piano room, staring into the dark pit where the massive instrument had sunk.

"He hasn't been well since Trill left," Lock explains. "He always seemed to be the strong one. The one we never worried about. But maybe not everyone carries loss the same way."

"Are you talking about Hatter?" I ask.

Lock gives a curt nod and points down the enormous tree trunk into the dark cavern below.

I climb down the rugged path, ignoring the bite of bark against my skin. When I reach the bottom, I glance around warily.

Before, it looked like the inside of a hollow tree. But now the space is covered in moss. Strange purple and pink flowers sprout in the corners of the room, seeping with yellow smoke. At first I think they might be poisonous, until I realize they're hydrangeas, rotting from the inside out.

All that's left of the grand piano is an enormous green mound.

Hatter is perched at the top of it, legs half buried in the moss. I think he's now a part of the piano, too. There are dark rings under his eyes. He doesn't just look like a ghost; he looks like he's being haunted by one.

I know that look. The broken sadness that feels like falling into darkness, further and further away from the surface.

It's how I felt the afternoon Mom and Dad told me Babung was really gone.

It didn't last long. It didn't need to. Because I started researching ghosts, and paranormal activity, and I knew—I just *knew*—I'd get another chance to say goodbye.

Hatter hasn't broken out of his grief. He's consumed by it.

I recognize it well enough to know there's nothing I can say right now to pull him out. So I sit beside him, hoping he'll be able to see that he's not alone.

Eventually, he turns his head. "You shouldn't be here," he croaks. "It's no place for a child."

"This kind of sadness is no place for anyone." I hold up the thimble, and Hatter's eyes drift to the glow in the center of my palm. "You're Charles Honeyfield, aren't you? The reclusive war veteran from my book."

"I . . ." He blinks.

"Take it—it belongs to you," I tell him, and he does.

A wave of color glimmers across his face, and Hatter transforms into a younger, brighter version of the person I first met in the Hollow. Even his mustache seems particularly well kept.

He stands, eyes glued to mine. "I understand now," he says, smiling peacefully. He glances up toward the opening, where Lock's faraway face peers down. "We will see each other again."

The moment Hatter—Charles—hands the thimble back, he fades away to nothing.

Something cracks deep inside the earth, and the mossy hill shudders before turning to a pile of ash that spills over my feet. The flowers become dust. The yellow smoke fades.

All that's left is me and the darkness.

I look around panicked, and clamber back up the tree as quickly as I can. When I reach Lock, he's still staring into the void.

"There was life in that piano," he says. "Life that only Trill knew how to reach."

I'm watching the walls, listening as the creaks and moans seem to erupt from every corner. Something is wrong. The monster isn't just awake—it's *desperate*.

I tuck the thimble into my bag with the other objects and take a nervous step away from the window.

I can hear it outside.

The monster is coming for the house.

Lock looks at me, uninterested in the noises that sound as if the house is being ripped apart. "I could never figure out how to possess an object the way she could. She didn't just touch the piano—she *became* the piano. She held on to its life, even in this dark place." He holds up a gray hand, staring through the translucent skin.

My eyes dart between Lock and the window. "The shadow monster is coming. I, I think this time I've made it angry."

But Lock doesn't hear me. "It would've been nice to possess a book like that." His eyes shine. "With all the stories in the library, I would never have to fear being alone." He shakes his head. "There's so much life in a library."

I turn, anxious to return to the living world, when his words send me reeling.

His library. His books.

A story . . . that holds *life without a heartbeat.*

"I know where to look next," I say with wide eyes.

In that moment, the monster thrashes at the window, making me shriek. Lock throws his hands up for cover before shrinking into a small boy and bolting back through the wall.

I stumble through the corridor, but the monster is more aggressive than ever, slamming itself against the glass with a feral snarl. It wails, and the horrible sound grates against my ears, making my head throb. I race down the stairs, and use the closet to retreat to the other side of the veil.

When I throw the door back open and crash against the floor, it isn't the monster that's waiting for me.

It's Mrs. Delvaux.

CHAPTER TWENTY-NINE

What are you doing?" Mrs. Delvaux asks, brow raised high.

I scrunch my bag with one hand, skeleton key wedged in the other, and try to slow my breathing. "I . . . er . . . got lost."

She laughs with her lips pressed together. "I used to love exploring this house when I was younger, too. Plenty of good places to hide—but mind you don't break anything. There are some ornaments upstairs I'd be very sorry to lose."

I nod too many times, hoping she won't pay too much attention to my bag, but it's the key her eyes drift to.

"Where did you find that?" She holds out a hand, and I have no choice.

I give the skeleton key to Mrs. Delvaux.

"I found it in the greenhouse," I say shakily.

She turns it beneath her nose. "You shouldn't be playing with this. This house has a lot of old keys, and I'd hate to lose track of one."

My shoulders feel weighed down by fear. If she takes the key . . . If I can't get back to the Hollow . . .

"I-I need it," I blurt out suddenly.

"What for?" she asks. "What's this one open?"

Salt settles in the corner of my eyes and I flinch. I'm not supposed to tell her. Hazel and I had a deal—and if Mrs. Delvaux tells my parents, everything will be ruined.

But if she takes the key . . .

"It's a special key. It lets me talk to ghosts, and it's the only way I can get a message to my grandma." I swallow the lump in my throat. "I promised I'd help her remember who she was—but she died before I got a chance to say goodbye. I *have* to keep my promise." To the ghosts and to Babung.

Mrs. Delvaux is quiet for a long time. I'm terrified of what she'll say, but I can't lose the skeleton key. Not when I've come this far.

With the key still in her hand, Mrs. Delvaux drops her arms and stares at me. Something stings in her eyes too, but I can't tell if it's anger or—

"You should go home," she says abruptly.

"But," I start, "what about the garden?" And the study, and the books, and the riddles, and everything I still need to do?

And what about the skeleton key?

Mrs. Delvaux's shoulders shake and she motions for me to leave. "This isn't a good time." Her bark rages through me, and when I leave the house, I feel like I've done something horribly wrong.

And I guess I have, because how am I ever going to get a message to Babung now?

I stab a fork through my egg, watching the yolk dribble through the white rice. Dad leans over with the spatula and drops two slices of teriyaki fried spam onto the egg before taking the pan back to the stove.

I shove the crispy meat around, not taking a bite.

Mom looks up from her to-do list. "You okay, honey? You seem quiet this morning."

I stuff my mouth with rice and make a noncommittal noise. Maybe it will be enough to stop her from asking questions.

I can't talk to my parents. Not about this.

Dad turns from the stove, sprinkling seasoning on his steaming bowl of rice. "Are you working on the garden today? The weather forecast says it's going to be pretty hot. Make sure you put on sunscreen."

I lean back, flustered. "Mrs. Delvaux doesn't want me there today." Maybe not ever again, after the way she looked at me.

I don't know exactly what I said wrong, but I know I upset her. I'm guessing it had something to do with the part about ghosts—and also the fact that I took her key without permission and had no intention of returning it.

Maybe she realized I've been hiding a secret all this time. Maybe she is the reason the Honeyfield ghosts lost their memories.

Mom and Dad exchange a glance.

"Did something happen?" Mom presses.

"It's not important," I mumble, still chewing. "I really don't want to talk about it."

Mom taps her pen against her list. "Well, maybe you and I could do something fun today? We could go to the park, and grab smoothies on the way home."

"I'm too old for the park," I snap.

"I didn't realize there was an age limit on grass," Dad says blandly.

"Yeah, well, you and Mom don't realize a lot of things." The moment the words leave my mouth, I know I went too far.

Dad widens his eyes at Mom, who purses her lips.

I stand up before they can tell me I'm being rude, or talking back, or whatever it is they're thinking. "I'm not really hungry. Can I go to the library? I have to return my book so I don't get a late fee."

Mom lowers her chin, watchful, but eventually nods. "Okay. Just—be careful. And make sure you're back home for lunch."

I nod and hurry to get my bag, leaving the sound of their muffled conversation behind.

000

I turn in *Roseheart: A Local History* to the librarian named Ruth at the front desk and watch as she tucks it into a nearby cart.

She passes my library card back and smiles. "Okay—you're all set."

I shuffle in place. "Do you know if there are any other books about the town's history here?"

Ruth's laugh is soft and light. "I don't know if this town is big enough to warrant *two* history books. But I can have a look for you." She types away at her computer for a few moments. "There aren't any other books on the town specifically, but it's mentioned in a couple of other books. There's one about award-winning gardens. And one about influential people in the Northeast during the nineteenth century—except it looks like that one was checked out a while ago and never returned. We could put a hold on it for you, but I'm not sure how likely it is that it will turn up after all this time."

I look up, frowning. "I remember seeing the gardening one when I searched on the library computer, but not the other one."

She nods toward the screen. "That's because it's under the town's old name—Rothbury. It changed to Roseheart in 1902 because of a rivalry with another town." She widens her eyes for dramatic effect. "It had something to do with the harvest festival. People were stealing pumpkins, and sabotaging pies . . . It was a whole thing. Lots of police involved, apparently, and Rothbury got a lot of bad press." She laughs. "Didn't you read about it in the history book you just returned?"

My cheeks turn pink. "I must've missed that part." I was so focused on the page about Honeyfield Hall that I hadn't actually finished the whole book.

"You know you can check the book out again, if you like," Ruth offers.

"With the gardening one as well?"

"Of course! Want me to write down the aisle number for you?"

I nod, and she pulls out a clean white card and jots some numbers and letters down. She hands it to me and taps the spine of *Roseheart: A Local History.*

"I'll keep this one at the desk for you. Just come back when you're ready," Ruth says.

I make my way farther into the library and find *Gardens of the Coast,* but on my way back to the desk, someone says my name.

"Eliot . . . um, hey."

I turn and find Sunny holding a library book against her chest.

She shifts her weight nervously, blond hair pulled in a high ponytail. "I haven't seen you in the neighborhood," she says.

I don't tell her I've been taking a shortcut every day to Mrs. Delvaux's just so I don't have to run into her and her friends.

"I've been busy," I say instead.

She nods, quiet for a few long seconds. "I'm sorry about what happened that day, with the bikes. It was a silly joke."

I open my mouth to say it's fine, but I realize it's not fine. It was mean, and if she'd played the joke on Hazel instead of me, I'd tell her so.

But I don't really know how to stick up for myself the way I'd stick up for a friend.

Maybe I need to work on that.

Sunny pauses, chewing her lip. "I remember what it felt

like to be the new kid in a small town. I should've made you feel more welcome."

I twist my mouth. "You were a new kid here?"

Sunny lifts her shoulders. "My parents moved here from Michigan when I was in second grade. It took a while to feel like I fit in."

My eyes catch the title of her book, and I make a face. "You like geology?"

She tightens her grip and flashes a crooked smile. "Oh, yeah. I got a rock polisher for my birthday a few months ago. I've been searching the neighborhood for quartz."

"Quartz is one of my favorites! It's a healing rock, but it's also good for protection when you're searching for ghosts." I hold up my bracelet. "I always have some with me."

Sunny beams and holds up a bracelet of her own. Hers is mostly white beads, with a rose quartz dangling from a gold charm. "Me too! Not for ghosts though. They just make me happy." She motions to the book I'm holding. "What are you reading?"

"Oh—I'm just doing some research on the town."

"Are you looking up gardens because of Mrs. Delvaux?" she asks quietly. "I heard you've been doing chores at her house."

"You heard?"

"Betty saw you," she admits. "Is it because we got you in trouble?"

I hesitate. "It's a summer job, actually."

She relaxes. "Oh. That's a relief."

I count the seconds and realize it's starting to get awkward, and I'd prefer to avoid having another marine animal meltdown. One was more than enough.

"I should go," I say quickly. "I'm supposed to be home before lunch. But—thanks for saying hi."

"Okay." Sunny nods. "Maybe I'll see you around the neighborhood sometime." She points to her book. "I'll let you know if I find any quartz."

I know she wasn't very nice to me the first time we met. And I know a shared interest in geology isn't going to undo what happened.

But I guess the apology means more to me than the anger.

I smile. "Okay. See you around."

I turn and make my way to the front desk, where I check out both books and wonder if it's a good thing to give second chances—and whether Mrs. Delvaux will decide to give me one too.

CHAPTER THIRTY

I t takes three whole seconds to process that Mrs. Delvaux is standing in my living room.

"You didn't show up this morning, so I thought I'd better check on you." She narrows her eyes. "Seems there may have been some miscommunication between us."

Dad gets up from the couch, smiling gently. "I'll give you two a minute."

Mom follows him into the kitchen, nodding politely to Mrs. Delvaux as she passes.

I swallow the knot in my throat. "I, I thought you didn't want me to come back."

"I'm sorry if I was short with you yesterday." Mrs. Delvaux's blue eyes still. Her hair is twisted into a low braid, and she's wearing a knitted cardigan over a long, black dress.

"You're the second person who's apologized to me today," I say matter-of-factly. Only I hadn't *actually* meant to say it out loud.

That's the problem with having too many racing thoughts— sometimes they forget the rules.

"Well, I sure hope mine's the better apology of the two," she says, voice hoarse. "I really don't like to lose."

I look away, embarrassed. "I didn't mean it like that. But—I'm the one who's sorry. I shouldn't have taken the key without asking."

"The key?" She frowns. "You thought I was upset about the key?"

I look up. "Isn't that why you told me to leave?"

She barks a laugh. "Not at all, girl. I asked you to leave because my emotions were getting the better of me. It's what you said when you were playing that game of yours, and pretending to talk to ghosts. The part about needing to say goodbye to your grandma."

My heart tightens. *She thinks it was a game.*

Maybe that's a good thing.

"When I was your age, I lost my father," she explains, voice heavy. "It was very sudden. I never got a chance to say goodbye either."

"I'm sorry," I say.

"I thought I'd gotten past the worst of it, but something you said brought it all back for me." She takes a deep breath through her nose. "I suppose there's no real finality to grief. You can bury it or shoulder it or conquer it, but it still finds small, quiet ways to reemerge."

I wonder if missing Babung will always hurt, or if someday it will get easier.

I wonder if I'll be okay when it does.

"Well, I certainly didn't come here to make anyone sad," Mrs. Delvaux says, folding her hands together. "I only wanted to tell you that you were very missed this morning, and I hope I didn't make you feel unwelcome. Yesterday had nothing to do with you—it was me letting my feelings get the better of me."

"Maybe that's a good thing," I say. "Maybe some feelings go after the best of you because the best thing *for* you is to let them out."

She chuckles. "You have an answer for everything. I like that about you."

I shift my weight, feeling the thump of the library books against my hip, and remember what's inside. Reaching into my bag, I pull out *Roseheart: A Local History*.

"Can I ask you something?" I crack the book open to the page with the Delvaux family. "Do you know who these people are?"

She takes the book and a smile spreads across her face. She runs a finger over the image. "These are my parents. And me."

"I thought it might be," I say. "I wasn't sure if you'd seen the photo before. But if there was a book that had a photo of me and Babung, I think I'd want to see it."

"My father died shortly after we moved into Honeyfield Hall, and my mother a decade later." She looks up, pointedly. "I'm sure you heard all about the *curse*."

"Nobody ever told me the story," I admit. "The book only says there was a tragedy with the Honeyfield family."

"It started with them," Mrs. Delvaux says. "One of their children passed quite young, and the sadness just seemed to follow the others. They said Mr. Honeyfield was so distraught that he put a curse on the house, so that no family would ever replace his. I don't believe any of his children married, and there were no grandchildren. Eventually the house went to my father—he was Mrs. Honeyfield's nephew, you see." She turns back to the photo, emotions splintering. "My father never believed in the curse, but he died in the house, and then my mother, and then my husband. And my son grew up wanting very little to do with me. So whether the curse is real or not doesn't matter—the fact is, there has never been a real family in Honeyfield Hall since the Honeyfield family."

I know Trill was Emma Honeyfield, and that Hatter was her son, Charles. But that leaves Lock and Pearl.

Were they *all* part of the Honeyfield family?

Mrs. Delvaux interrupts my thoughts. "The well in this photo . . . I remember it was *very* deep. You could shout your name and the echo felt like it lasted a whole minute." Her smile falters. "I sometimes used to shout to my father, thinking if I tried hard enough, eventually he might shout back."

I grimace. "Do you think I'm silly for trying to find my Babung?"

"Not at all," she says. "I'm only telling you this because I want you to know that I understand."

"My parents don't understand," I say. "They don't even like me talking about her."

Her eyes glint. "Some people shout into the well. Some people pretend the well isn't even there. But someday, we all meet in the middle." Her mouth wrinkles. "Give it some time."

"I don't remember seeing a well in the backyard."

"It was filled in a good twenty years ago. Too many local kids kept sneaking into the yard, and I was worried there'd be an accident."

I try not to look too guilty.

She hands the book back. "You've done plenty to fix up the mess of the strawberries. And while the offer of the summer job still stands, I understand if you'd prefer not to spend your vacation with an old woman and her marigolds." Her normally hardened gaze softens. "There's no pressure to come back to work unless you really want to."

I take the book. "I'll be back tomorrow."

Her blues eyes twinkle. "Marvelous."

Mrs. Delvaux moves for the front door, but I hold up a hand to stop her.

"Wait—I have something for you." I set the book down, race up the stairs to my room, and return with two pieces of quartz. I hold them up in my palm. "There's one for you and one for Hazel. She was having bad dreams, and rose quartz is supposed to help. It also helps with bad energy caused by grief." I shrug. "And if you don't think you need it, that's okay—someone reminded me today that it's okay if it just makes you happy looking at it."

"That's very sweet," Mrs. Delvaux says, and takes the stones. "Thank you, Eliot."

I follow her, and we both stand near the threshold, watching each other.

"The sadness and the loss never fully go away. But the coping gets easier." She lowers her chin. "The memories still hurt, but they don't hurt everything around them. Do you understand what I mean?"

"I think so," I say, although I'm not sure *what* to think. Of all the people I've met, I didn't expect Mrs. Delvaux to be the one to see me so clearly.

Does grief make people feel like they know each other?

"Losing someone as a child is different," she adds, the pain in her voice rigid. "Children remember things so fiercely— your whole life fits in so few years. But as you get older, memories become more like snapshots. Pieces, rather than a whole puzzle."

I stare at my feet, trying not to let the hurt bubble up through my chest.

"Your grandmother would want you to be okay," Mrs. Delvaux says. "You can hold on to your memories as tight as you like. But they exist for remembering—not for dictating your future."

I watch her disappear down the road, thinking about how

she isn't scary, or mean, and she certainly doesn't put curses on children. She's someone who doesn't want to be alone, but can't figure out how to say the words.

We're different in almost every other way, but the loneliness? We have that in common.

CHAPTER THIRTY-ONE

’m running through the misty nothingness, and the monster is close behind me.

It's not just after the memories—this time, it's after *me*.

Waving my hands in front of me, I try to clear some of the fog, but it curls around me, sticking to my flesh like it's going to smother me whole.

Behind me, the monster picks up speed, footsteps thundering against the cloudy earth.

I run so hard my sides ache and my calves hurt and my bones feel like they're ready to snap. I run toward the empty horizon, hoping somehow—somewhere—I'll find a way to make all of this right.

My foot hits something hard, and I stumble forward. But the earth is no longer a gray mist—it's a black hole.

I fall down the well, my scream echoing around me. The monster stares down, fangs bared in triumph, and I crash into a pool of starlight.

I launch myself awake, clutching my blanket around me as I emerge from the nightmare. The ticking of the clock grounds me, and I follow the dim glow of the streetlights peeking through the curtains.

The library books are still sitting on my nightstand. I looked through them right before bed, hoping something would spark an idea, but so far, nothing.

The book about gardening had photos of Honeyfield Hall taken sometime in the 1970s. There was one of the rose garden and all its multicolor blooms, and another of an enormous tree surrounded by hydrangeas. There was even a better-quality photo of the well, when it was surrounded by yellow and white flowers and looked like something out of a fairy tale.

Maybe that's why you dreamed about it, my mind reels.

I start to rub my temples, pushing away the images of the well in my head, when my stomach drops. The well in my dream . . . I can still picture the starlight, and the echo that surrounded me like a vortex.

I carry the stars but cannot fly, and will always answer your call.

"You're a clue," I whisper to the darkness. To the image of the well still seared in my mind.

But just as the riddle clicks into place, I recall what Mrs. Delvaux told me, about the well being filled in because it was too dangerous.

If the well was destroyed, what happened to the treasure that was hidden there? Would it have been destroyed, too?

I wrap my arms around myself, fingers digging against my ribs. I have to hold on to the hope. I have to believe that whatever was hidden—whatever memory that's been lost—can still be found.

Lost doesn't have to mean forever.

Does it?

I lie back down, pull the blanket over my shoulders, and stare at the shadows on my wall until I fall back asleep, hoping the next dream will provide more answers than the first.

CHAPTER THIRTY-TWO

A book and a well; two potential answers to the riddles.

But right now, I'm only thinking about one of them.

I stare off toward the greenhouse while Mrs. Delvaux finishes planting the last of the lettuce seeds. The photo inside the history book was taken somewhere around here; I recognize the paving and the outer wall of the house.

I'm thinking of a reason to go snooping around when the universe gives me one in the form of a cat.

"Not again," Mrs. Delvaux hisses through her teeth.

Dorothy bursts from the back door and makes a break for freedom, fleeing toward the side of the house with record-breaking speed.

"I'll get her," I volunteer, jumping up before Mrs. Delvaux can argue.

I race toward the greenhouse, eyes scanning ahead to where the cat disappeared. The remains of the well are easy enough to find. Some of the stonework is still here, shaped like a perfect circle.

Sand overflows from the rim, creating a small mountain in the middle of the broken cobblestones.

There aren't any clues here. Not unless they're buried far, far beneath the earth.

I try not to feel too defeated, and make my way to the greenhouse instead, where an enormous tree sits in a wide patch of grass. Dorothy is perched on top of a stone embedded just above where the roots must be.

"You're going to get in trouble," I warn. "Mrs. Delvaux doesn't like you going outside."

Dorothy yawns and licks her lips.

I gently scoop her up in my arms, and my eyes fall to the inscription on the stone.

"TO DIE WILL BE AN AWFULLY BIG ADVENTURE." —J. M. BARRIE

Overhead, the leaves dance in the branches, sounding like a dull rainfall. I stare at the stone and the words, wondering how long it's been here, when a voice interrupts my thoughts.

"I take it your quest is going well?" Graham asks, appearing from behind the massive tree trunk.

In my arms, Dorothy hisses.

Graham lifts a brow. "Yes, I am *quite* aware of the time, thank you." He tips his hat, and Dorothy settles.

"You can talk to cats?" I ask blankly.

Graham flashes his teeth. "Depends on whether you believe cats have a soul or not."

Dorothy's tail brushes against my skin, and she closes her eyes sleepily.

"There's still two memories left to find." I twist my mouth. "I think I figured out the riddles, but one of the memories might be buried, and the other is a book—and I have no idea which one."

"Ah." He steps over one of the protruding roots, lithe as a dancer. "That is a predicament." He motions to the stone at his feet. "I have heard on good occasion that the best thing to do when you don't know what to do is read a book."

"There are probably hundreds of books in this house."

"It couldn't hurt to read them all," he suggests. "But I imagine time is not on your side."

"Last time I was in the Hollow, it looked like the house was starting to unravel," I explain. "Is that possible?"

"It's starting to resemble the only thing left they know—a resting place."

I think of the soil, and the tree roots, and the ash. "You mean like where they were *buried*?" I look at him, horrified.

"It was a house before, because that's what they remembered. Now it is becoming the earth."

"What happens when they can't remember anything at all?"

Graham lifts his shoulders. "If you have no memories left—not of who you are or where you are—I suppose there's nothing left to ground you to any one world."

I shake my head like I don't want to believe it. "But you don't just stop existing. Just because you forget, that doesn't mean you're not still here." I think of Babung when she was alive. Here, but not the same as before.

"That's because there's still someone around to do the remembering," Graham says. "But what happens when a ghost is forgotten completely? By themselves and everyone left in the living world?"

I hold Dorothy close to my chest. "I won't forget them." Just like I won't forget Babung.

I'll keep them alive with all the memories I have of them.

He nods slowly. "Nobody has forever, Eliot. Not even you."

"Maybe not." I stare at the grass stubbornly. "But I'm still not ready to give up."

He chuckles lightly. "I'm glad to hear it. It's been a long time since I've been so invested in the ongoings of a living soul. I am curious to see how this all plays out." He stares down at the stone again.

I narrow my eyes. "Why does it feel like you're helping me? I thought you said that was against the rules."

"Yes, that is technically true." He looks around, waving a hand at the empty space. "But we're not on the other side of the veil, and *you're* not a ghost."

"And I won't remember this anyway," I finish for him.

"You won't remember *me*," he corrects. "But perhaps there are other things you can hold on to. You've been doing well enough so far." Graham's golden eyes watch me for a moment, before he steps behind the tree and vanishes completely.

I stare at the bark of the tree, listening to the flutter of leaves overhead.

It's peaceful out here. Of all the trees on the property, this one is by far the most beautiful.

I look down at Dorothy. *That's why I'm standing here— to bring the cat back*, I think.

I glance at the stone one more time, thinking of why the name J. M. Barrie sounds so familiar, and by the time I reach the porch and stick Dorothy inside the house, I realize it's a quote from *Peter Pan and Wendy*.

A *book*. And maybe the clue to the next memory.

CHAPTER THIRTY-THREE

There are at least a thousand books in the upstairs study. Probably more.

None of them are organized—not by author name or title or color. I stand on tiptoe, straining to read the highest shelf, while Hazel searches through the books on the opposite wall.

"Any luck?" she asks, crouching low.

I shake my head. "No. But this is making me dizzy."

"I wonder if anyone even reads these," she says. "Some of them look *really* old."

"I haven't seen a single title I recognize," I add.

She frowns, straightening. "You're right. I don't think any of these are even children's books."

I retrace the last row, reading the spines in my head. All of these books are about poems or gardening or history. There's nothing here that's aimed at kids.

Definitely no *Peter Pan and Wendy*.

My stomach drops, but I turn to look at Hazel. "Isn't there a bookshelf in your room?"

Her forehead crumples like she isn't quite sure. "I, I think so."

There was nothing about Babung's house I wasn't sure of. I memorized every corner. Every shelf and ornament and knickknack. I knew it by heart, just like I knew Babung by heart.

"You're thinking about your grandma right now, aren't you?" Hazel asks quietly.

I look away. "How did you know?"

"Your face changes when you think about her. Even though I can tell you're sad, there's a light there, too."

"I didn't know I was so easy to read."

Hazel grins, and points to her own face. "Try me. What am I thinking?" She forces her mouth into a straight line, even though it looks like she's about to burst out laughing.

"Um. I don't know." I scrunch my nose. "Peter Pan?"

"Yes!" Hazel shouts and claps her hands together. "Holy Amazing Mind Reading Skills!"

"I mean, we literally just combed through five bookshelves looking for it," I point out.

Hazel shrugs. "If you're easy to read, then I want to be easy to read. We're partners, remember?"

I blush a deep burgundy. "Yeah. I remember."

Hazel motions for me to follow her, and we turn down the corridor and make our way into her bedroom. It feels just as empty as it did last time. Even the bed is perfectly made, like it's more of a hotel room than a twelve-year-old's room.

But I do notice the rose quartz sitting on the bedside table.

I'm glad Hazel isn't looking at me—if she were, she'd see that I'm glowing from the inside out.

We stand side by side in front of the bookshelf, eyes scanning from right to left and back again. And then I see it, wedged between a copy of *Black Beauty* and *Grimm's Fairy Tales*—a worn copy of *Peter Pan and Wendy*.

Taking it from the shelf, I dust the cover and study the binding. There's some water damage, and most of the pages have turned golden-brown. But there's nothing especially peculiar about it. Nothing to signal that it's part of a memory.

Not until I open the cover and see the card that's been left inside.

It has the word "reception" written at the top in black ink, with an address and date that's too smudged to make out. The name Emma Delvaux is written in fancy cursive, followed by a list of dances—and the name August Honeyfield is written in every blank space.

"What is this?" I ask.

"A dance card," Hazel replies easily. "Girls used to tie them to their wrist, and boys could write their name in the blank spaces if they wanted to claim a dance. It's a ridiculous tradition."

"What, like calling dibs?" I make a face. "What if you didn't *want* to dance with the person?"

Or if a girl wanted to ask the boy to dance?

Or if they didn't want to ask a boy at all?

Hazel purses her lips. "It's not really fair, is it?"

"No. It's not." I look at August's collection of signatures. "He must've really wanted to dance with her."

Hazel snorts. "I can't tell if it's sweet or rude. It's bad manners to write your name more than once—doesn't really give anyone else a fair chance."

"In Emma's memory, there was a boy," I say, remembering the trinket box, and the wish. "I think they were in love. If it was August Honeyfield, maybe that means they were in love for their whole lives."

Hazel makes a face. "So you're firmly in the 'it's sweet' boat, huh?"

"I didn't realize you were so anti-romance."

"I'm not," Hazel huffs. "I just think it would be a lot more romantic if there were no dance cards or rules or parents telling their kids what to do. And preferably one of them would be a pirate, and the other a mermaid."

I lift my eyebrows. "Or if they were *both* mermaids, from warring mer-kingdoms."

She nods enthusiastically. "Whose families are sworn enemies, because one side used their magic to curse the other side with fish tails!"

"And they're both heirs to their kingdoms," I add, laughing.

She lifts her hands. "Both destined to be crowned queen and—" She hesitates, mouth parted.

So I finish for her. "Queen."

Her eyes brighten. "Yeah. Queen and queen." She stares at the shelves. "I'd love a story like that."

My eyes fall back to the dance card. If it were Hazel's, I think I'd want to write my name on every dance, too.

I tuck the card in my bag, and clutch the thought close to my heart.

"If this is August's memory, you'll be able to reunite them," Hazel says, voice suddenly soft. "They won't have to be alone."

"If Lock is August, then after I give him the card, he'll disappear. It means Pearl will be the only one left." I chew my thoughts. "What if her memory was really destroyed with the well, or impossible to reach? What am I supposed to tell her?"

I don't want to let her down. I *promised*.

"Maybe telling her who she is will be enough," Hazel suggests. "You think she's August and Emma's daughter, right? So just tell her that part."

"What if it's not enough?" I ask.

Hazel's quiet for a while. "I know you miss your grandma . . . But why is it so important that you talk to her again?"

I look away. "I didn't get a chance to say goodbye. She'd already forgotten me, and I was so busy trying to think of things to tell her—ways to make her remember—that I guess I didn't realize how short we were on time. My parents just sat me down one afternoon and said she was gone.

"I want to say goodbye properly—but mostly I want to make sure she isn't stuck somewhere not knowing she was loved. Because if I can remind her of all the things that made her special? That made *us* special? Then she won't be alone in the afterlife."

"What is it you want to tell her?" Hazel asks.

I shrug. "Everything that mattered. Like how she used to name her orchids after all the names she'd call me—Eliot, and Eliot-Chan, and Usako—with a number at the end because her orchids started to take over the backyard. I want to tell her about mush, and her jade frogs and crocheted rabbits. I want her to remember how great she was at listening, and how I always felt like I could tell her anything and she'd only love me a thousand times more. I want her to know that even when she got scared near the end, that she was loved more than she could've possibly realized—and that I wasn't a stranger. I was her favorite."

The salt in my eyes burns, and I wipe my cheek with the back of my hand.

"Those are all the things you told me about," Hazel says. "I like those memories."

"Yeah. So do I."

"Don't worry. We'll save the Honeyfield ghosts—and they'll take your message to your grandma." Hazel offers a smile full of hope. "Batman and Robin always win. It's just the rules."

I half laugh, half sniffle. "We still need to get the skeleton key back. I can't do anything without a way to the Hollow."

"I can try to ask for it back, but there's no guarantee it will work. Me and my grandma aren't like you and Babung,"

Hazel says. "I doubt she'd ever go through this much trouble to try and help *me* in the afterlife."

"I think you two are more alike than you realize," I say.

Hazel snorts. "If that were true, she'd stick up for me when it came to my parents. She'd tell them to stop controlling every single thing I do, and every place I go. She'd make me feel welcome here instead of acting like I don't even exist. And—okay, maybe I don't always make it easy, but I feel like all they want is for me to be someone I'm not."

"I didn't know your parents were like that," I say. "But I think all your grandma really wants is for someone to *want* to be around her."

Hazel's face falls. "Ah. So that's what you mean when you said we're alike."

I shrug. "I don't think it matters how old you are—it's hard being lonely."

Hazel turns her face toward me. "I know you miss your grandma, but I hope you know I'm here if you ever want to talk. Even if it's not exactly the same."

It isn't the same. No one can ever replace Babung, and I wouldn't want them to.

But Hazel is *Hazel*. And no one can replace her, either.

"Thank you," I say softly. "I feel the same way about you, too."

Hazel grins. "See? We're perfect for each other."

This time when my smile goes in every direction, I don't fight it. I let the joy take over my whole face.

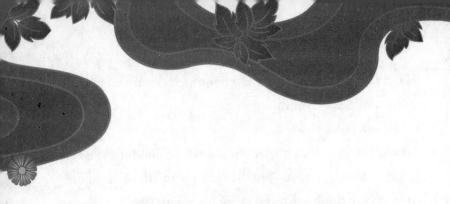

CHAPTER THIRTY-FOUR

I sit outside pulling weeds from the cracks in the paving stones. Clumps of green sprout everywhere, following the crooked lines like they're trying to break free.

"Powerful things, aren't they?" Mrs. Delvaux trails a finger above one of the jagged lines. "Some plants search for weaknesses, you see. Cracks, poor structure . . . If given enough time, climbing ivy can take down an entire brick wall."

I drop the weed into the bucket. "You know a lot about plants."

"That's what's supposed to happen when you get old. You learn things."

"Some people get old and don't *want* to learn anything," I point out.

Mrs. Delvaux snorts. "Yes. That's what happens when you care less about understanding than you do about being understood."

Frowning, I sit against the outbuilding. The stone wall is cool in the shade, and it gives me shelter from the sun. I lean my head back, staring up at the corner pillars, and see a pair of initials carved into the rock face.

EH + AH

I sit up, squinting hard at the letters, eyes trailing along the roof of the building. Giant shrubs block what used to be a window, and it's too dark to see inside. But whatever it is, it's really, really old.

"What was this gazebo for?" I ask, peering into the shadows.

"It's the original well house," Mrs. Delvaux remarks.

My heart thumps. "Well house?"

She nods. "I told you we filled in the one near the house, but this one dried up years before. It's probably long past its time to come down, but it'll cost a great deal to demolish. I supposed I haven't been in much of a rush to do anything about it, being as it's been locked up for decades." She makes a face. "Might be easier to just leave it until I die, and it can be the next owner's headache."

I look at her wide-eyed, but she only laughs harder.

"Don't worry. I haven't made any reservations for the next life quite yet." She stares up at the brick building, gaze full of nostalgia. "I really loved this house as a child. Before my father died, I thought it was the most magical place on earth. So many places for hiding, and playing games . . ."

I stand up, looking around the corner where the wrought iron door is sealed shut. I give it a tug, but it's locked.

Mrs. Delvaux makes a noise of surprise and reaches into

her apron pocket. "After you found that key, I went through every drawer in this house trying to collect the old ones. Thought it would be good to keep them in the same place."

She pulls out a brass ring with half a dozen keys attached to it. I recognize the skeleton key immediately, and all the air rushes out of my throat.

My heart isn't just thumping—it's ricocheting off every rib.

She pinches a black one with her fingers and holds it up. "Here it is—the key to the old well house."

Mrs. Delvaux shuffles around to the door and slides the key into place. The lock gives way with a heavy *clunk*. She pulls the door back and the hinges let out a horrible groan.

We step into the cool space, and I peer nervously into the well. It's deep—far deeper than the one I'd dreamed of. I don't know what makes me more nervous—the fact that a monster could be living at the bottom, staring back at me, and I'd never know, or that Mrs. Delvaux is standing behind me with the skeleton key nearby and it might disappear again at any moment.

I stiffen, gripping tight to the stone.

Mrs. Delvaux doesn't pay me any attention at all. She just rubs her shoulders like she's fighting off the cold.

Outside, a car pulls up to the house, tires crunching against the gravel until the vehicle slows to a stop.

"Who on earth . . . ?" Mrs. Delvaux peeks through the overgrown shrub and spots the silver car in the driveway.

"I didn't think they were coming today," she says to herself more than me, and wanders off to greet her visitors.

I don't waste any time: I search every corner of the well house for clues, steering clear of the black pit. An object in the rafters catches my eye, and I use the crevasses in the stone wall to lift myself up, high enough to reach it.

I jump, snatch the item from the wooden beam, and half stumble to the floor.

It's a chess piece, shaped like a horse's head, and carved out of white stone.

I look toward the doorway to make sure Mrs. Delvaux hasn't returned, when I see the set of keys sticking out of the lock.

Whether it's a trick or good luck, I don't ask questions. I take the skeleton key from the ring, shove both items into my bag, and hurry for the porch before Mrs. Delvaux spots me.

Once I'm inside the house, I search for Hazel. She isn't downstairs, so I go up to her room, knocking on the door impatiently.

"Hazel!" I half growl, half whisper. "It's me!"

Footsteps sound nearby, thumping across the floor with angry force, and then the door tears open in one swift movement.

A girl stares back at me. Red frizzy hair, brown eyes, and a horrible scowl, she looks nothing like Hazel. She *isn't* Hazel.

"Um," I stammer, "H-hi."

She pouts. "What do you want?"

"Is, uh, is Hazel here?"

"Is this a joke?" She rolls her eyes. "If my grandma sent you up here to try to force some pointless part-time friendship, forget it. Like I've told her a billion times, I already *have* friends, and I hate this town."

I stare back, baffled.

What is happening? Where is Hazel?

The girl groans. "Seriously, the people in this neighborhood are *so weird*," she says. "I can't wait until my parents sell this dump and I never have to come back."

And with that, she slams the door in my face.

CHAPTER THIRTY-FIVE

Walking down the staircase feels like walking through a fog. I don't understand—who was that girl? Why was she in Hazel's room?

Why do I feel like there's a missing piece to this puzzle that I'm still not seeing?

I pause in the living room, listening to the voices out front growing louder and louder. Mrs. Delvaux is arguing with someone. With *two* someones, judging by the number of shadows in the window.

"I am not selling my home!" Mrs. Delvaux growls.

A man lets out a noise of frustration. "You clearly can't manage it yourself, Mom. You can't even afford the upkeep. For crying out loud, you've got some neighborhood kid doing the gardening for you!"

"You have no right to tell me what to do with my own house!"

"Let's all take a step back," another woman says. "I think what Ted is trying to say is that it might be worth selling the house now while it still has some value, rather than wait for it to depreciate even more than it already has."

"That's exactly what I'm saying," the man huffs.

"The only time you come to visit me is when you need someone to look after Hazel," Mrs. Delvaux yells, hurt. "And you have the nerve to come down here and ask me to *move out*? This house is the only family I have left!"

"We *are* your family, Mom," Ted argues. "That's why we're here, trying to have a conversation."

"No," Mrs. Delvaux snaps. "You're here because you want the money from the house sale. That's all you've ever cared about. You've been sitting around for years, waiting for me to die. And now that I'm not doing that fast enough, you want to kick me out of the only home I've ever known."

I step away from the window. This conversation sounds private; I shouldn't be here. Not when Mrs. Delvaux is so upset.

When I reach the porch, I pull the door handle as gently as I can, trying not to let it make a sound. I don't want to draw any attention. Especially when I'm walking away with the skeleton key.

I hesitate, staring at the lock.

On this side of the veil, I'd be imposing. But on the other . . .

I have the final two pieces of treasure. The last two memories for Lock and Pearl.

I don't know what's going on with Mrs. Delvaux and the

person in Hazel's bedroom, but I know I'm running out of time to finish what I started. Right now, there are two souls that need to be set free.

I turn the key in the back door, and step into the house.

Everything is different.

Ash swirls around me, making me dizzy. A thick, gray mist sweeps through every room, slipping through mangled branches and tree roots that have replaced every wall and floorboard. The ceiling is a mess of shredded twigs that loom above like thick spiderwebs. I doubt it's doing much to keep the monster out, if it's doing anything at all.

I turn in place, scanning the fog for the other rooms, but I'm not sure they exist. There's just an emptiness rolling in from the windows, swallowing whatever was left of the downstairs.

I turn for where the staircase once was, and find a mountain of soil flooding through the hall. I claw my way to the top of it, reaching over protruding roots that weave between one another like fingers, replacing whatever is left of the former walls. It's a struggle to climb, but I have to get to Lock and Pearl.

The second floor is unrecognizable. All the doorframes are slanted or missing altogether. Most of the external walls have been ripped away, leaving broken bits of splintered wood behind.

I search the rooms one by one, and when I reach the end of the crooked hallway, I find the last two ghosts.

Pearl sways in the middle of the only room that seems to

have a stable floor, wearing a dress that looks as if it's been dragged through a filthy street. Her normally meticulous hair looks like a wild bird's nest, and to my horror, I think something might be crawling inside of it.

She counts her fingers like she's working out a problem. Every time she gets to her last finger, she pauses and starts over again.

Lock paces wildly, flailing his arms around like he's shouting curses at the walls. "We still don't have the last *one*! We'll never finish it—not without all the pieces." He spins toward me suddenly. He's a young boy again, stomping his feet as he yells, and for a moment I see the boy from Hatter's memory in his frown. "She missed one. I tried to remember—I waited for her to come back. But she forgot to count them *all*."

"I, I don't know what you're talking about," I say, looking between them.

Pearl laughs deliriously, still counting her fingers. "One is missing, one is missing . . ."

"We couldn't hold on to everything," Lock says, jumping from boy to man with every passing second. "The house wouldn't last—so we gave it up faster. Stayed in this room, and tried to remember the message."

"Wasn't there a girl?" Pearl's voice turns childlike. "Weren't we supposed to tell her something?"

I frown. "Did . . . did you have a message for *me*?"

Lock paws at his head, thumping his skull like he can't quite remember.

I decide it doesn't matter. Not when they're so distressed. "Don't worry," I say gently, pleading with my hands for him to calm down. "It's okay now—I brought these." I reach into my bag and draw out the glowing dance card and chess piece, and the memories sweep over me like a wave, taking over my senses.

A middle-aged man sits at a chessboard, staring at the pieces. His son doesn't like chess; he prefers studying animals, and being outside. And as much as he doesn't mind that his son enjoys the outdoors, he does wish he enjoyed chess a *little*.

The sitting room door cracks open, and a girl pokes her head through the opening, hair in blond ringlets.

The man opens his mouth to say hello, when he hears the noise down the corridor. Loud voices, one on top of the other, disagreeing over something he's clearly missed.

"What's all that about?" he asks the girl.

She sighs, voice too mature for her age. "Ribbons and lace, and whether they're even necessary."

"I suppose I can guess as to which side your mother is on," he notes with a wink.

The girl giggles.

He motions to the chessboard. "Fancy a game, Peggy, dear?"

The girl pauses, peeking back through the doorway. When

she's certain the others are preoccupied, she skips toward her father and plops down into the opposite chair.

They play for half an hour. The man tries to lose on purpose, just to help keep the game going for longer. And the girl grins and grins every time she takes one of his pieces.

"Yes!" she announces triumphantly. "I got your horse!" She snatches up the white knight and sets it to the side of the table.

The man chuckles. "Promise me we'll still play chess together—even if your mother forbids it during the social season."

"I promise," the girl says, "as long as *you* promise I can always take your horse. They're the best-looking pieces, you know."

The man smiles. "I'm sure we can arrange that."

The memory shifts to another. The man is much younger now, not even able to grow a beard. He hooks a finger around his collar and pulls, loosening the material. He's only worn a suit once before, and it wasn't as tight as this one.

He knows Emma's parents will be watching, hoping to keep their daughter distracted with much wealthier suiters. Not that the man doesn't have money of his own. But his is *new* money, built from luck and hard work, and a few calculated speculations.

The Delvaux family does not approve of new money.

But the young man has a plan.

He spots her across the room, dressed in a blue and white gown and her hair bound in ribbons and pearls. She looks beautiful. But Emma Delvaux always looks beautiful.

The young man hurries across the ballroom, even as the music already begins to play, and skirts around the crowd to the back of Emma and her parents. There aren't any pick-pockets in his family, but he grew up with older brothers, and sometimes it was helpful to be quick and silent.

He slips the dance card from Emma's wrist, and steps away to write his name inside.

And he does—over and over again, in every empty space, next to every available dance.

Smiling, he walks back over to Emma and whispers over her shoulder, "I think this belongs to you."

She turns, piercing blue eyes shifting from surprise to recognition. It's been a while since they've seen each other. Her parents made it a point to keep them apart, and the older she got, the easier that was to do.

The young man had been busy making a name for himself. He'd promised Emma he'd do whatever it took to prove to her parents he was worthy of her hand—and if that didn't work, then they'd sail across an ocean together, just like they said they would all those years ago.

Emma takes the card, eyelashes fluttering when she realizes what he's done. "August!" she whispers, slightly alarmed, but mostly amused. "Do you have any idea what people will say?"

He grins. "That we're genuinely happy, and not just pretending to be."

Her face lights up, and there's no question that they're both completely and wholeheartedly in love.

They dance the entire night together, and soon everyone else in the room knows it, too.

When the memory vanishes, it's just me and the ghosts standing in the Hollow.

"But—I don't understand." I stare at the glowing items in my hand. "They're both *your* memories," I say to Lock—or rather, August Honeyfield.

He blinks, confused, but I hand them over because it's the only way he'll understand.

All at once, his face shifts into a strange contentment, and then he ages rapidly until he's once again a middle-aged man with gray hair and tired eyes.

"Yes," he says softly. "I remember." He holds up the chess piece, eyes glistening. "I chose this memory for Margaret. For my little Peggy." He reaches out a hand, winding his fingers through Pearl's.

A brief moment passes before her eyes grow large and she gasps with a hand to her mouth, and then she remembers, too.

"Hello, Father," she says, beaming.

Lock hands the memories back to me, bowing his head with gratitude. "They belong with the others."

I watch the two ghosts embrace, smiling with all the love in the world, and then they vanish into nothing. One single moment, traded for another.

There's no time to recover—because the second they're gone, the house trembles violently, and the monster bursts through the weakened branches.

It slams against the tree-lined floor, stopping several feet away from me, and roars.

I shove the objects back into my bag and run for what's left of the staircase. The monster reels, black smoke twirling around its body like venomous ribbons, and it tears down the hallway after me. The surrounding branch-threaded walls explode, blowing splintered bark and clumps of soil in every direction.

If it keeps this up, it will destroy Honeyfield Hall in a matter of minutes.

But maybe that's the point.

There are no ghosts left, which means there are no memories left for the monster to hunt. No reason for the Hollow to still *exist*. One way or another, this place was fated to disappear.

And I need to get to the other side of the veil before it does.

I spot the mountain of soil leading downstairs and race for the edge, just as the monster crashes into the wall beside me. I duck, terrified, and trip over the top of the hill, tumbling down mulch and dirt. I dig my heels into the soil, trying to slow down, and barely miss the curve of a tree root waiting at the bottom step.

I scramble to my feet, heart hammering out of my rib cage, and throw my hand into my pocket to retrieve the key.

But it's gone.

Panicked, my eyes scan the heavy mist. It must've fallen on my way downstairs. I scrape my fingers against the earth, searching for metal, moving faster and faster the more frantic my heart becomes.

The monster rips apart the earth-covered incline behind me. Rotted planks of wood clatter through the air.

What happens if the monster reaches the doorway? What if I can't get *home*?

My fingertips brush something cool, and I wrap my fingers around the key and pull it toward my chest. I'm about to stand when I look up at the fireplace across the fog, sitting in the place the living room once was—except now, the room is only mist and stretches of faded gray.

But the fireplace remains.

There's a brick missing in the corner, where no one would notice it if they weren't looking from the ground up.

And I know it doesn't make sense—I know it's *impossible*—but I swear there's a crocheted rabbit hidden in the tiny alcove. The one Babung made for me. The one I sacrificed to the monster.

I gasp, but there's no time to grab it.

The monster throws itself onto the floor. The ground

rumbles, and the earth splits apart. I'm racing for an exit, cold air snapping against my lungs, and I slip through the back door and use the key in the lock.

The last thing I hear before the *click* is the sound of Honeyfield Hall blowing apart.

CHAPTER THIRTY-SIX

I get on my bike and pedal home as fast as I can. Terror still courses through my bloodstream, but it's my mind I'm struggling to calm down the most. All of my thoughts are spinning around and around, like they're caught in a vortex. Like they're all pieces of a puzzle that still don't make *sense*.

Why was the monster still chasing me when there were no memories left? Who hid the rabbit in the fireplace? And where was *Hazel*?

I need to talk to her. I need to talk through everything I've just seen.

I don't know what I expected would happen once I returned all the memories to the ghosts. It's not that I thought the clouds would part and light would stream down and Babung's ghost would appear—but I thought it would feel more *final*.

Instead, it feels . . . unfinished. Like there's something missing. Something I'm still supposed to do.

I turn down the old railway line, wind beating against my face, and make a left onto my neighborhood street. When

I'm home, I park my bike in the garage and race up the stairs three at a time.

I sit on my bed and dump the contents of my bag across the bedspread, lining them up in a neat row.

The chess piece, the dance card, the thimble, the ornament box, the skeleton key, and the poem.

What am I missing? What didn't I *find*?

The ghosts said to keep the items together. But maybe they didn't just mean in my bag. Maybe I'm supposed to put them somewhere else—somewhere important.

I think of the missing brick in the fireplace again, but I can't figure out how it fits in with the rest of the puzzle.

I scratch my shoulder, too focused on the items to realize Mom's opened my door and is standing a few feet away.

"What's all this?" she asks.

"It's nothing," I say, stuffing the objects back into my bag to hide them from Mom's gaze.

She sits on the edge of my bed. "I think it's nice that you're so interested in this town, you know. If this is a history project, and you don't want me to know because you're still trying so hard to hate this place . . . Well, just remember that it's okay to change your mind. I'm not going to say 'I told you so.'"

"You kind of just did," I say blankly. "And this isn't a history project."

"Well, then tell me about it," she says.

"I can't."

"Of course, you can—you can tell me anything. I'm your mom."

Maybe it's the fact that I've been chased by a monster and my best friend is missing, but I don't hold any of my words back—I let them burst out of me like a volcanic eruption.

"I can't tell you anything because you never understand me! You just want me to not talk about Babung, and pretend to be happy, and *move on*. But I'm not ready to move on. I have unfinished business. And Babung is still out there and I don't even know if she got my message and—"

"We talked about this." Mom looks exasperated. "This is exactly what I was afraid of."

I cross my arms. "What's that supposed to mean?"

"I didn't want you searching for ghosts because of what I thought it might do to you when you realized it was all make-believe. That ghosts aren't *real*."

"Yes, they are. I've *seen* them."

"Oh, Eliot." Mom holds her palms up, pleading. "I love your big imagination. But this—this is too much. You're making yourself upset, and you don't even see it."

"*I* don't see it?" I motion to the altar that's still sitting on my dresser. "*You* never see *me*! If you did, you'd know that looking for ghosts is the one thing that's kept me hopeful since Babung died. You'd know that the thing I've been most sad about isn't just that I lost her—but that you won't even let me *remember* her. And you'd see that it hurts me that you and Dad won't talk about her. *Why* won't you talk about her?"

"Because I'm worried about you!" Mom's eyes fill with tears. "I don't talk about her because I don't know *how* to talk about her. I don't know what to say that will make you feel better and also help you process that you're never going to see her again. Because you're not, Eliot, no matter how badly you wish it were possible.

"I'm sorry you couldn't make her remember things. I know how much it hurt to see her forget your face, again and again, and then for good. It's why we tried to protect you as much as we could. We tried to give you the good days instead of the bad ones. But those last few months . . . They were hard on all of us."

"They were hard on *Babung*," I argue. "The least you could do is carry on her memories instead of letting her disappear forever."

Mom pulls her face back. "That's not what we're doing. But we all grieve in different ways."

"Maybe talking about her is how *I* grieve!"

Mom motions to the altar. "You're looking for Babung's ghost like you think she's still going to come back and be a part of this family. Grief is accepting when someone is gone. And she is. I know it's awful, but Babung is *gone*." Tears pour down Mom's cheeks. "I'm trying my best, Eliot. There isn't a manual on how to do this. How to help you. I'm just—I'm just trying my best."

"Yeah, well, so am I." I push myself off my bed, shoulders shaking. "And looking for Babung is just something I need to do."

Mom doesn't stop me when I leave the room, and Dad doesn't stop me when I get on my bike and race down the driveway.

I think I hurt them.

But they hurt me, too. And maybe that doesn't make it okay—to fight hurt with hurt—but I'm ugly sobbing and my heart can't repair itself and I guess hurting is the only thing I know how to do.

CHAPTER THIRTY-SEVEN

August Honeyfield's grave sits on top of a hill. It isn't difficult to find—it's one of the tallest in the cemetery, covered in dead ivy. I pull the tangle of branches aside to read the name engraved on the stone, and the inscription that's been weathered with time.

A loving husband and father.

Most of the graves say the same kind of thing, but I think in August's case, it was true.

Are they all together now, on the other side of the veil?

Was giving back their memories enough to help them move on?

I'm not so sure. Because *memories* aren't the same as *unfinished business.*

There was something they were all supposed to do. Something they needed to be reminded of.

I know there's a missing piece here—I just can't figure out what it is.

I let go of the branches, and a few thorny twigs scrape against the stone. My eyes drift toward the surrounding headstones. Emma—*loving wife and mother*—is buried beside her husband, followed by Charles Honeyfield and Margaret "Peggy" Honeyfield—who I came to know as Hatter and Pearl.

A snap of twigs draws my eye, and I see a fifth grave nearby—older than all the rest, and half-buried beneath an aggressive hawthorn bush. I squint, trying to read the faded letters, and the moment I make out the name, my entire body goes rigid.

Hazel Honeyfield.

It . . . it can't be.

My skin feels hot and cold all at the same time. I blink once. Twice.

The gravestone says Hazel Honeyfield died when she was only twelve. But that would mean . . .

That would mean . . .

"I wondered when you'd figure out that part of the mystery," Graham says beside me.

Even though it feels like he appeared out of nowhere, he's standing like he's been there for a long time.

I look between him and the grave, mouth parted. "This has to be a mistake."

Hazel . . . She can't be . . . It's not *possible.*

"There were only four ghosts in Honeyfield Hall," I say, firm. "I met them all—Lock, Pearl, Hatter, and Trill. Hazel . . . she was never in the Hollow." She was in the real, living world, with *me.*

"And how many riddles are on your list?" Graham's golden eyes catch the sunlight.

I frown, pulling the parchment from my bag, and read every word for what seems like the thousandth time.

I hold life without a heartbeat,
I have a face but cannot see,
I give hope on the coldest nights,
I have roots but am not a tree.
I carry the stars but cannot fly,
and will always answer your call,
I am the keeper of all that was stolen,
and the master of Honeyfield Hall.

I read the third line out loud. "I give hope on the coldest nights." The realization thunders through me, making me dizzy. "I didn't solve all the riddles. I'm still missing a memory."

Graham doesn't reply.

"*Hazel's* memory." I hear the tremble in my voice, rattling like a small stone in a glass jar. "Because Hazel . . . Hazel is a ghost." My eyes burn. "Why didn't she tell me?"

"You assume that she knows," Graham says. "But ghosts have a habit of forgetting things in the Hollow. And Hazel has been there a very, very long time."

I shake my head. "But she isn't in the Hollow. I've seen her—she looks nothing like the other ghosts. She's *real*."

Graham stares at the grave. "What do you think would happen to a ghost who forgot so much, they couldn't even remember they'd died?"

"No riddles," I plead, eyes stinging. "What happened to Hazel?"

His golden irises soften. "She forgot too many things, and wandered too far from the house." Our gazes meet. "Now she doesn't remember which side of the veil she belongs on."

"She thinks she's Mrs. Delvaux's granddaughter."

"She found an identity to tether herself to. I suppose it's why she appears so real to you."

"But, but Mrs. Delvaux—" I shake my head, thinking back to all the times I've seen them together.

I think of the screaming upstairs, and the time Hazel knocked the teapot over—and I realize I've never actually seen them *interact*. Not really. All the times I heard Mrs. Delvaux speaking to her granddaughter . . .

It was the *other* Hazel. The one with frizzy red hair, who acted like she didn't know me at all.

The tears pool in my eyes. "You could've told her," I say, fighting the scratch in the back of my throat. "She deserves to know the truth."

"Sometimes the truth does more harm than good. Especially when it's impossible to hold on to." Graham turns to me. "Perhaps it's a kindness to let a friend live in a world that feels safe to them."

Memories of Babung flash through my mind. There were so many things she forgot in such a short time. At first it was little things, like thinking we were always driving a new car she'd never seen before, and forgetting the names of foods she'd eaten a thousand times. But that's how I'd always known Babung—a little forgetful, but she'd always laugh when you corrected her.

Eventually, the little things turned into big things. Sometimes Babung would hang up the phone abruptly, because she'd forget she was in the middle of a conversation. She'd muddle up dates and names and places. She was happiest when she stuck to a routine, like tending to her plants or crocheting little animals, and she'd get frustrated doing new things.

Then the big things turned into *bigger* things. Babung thought Mom and Dad were a lot younger. She thought Grandpa was still alive, and cried every time someone had to tell her he'd passed away nearly twenty years ago.

And she had no idea who I was at all.

Would it have been kinder not to correct her? Did I make a mistake trying to remind her who I was, again and again?

Is it a mistake that I'm still trying to do that now?

My cheeks get hot. "Maybe Babung was never going to remember things when she was alive. But there has to be different rules in the afterlife. Otherwise, otherwise—"

Otherwise it means Babung will never remember me.

I'll be a stranger to her, for all eternity.

And if one day I get older and forget things too, it will be like Babung and I never existed together. It will be like none of what we shared, or how we loved, will even matter.

We may as well have been strangers in real life, too.

"Some stories have already been written. We can't change them, no matter how much we want to," Graham says.

"No." I set my jaw. "That can't be true. If it were, I wouldn't be able to help the ghosts. But I'm changing things. I already gave four of them their memories back."

"Ah. But perhaps *that* is what's written."

I stare at Hazel's grave, wondering if finding the ghosts wasn't a way of helping me find Babung—it was a way to help *her*. Hazel Honeyfield. The first of the family to become a ghost, and now the last to move on. Stuck on the wrong side of the Hollow.

Whatever led me to find the skeleton key, and meet Hazel . . .

I think it was always to help her find her way home.

I need to make sure she remembers everything, so she can rejoin her family on the other side of the veil.

Just like how it should be.

I wipe a tear with my sleeve. "Hazel is going to disappear," I say solemnly. "When I find her memory, and hand it back to her, she won't be able to stay."

I'm going to be alone again.

My entire body quakes, and I wrap my arms around myself like I'm trying to keep myself from breaking apart.

"Everyone leaves this world one day," Graham says, eyes

flashing. "That's what it is to be mortal." He turns his back to me, and stalks down the hill.

"I'm not ready to say goodbye," I call after him.

Graham stills, but doesn't look over his shoulder. "Is anyone ever ready?" And then he disappears.

I stare at the bottom of the hill, trying to hold on to a thought as hard as I can, until I realize I can't remember the thought at all.

But when I look back at Hazel's grave, I know what it means, and what I have to do.

Even though saying goodbye and losing my friend is going to shatter what's left of my heart.

CHAPTER THIRTY-EIGHT

My pillow is soaked with tears. After the graveyard, I should've gone straight to Mrs. Delvaux's, found Hazel, and told her the truth. But I just couldn't do it.

Not yet. Not tonight.

There's a knock at my bedroom door, and Mom and Dad walk in with a mug of hot chocolate. It's topped with a mountain of whipped cream *and* chocolate sprinkles.

It's a drink that either says "We're sorry" or "We need to have a serious talk."

I'm not prepared for either, but I don't have the energy to argue. I shuffle upright and tuck my legs against my chest.

Mom hands me the drink, and they both settle at the edge of my bed.

"Hey, kiddo," Dad says with a weak smile.

Mom folds her hands in her lap. Her eyes are all red, like she's been crying for a while. "I'm so sorry about earlier, Eliot. I should've handled that better. I just get so worried about you sometimes, and when I don't know how to fix something, it scares me."

"I don't need to be fixed." I stare at the whipped cream that's starting to melt around the edges.

Mom nods, slow and unsure, like she's gearing up for something. "The last thing I'd ever want is to fail you as a mom." She lifts her shoulders. "Lately, I just can't seem to figure out the right thing to say. Everything I try only makes things worse."

"I don't need you to say anything. I need you to *listen*," I say.

Mom's eyes water. "Okay," she says. "I'm listening now."

Dad nods beside her. "We both are."

So I tell them how I feel. I tell them how much I miss Babung, and how angry I am that she's gone, and that there are strangers living in her house, and that we're miles and miles away from all the places she used to visit.

I tell them I'm sad they don't seem to miss her the way I do.

I tell them how even though I'm angry and sad, I want to be okay someday, too.

And I tell them that I don't care if they don't believe in ghosts—I do, and I believe I'll see Babung again someday. But I know it might be a long time before that happens, and I'm terrified of having to spend a lifetime not talking about all the things she did that made her wonderful. The things that made *our* lives wonderful.

I tell them I want to hear all the stories they have about her too—and that I don't care if there were good days and bad days. Because they made up Babung's life—and I want so badly to remember her life.

When I finish, Mom and Dad reach out across the blanket, like closing the distance between us is as simple figuratively as it is literally.

"I'm sorry we got this all so wrong," Dad says. "Babung had an amazing life that was full of love. And even near the end, I think that's what she wanted *us* to remember most."

Mom takes a breath. "If you need to hear more stories about Babung to feel her presence, then we can fix that. I promise."

I nod, staring at the threads of my blanket. "It's not fair. What happened to her—it just wasn't fair."

"I know," Dad says quietly. "But the truth is, sometimes people get sick, and their memories start to go. I could teach you all about cells and aging and all the rest of it, but it won't matter. If you're looking for fairness, you won't find it. It's just life—and life can be beautiful, but it can also be sad."

I hold the mug tight, thinking not just of Babung, but the Honeyfields, too.

There's so much loss . . . but also friendship and love and laughter. I know I'm going to have to say goodbye to Hazel, but would I give up ever knowing her if I could avoid having to lose her?

I know I wouldn't. I'd be her friend again and again if I could. Even if the goodbyes got harder every time.

Babung lived a rich life that was full of light. It isn't fair that she forgot about me, but if that's the way her story was written, then I'm only grateful I got to be such a big part of it.

We had the time we had—and I will treasure it forever.

"Maybe—maybe remembering her is more important than looking for an explanation," I say. "Remembering her feels like the best way to keep her alive."

"You're right," Dad says. "You're so right."

Mom's smile is cautious, but a little hopeful. "You know, she did say some funny things, even in those final weeks. She used to make us all laugh—even the nurses."

"Really?" I say. My smile is a little hopeful, too.

She nods. "I don't know where she thought she was, but she was always telling the doctors to 'get up and dance,' like she was having a house party."

Dad laughs, loud and loose. "She had this thing about banana milkshakes. She was always asking us to bring her one, and every time we did, she'd get so excited and say it was the first time she'd ever had one. She was about as excited as you used to get opening Christmas presents!"

"Do you remember when you used to lecture her about eating all her food?" Mom smiles and looks at me. "Babung would pretend like she'd forgotten to turn on her hearing aid and ignore him, but as soon as your dad would leave the room, she'd look right at me and wink."

"She had a good sense of humor," Dad explains. "That's how she coped with things, even from when I was a kid."

"I like hearing stories about her," I say, staring at my blanket. Maybe it's my way of coping—feeling like she's still around, in whatever way possible.

Mom rests a hand on my knee. "Then how about we tell you more of them."

"I'd like that," I say.

Dad smiles mostly with his eyes. Mom leans in and hugs me, not caring when hot chocolate splashes onto the blanket. She just wants me to know she's here. That they both are.

They spend the night telling me stories about Babung, and her life before I knew her. It's the closest I've felt to her—and my parents—in a long time.

When I wake up in the morning, I find Babung's jade frog sitting next to the Obon altar on my dresser. A gift from my parents—and maybe somewhere out in the universe, it's a gift from Babung, too.

CHAPTER THIRTY-NINE

I return to Honeyfield Hall the next morning. The closer I get to the front door, the more it hurts. But I do it anyway, because sometimes when you care about someone, you have to care about what they need more than what you want.

I wish I'd figured that out a little sooner with Babung. She needed people who let her say the wrong thing and didn't push to correct her. Who just let her exist in a world that felt safe, and familiar, even if it wasn't always.

But I can do better. Starting with Hazel.

I take a deep breath, and knock on the door.

Mrs. Delvaux appears with her gray hair brushed into a tight bun. She ushers me inside, and when she speaks there's a croak in her voice, the way Mom's gets when she's been crying.

"I have to admit, I'm not in the gardening spirit today," she says. "How would you feel if we took a day off and ate a piece of carrot cake instead?"

I stand in the front hall, bag hanging at my side. "Cake sounds great."

Mrs. Delvaux leads me into the room with the pink-rose wallpaper. She's been watching something on TV in black and white, and it's been paused in the middle of a scene with a woman crying. Except she's crying in the most glamorous way imaginable, with her makeup perfect and not a crumpled frown line in sight.

It's not what a broken heart looks like. Real hurt is ugly and messy and makes snot come out of your nose for no reason.

Rainbows come *after* a storm. Maybe it's like that when you're sad, too.

I guess I'm not quite there yet.

"Have a seat," Mrs. Delvaux urges.

I sit in front of the small coffee table, and Mrs. Delvaux vanishes into the next room and returns with a plate of carrot cake. She sets it down in front of me and takes a seat on one of the sofas closest to the television.

"My grandma used to watch black-and-white movies too," I say. "I always liked them. Everyone had perfect hair."

She hums. "The magic of television. My son hated all these old movies. He said they were boring. He was a big fan of that one show though—what was it called?—the one with the birdman."

My heart sinks. "Batman?"

"Yes, that's it. He preferred the movie though."

"Holy Hole in a Doughnut," I say, voice cracking. So that's where Hazel got it from. She watched the show with Mrs. Delvaux's son.

She lets out a soft chuckle. "He was obsessed with the characters. Had all the posters and toys and tin lunch boxes. Some of it's still up in the attic."

I swallow the knot in my throat and stare into the next room, where I can see the edge of the fireplace. The one with the hidden alcove.

"I know it's old and falling apart in some places," Mrs. Delvaux says suddenly. "But it's mine."

I turn sharply, and realize she's not talking about the fireplace—she's talking about Honeyfield Hall.

"There was a time my son couldn't wait to move out and get away from me. And now . . ." She presses her lips into a tight line.

"I don't think you should sell the house," I blurt out suddenly.

Mrs. Delvaux lifts a brow, and my cheeks turn pink.

"I, I overheard you talking about it yesterday," I say. "I'm sorry. I wasn't trying to eavesdrop. But this house is amazing, and it's full of memories and stories, and I know you think there's a curse on it, but maybe the luck here is going to change soon." Maybe when all the ghosts move on, the curse will too. "If you love this house, you should hold on to it."

Home wasn't a place to me, but to Mrs. Delvaux, this house is her whole world.

She shouldn't have to give it up.

Mrs. Delvaux whistles through her teeth. "I have no

intention of selling this place. Certainly not for a son that doesn't even come to visit me unless he needs something. Don't worry—there's plenty more time to fix up that garden, in case you thought you were about to lose your job."

"Oh." I tangle my fingers together. "I didn't care about the job. I just didn't want you to be sad."

She looks at me, expression softening. "You should know that after the argument I had with my son, Hazel went with her parents. I'm . . . not sure she'll be back anytime soon. I know you two were becoming friends, so I'm sorry to be getting in the way."

I don't say anything. I'm not sure there are words for how I'm feeling.

Mrs. Delvaux continues, absentmindedly. "I used to dream of this house filled with the laughter of friends and family, the way it was when my parents and I first moved in. I thought it might happen once I had a family of my own—and that maybe that loneliness I felt in my grief didn't have to be forever." She shakes her head like what she hoped for never came to be.

I don't know why some people get families who love them, and other people get families who don't want to be around them. Or why some people *want* a family but aren't able to have one, and others *don't* want one and have one anyway.

I guess we don't get to pick that part. It's just the way life writes our stories.

Mrs. Delvaux tucks her lip in, and stares at the frozen screen like she's holding back a tsunami of emotions. I thought I was lonely after Babung left, but Mrs. Delvaux?

She's been lonely most of her life.

"I wonder what the point is," she muses under her breath. "To live so long for no reason at all."

"Maybe," I say slowly, "the point is just to keep making new memories, and to hopefully find the people who make them feel special."

Mrs. Delvaux closes her eyes, not saying anything for a while. When they open again, her blue irises shine like glass. "I can see why your grandmother cherished you so much. You've got a good heart, Eliot. Even if you did let the neighborhood kids talk you into pulling a prank on me." The humor in her gaze lasts several moments, and then she un-pauses the movie and we sit together until she drifts off to sleep.

I get up to find Hazel. I'm not sure whether to call her the real Hazel or the ghost Hazel, but I guess both are true.

Standing in the center of the parlor room, Hazel stares blankly at the wall. My footsteps creak against the uneven floorboards, and she snaps her head toward the sound. Even though she sees me, she looks like she hardly recognizes me, blinking several times before her familiar smile returns.

I didn't notice it before. The *pause*. Every time I came back from the Hollow, and saw the monster—it was always there. The hesitation knotted in her brow, like she was trying to remember me, and this place, and who she was.

Now the pause is all I see.

Hazel has no idea she's dead. And I have to be the one to tell her.

"Did you figure out any more of the riddles?" Hazel asks, stepping toward me.

Everything feels cold. I don't know if it's fear or nerves, but it's making my entire body twitch.

"There's one more left," I say quietly. "I . . . I miscounted before. I was missing something." It's what Lock and Pearl were trying to tell me the last time I saw them.

Hazel crosses her arms. "Which one did we miss?"

Still "we." Still thinking we're partners on the same team.

I hate how much this hurts.

"*I give hope on the coldest nights*," I recite. "There were five treasures, not four. And I know where it is."

"You do?" Hazel brightens. "That's wonderful!" She hesitates, then frowns. "Wait—why do you look so worried?"

"I just . . . I don't like goodbyes, I guess."

Hazel drops her arms. "But you're also finally going to get a message to your grandma. This is a *good* thing."

I stare at the floor. How do I tell her the truth? How do I explain to her that she died a long time ago? That it's *her* I have to say goodbye to?

"Hazel," I start, but I can't finish my sentence. I can't even finish the thought.

She steps forward. "It's okay, Eliot. You're helping the ghosts move on—that's the best kind of goodbye you could give them."

Except moving on is one of the hardest things a person can do—not for the ones who leave, but for the ones who are left behind.

"The last treasure . . . It's in the fireplace," I say finally.

"Fire." Hazel grins. "Of *course*."

"Come with me," I say, and motion toward the next room. "I think we're supposed to find this last one together."

I lead the way out of the parlor room, to where an enormous stone hearth sits empty. A cold draft snakes its way through the room, but I'm focusing too intently on the object hiding in the secret alcove. It's not a crocheted rabbit, because the treasure was never on the other side of the veil.

Someone was trying to get me a message. They wanted me to find the last clue.

I reach up and find a small ballet shoe, wound tight with a frayed ribbon, the off-white color coated in layers of ash.

Dusting it off with my hand, I hold the shoe up to Hazel. "I think this is yours."

Hazel makes a face. "Mine?" Her laugh is unassuming. "I think I'd remember hiding a ballet shoe in the fireplace. I mean, talk about a fire hazard."

My body is shaking and I don't know how much longer I'll be able to find the strength to do this, so I push the shoe into her hands, hoping she'll see the memory and understand. Maybe that way I won't have to explain it to her.

But the moment the shoe touches her fingers, it slips right through her flesh and falls with a *thud* against the floor.

Hazel's smile fades. She looks at her fingers. Stares at her palms. Tries to figure out what just happened.

I stiffen. I thought handing the memory over would work. And then it dawns on me: All the other ghosts got their memories back in the Hollow. Hazel is still here, on the wrong side of the veil.

I'm trying to give her a memory she isn't able to hold on to. Not yet.

"I don't—" Hazel's face shifts between every emotion in existence. "It must've slipped," she says, trying to make sense of it, exactly the way she did when she dropped the teapot.

Only back then, I didn't know she was a ghost.

"Hazel," I start, voice quaking. "There's something you need to know."

She laughs again, even though there are tears in her eyes. "I'm just clumsy, that's all."

I bite my lip. Shake my head. "No. That's not all. You—you're one of the ghosts, Hazel."

The skin on her forehead crumples. "That's ridiculous. I'm, I'm Hazel. I—" She huffs, flustered. "I *know* who I am."

I lift my shoulders. "You *are* Hazel. But not Hazel Delvaux—you're Hazel Honeyfield. You got lost in the Hollow, and found your way here." When she doesn't say anything, I add in the gentlest voice I can muster, "You died. A really, really long time ago."

"That's not true," Hazel argues, face turning red. "I live here. This is my *house*."

"Exactly," I say seriously, holding out my hands like I wish I could help her calm down. "You live here. But the other Hazel doesn't. She barely even visits. But you're here every single day."

Hazel presses her hands to the sides of her head. "That . . . doesn't make sense. I remember things. I remember *you*."

My eyes burn. "What do you remember before me?"

Hazel's expression splits, and her understanding shatters. I remember that look; it's the same look Babung had, every time I told her who I really was.

Every time she realized she'd lost all sense of time.

Hazel clenches her teeth, and a deep, guttural sob rages through her. She bends at the waist, every sharp breath visible across her back, and grabs her hair. The panic takes over, and Hazel steps back, frantically looking around the room. For an explanation or a sense of safety, I don't know—but she's desperate. I think if hope were an object, she'd devour it whole.

I see it then. The flash in her eyes. The pain, and fear, and *desperation*.

It's the same flash that exists in the Hollow, right in the heart of the monster.

My breath leaves me, and the final puzzle piece clicks into place.

Hazel *is* the monster.

It's what she left behind once she stumbled back to this side of the veil. Two parts of a whole—and the reason the monster is so desperately searching for memories.

But not just any memories—she's looking for her own. For the part of her that's missing. The part of her that's right in front of me.

I stretch out my fingers, but Hazel is too frantic to sense me. "I know how to fix this."

Hazel cries out, still searching the room for understanding.

I pick up the ballet shoe from the floor, clutching it tight to my chest. "I need to take this to the Hollow, so you can have your memories back. But I think this time, you need to come with me."

It didn't work before, when I opened the door with Hazel beside me. Neither of us could see anything. The skeleton key wouldn't let us in.

Maybe it's because Hazel wasn't ready to go back—not without her memory. Her unfinished business.

And now that it's in my hands . . .

"This will work," I promise my friend.

I take out the skeleton key from my bag and use it to open the door to the hallway. When the lock clicks, a white light appears like it's bleeding through the frame.

I look back at Hazel and hold out a hand. "I don't know what's waiting on the other side of this door, but I trust you, and that means I trust the monster." I pause, watching her. "Do you trust me?"

Hazel looks up, peeling her fingers from her hair. Her blue eyes shudder, but she nods.

She reaches for my hand, and for a split second I know I feel her. The warmth, and laughter, and friendship.

Hazel is a ghost, but she's the realest friend I've ever had. As real as Babung was.

Then her fingers drift through mine, but it doesn't matter, because she follows me into the Hollow.

CHAPTER FORTY

There is nothing left of Honeyfield Hall except the doorway we arrive through. Remnants of the building sift through the air like snowflakes, and the landscape is covered in a colorless fog.

Across the space, the monster bellows in despair.

I'm not afraid. Not of Hazel—not in any of her forms.

She was searching for her family. For her *memories*. And she was willing to tear the house apart to find them. On the other side of the veil, I've been doing the exact same thing.

I hold up the glowing ballet shoe, and the memory takes over.

A young girl stands with one hand on the ballet barre and the other curved in front of her. She hates dance lessons, and she makes a face every time her teacher tells her to straighten her back or point her toes.

Ballet is her mother's dream.

The girl doesn't dream of theaters and costumes and the

adulation of society. She wants to go on adventures in the forest, and search for long-lost pirate treasure. She wants to wear trousers like the local farmhands, and watch the stars from a rooftop. She wants—

Her eyes drift toward Maisie Austen. She has raven-black hair and all the grace of a far superior dancer.

The girl never wanted to take ballet lessons. But when she saw Maisie, she thought maybe she could learn to *like* dancing, even just so she and Maisie could become friends.

Except she is too nervous to ever talk to her, no matter how hard she tries to build up to it.

"Hazel," the dance teacher snaps. She even *scolds* with grace. "You're distracted again. How is it possible you can hardly manage a moment without disappearing into a dream?"

The girl's face flushes when everyone in the room turns to stare. The attention makes her feel sick. Especially when Maisie glances her way.

She'd wanted Maisie to notice her, but not like this. Now she'll never want to be her friend; she'll be too busy remembering her as the girl who couldn't pay attention in class.

The moment there is an opportunity to flee, the girl runs to the changing room and sinks into the corner, biting the edge of her lip as she tries not to cry.

"Are you okay?" a voice asks.

Maisie is standing a few feet away, one hand on the hip of her pink leotard.

The girl wipes her eyes quickly. "Oh, yes. I'm fine." But she isn't fine. She wants to sink into the corner and never appear again.

Maisie sits on the floor in front of her and points to the girl's shoe. "There's a proper way to tie them, you know. I can show you, if you like."

The girl nods, pushing her foot out slightly. Maisie unties the ribbons, and crisscrosses them around the girl's leg. She always ties it like she's in a hurry, but Maisie is careful. Like tying ribbons is one more part of a dance.

"I know Madam Blythe can be strict, but she really knows a lot about ballet," Maisie says. Her green eyes are flecked with spots of amber. They remind the girl of a gemstone she saw in a museum once.

"I don't know if I'm meant for ballet," the girl admits, stiffening when Maisie winds the ribbons around her calf. "I'm not very good at it. Not like you."

Maisie sits back, tilting her head. "That's because you don't try. But I bet if you did, you could be great." When the girl makes a face, Maisie adds, "Madam Blythe only picks on the students she thinks has potential."

"You're only saying that to be nice."

"No," Maisie corrects. "I'm only nice to people I don't care about. If I like someone, I give them the truth instead."

If I like someone . . .

The girl's blush turns scarlet. Maisie stands and reaches out a hand.

"Come with me. I'll help you with your posture, and you'll be dancing a solo in no time at all," she says with a smile.

The girl follows her back to the dance hall, and all the while she thinks about how she can never give Maisie the truth, no matter how much she likes her.

Who in her family would ever understand? Where would she ever fit in with her mother's society friends?

The girl's truth is too big, and the world around her is too small.

But her heart is beating like a hummingbird's after Maisie touched her hand. Maybe this is what flying feels like.

If it is, she hopes she can stay in the clouds forever.

I hold up the glowing shoe, feeling the memory flood through my heart. Turning to Hazel, I hesitate, fist frozen between us.

"I'm sorry it took me so long to see you," I say.

Hazel doesn't respond. But when the shoe touches her palms and she cups the glowing memory to her chest, her face softens, and she no longer looks like the twelve-year-old from behind the screen door.

She looks like someone who's been waiting to go home for a very long time.

A tear slips over her cheek. "I remember, Eliot. I remember everything."

I force a smile, even as my heart cracks in two. But she doesn't disappear—not yet.

Hazel reaches for my hands and squeezes. Despite everything,

I can feel her. "I never got to live the life I wanted when I was alive. But you've got so much time ahead of you, to be whoever you want to be. So don't be afraid to tell the world who you are—and especially your parents. Because anyone who sees the real you will love you just as much as I do."

The monster straightens, sensing the final memory, and charges toward us.

Hazel closes my hands around the shoe. "You have to give this to my soul." She nods to the approaching darkness. "Make me remember."

I brace myself as the monster pounds across the mist, inching closer.

Hazel leans toward my ear, and I'm sure I feel the heat of her breath against my cheek. "Don't be afraid. It won't hurt you—because *I* would never hurt you."

The only thing I'm afraid of is saying goodbye, I want to whisper back.

But this was never about me. It's about setting the Honeyfield family free.

I gather up my strength, and face the darkness head-on. It rears up, ready to charge, when I hold up the glowing shoe. I take a step forward. And another. And another.

The monster lowers its head, hollow spaces in its eyes stretching into two empty voids. There's no sign of Hazel. Not yet.

"Here," I say to the monster. To my friend. "Everything is going to be okay."

The moment the monster touches the shoe, the creature rears its head, howling at the surrounding mist, until the black smoke whittles away, piece by piece.

When the darkness fades, Hazel is all that's left. Her skin glows with warmth. There's life in her eyes—richer than anything that exists in my world.

A whole soul, no longer lost, and no longer without any idea of who they are.

"My family—they're waiting for me." Hazel stares off into the nothingness.

I nod too many times, because it's all I can do to hide the fact that my very heart is splitting down the middle.

She tilts her head toward me. "Don't be sad, Eliot. Now I can take your message to your grandma. I'll make sure she remembers everything."

I choke on a breath. This is what I wanted. This is *all* I wanted.

But what I wanted, and what I want now . . .

"Can you, can you do me a favor?" I ask.

"Anything," Hazel says.

"If my grandma is in the Hollow somewhere, can you help her? But if not . . . If she's already moved on to the other side . . ." I look up, voice quaking. "Then don't try to make her remember what she can't. Babung deserves to rest in peace. And if she's already forgotten me, then all I really want now is for her to feel safe."

"You're going to stop looking for her?" Hazel asks, solemn.

I nod. "It's the right thing to do. For Babung."

After a while, Hazel lifts a hand. "Come with me. I need to show you one more memory, so you'll understand what you still have to do."

I thread my fingers through hers, and we walk through the mist. The tallest tree in the garden appears, glowing just like one of the memories.

It's the tree from the gardening book. The one surrounded by hydrangeas.

"I thought I could only find memories in the living world," I say.

"This memory is no longer lost," she replies. "It's *ours*."

With our hands still clasped, Hazel places my palm against the bark of the tree, and the nothingness morphs into color and texture. Around me, a memory appears.

Hazel watches her father place the box on the table. He's smiling in the corner of his mouth, the way he does when he's up to something.

Her mother flattens her skirt. "What is this all about, August?"

"It's a time capsule," he announces.

Hazel perks up immediately. Even Charlie and Peggy look curious.

Emma blinks. "Is it supposed to do something?"

August laughs, good and loud. "I promised you we'd have a family who was truly happy, and I think we need a reminder that we *are* happy. Even in this chaotic, ever-changing world." He pulls a dance card from his pocket. "We each pick something that means something to us. Something that reminds us of a memory that gives us the most joy. And we're going to put it in this chest, and bury it under the biggest, most beautiful tree outside."

"Yes, but—" Emma looks flustered. *"Why?"*

Hazel knows the answer. It's right there on the table. "So our memories will last forever. Even when we're gone."

Her father nods, and slips the dance card into the chest. "Remember—only the very best memories." He winks at Peggy. "Maybe I'll give you a hand, little one."

They meet again, hours later, and place all their items in the chest.

"Can I dig the hole?" Hazel asks, fighting a cough that's rattling deep in her chest. It's been there for a few days, but the doctor says it isn't serious.

She's only twelve. How serious can a cough really be at twelve?

"Of course, you can," August says, even though Emma makes a noise of protestation. "We can all dig the hole together. Because that's how families should be—they may have to work to be happy sometimes, but they always find their way back to one another. And the love . . . That's forever."

Emma sighs. "Fine. But *after* dinner. The Harolds are coming over, and we don't want to be covered in soil. They'll think we're farmers."

Hazel would've liked to be a farmer, but she wants to dig the hole even more.

Except after dinner, she feels dizzy. Too dizzy for digging.

Her fever comes the next day, and then the cough gets so bad, the doctor changes his mind about being worried.

And somehow during all the commotion, the box gets locked away in the attic, and forgotten with time and grief.

Our hands fall away from the tree, just as the memory fades.

"I need to bury the memories," I say, understanding. "That's your unfinished business."

Hazel nods. "Don't leave anything out. They're meant to stay together."

"I'll take care of it." I look over my shoulder at the only door still standing. "I just need to think of something to tell Mrs. Delvaux. I can't dig up her yard without permission."

Hazel's laugh is light. "Show her the poem, and tell her what needs to be done. She'll believe you."

"How do you know?" I ask.

"Because what she did to us wasn't on purpose." Hazel smiles. "You'll understand soon."

I turn back, and catch sight of the other ghosts standing beyond the tree.

August, Emma, Charles, and Margaret. They're all here. Waiting.

"I guess it's time for you to go?" My voice cracks.

I'm not ready. I don't think I'll ever be.

But death has a schedule to keep.

Hazel shakes her head. "It's time for *you* to go. We'll still be here, until you bury the box."

I blink away tears. "Will I see you again?"

Her eyes shine. "I hope so. But not for a long, long, long time." She pushes her forehead against mine and scrunches her nose. "Live a good life, okay? Be brave, and be free."

"I'll try," I say.

Her laugh is a breath. "Thank you for being my friend, and for always seeing the best in me."

The best is all there is to see, I want to tell her, but I'm crying too hard for words.

I pull away even though I don't want to, and wipe my tears with my sleeve. "Thank you," I finally manage to say. "For everything."

Goodbye, Eliot, she mouths, stepping back into the mist.

I walk toward the door, worried that if I look back, I'll fall to pieces. But when I pull the handle, I realize I can't go without seeing her one last time.

Except she's already vanished into the fog. Here one second, gone the next.

And I guess that's how it was always meant to be.

CHAPTER FORTY-ONE

I stand in the living room with the wooden chest in my hands. Mrs. Delvaux peels her eyes open and studies me.

"What's that?" she asks, frowning.

"It's a time capsule." I search for the right words. "It was supposed to be buried a long time ago. And the only way to help the Honeyfield family is to make sure it's buried now, in the garden by the big tree."

"The Honeyfield family?" she repeats. "What are you talking about?"

Hazel said I can trust her with our secret. So I do.

I take out the parchment from my bag and hand it to Mrs. Delvaux.

Her frown moves across her face, from her mouth, to her jaw, to her forehead. "Where did you find this?" Her voice is hollow.

"In the attic. Hazel showed me." It's sort of true, and sort of not true, but I don't know how to explain the rest.

The loss . . . It's still too raw.

"I haven't seen this in years. I was only a child when—"

Mrs. Delvaux looks up. "Did you find everything that was inside?"

I nod, open my bag, and remove the contents one by one, setting them inside the chest. The dance card. The chess piece. The ornament box. The thimble. And the ballet slipper.

Mrs. Delvaux looks over them in disbelief. "I just never thought . . ." She shakes her head. "But you're missing one."

I step toward her, reading the poem over her shoulder. "But I figured out all the riddles."

She points to the last two lines: *I am the keeper of all that was stolen, and the master of Honeyfield Hall.*

"But," I start, "isn't that you? The person who hid the treasure?"

"I did hide the treasure. But I'm not the answer to the riddle." Mrs. Delvaux smiles. "Follow me," she says, and leads me up to the study.

Surrounded by bookshelves, she shows me the desk in the center of the room.

I look around confused. "I don't understand—this is the answer to the riddle?"

"It was my father's study," she explains. "He was the master of this house, long before I was." Mrs. Delvaux looks around, breathing in the memory, and looks at me. "I found that box in the attic when we first moved into this house. My father was so busy at the time, and he seemed so worn out. I thought I'd make a treasure hunt for him." The sadness rushes out of her like a wave. Like something caught in a cycle.

"That's why you wrote the poem, and hid all those things."
It was a treasure hunt. A game. Not a curse, or something intentional—but something crafted out of love.

No wonder Hazel said I could trust her.

Mrs. Delvaux nods. "Yes. But my father never stopped being busy, and then he passed away quite suddenly, and I forgot all about the game I'd set up. It didn't seem important anymore."

"It *is* important," I say. "Those things . . . They mattered to someone. A whole family, who wanted them to be buried together."

"If that's the case, I'm sorry I misplaced them for so long," she replies, then nods to the small drawer just below the table. "I left this room just as my father left it. It's been a tomb all these years. Maybe this house has been that, too." She sighs. "The answer to the last riddle—it's in there."

I slide the drawer open, and find a single photograph.

I know Hazel's face right away. It doesn't matter if the photograph is in black-and-white—I can see her blue eyes as clearly as I can see all the other members of her family, staring up at me from the snapshot. August, Emma, Charles, and Margaret.

The Honeyfields, before the sadness and tragedy and grief.

Mrs. Delvaux steps around the table and looks over my shoulder. "Is that the family?" she asks, like it's the easiest question in the world.

All I can manage is a nod.

"They look happy." She doesn't pull her gaze away. "We better hurry up and bury their things, so they can stay that way, hmm?"

000

I dig a hole in the garden, right beneath the Honeyfields' favorite tree. With every item returned to the box—including the photograph, which probably hurts the most to let go of—I set it deep in the hole.

Mrs. Delvaux waits with me while I shovel soil back over the trunk. She doesn't say a word. Sometimes silence is the best thing you can offer someone.

When the earth is mostly flat, I set the shovel down and smooth out the top soil with my hand. *Now you'll never forget*, I mouth to the earth.

And if there's ever a time when they stop remembering, I'll just have to remember them twice as much.

I meet Mrs. Delvaux on the porch steps. She's still staring at the tree in the distance, with a different kind of mourning in her eyes.

For her dad, maybe. The way I still see Babung everywhere I look. Like we're still haunted by a ghost.

Except I'm not afraid of ghosts. They're a comfort. They mean that maybe someday, we'll get to see where the lost ones go.

I take the skeleton key from my bag and hand it to Mrs. Delvaux. "Here—I don't think I need this anymore."

She sniffs, turning the key in her hand. "I tried this key in every lock in the house. And do you know what?" She lowers her chin. "It didn't open a thing."

I frown. "But—that's impossible. I've used it, more than once. I found it in the greenhouse, and it was just sitting there on the ground, like . . ."

Like someone wanted me to find it.

Mrs. Delvaux hands the key to me. "I don't think it belongs to Honeyfield Hall. I think it belongs to you."

I take the key and squeeze it tight in my fist before slipping it into the safety of my bag.

"It's hard letting go," Mrs. Delvaux muses, gaze drifting over the garden, and everything we've planted together. "But I'm here. If you ever need a place to sit in the quiet, or bury a memory or two."

"Thanks," I say, shoving my hands into my pockets. "If it's okay with you, when school starts, I'd like to still help with the garden now and then. You don't have to keep paying me. It's just nice to watch things grow, I guess."

"You're welcome anytime." Mrs. Delvaux nods toward me. "I find I'm enjoying the company far more than the gardening anyway. And there's always cake, which goes well with homework." She holds up a finger. "That reminds me . . ."

She disappears into the house, and returns a little while later with an old library book. The cover is a collection of sepia faces, and the title reads *Influential Faces of the Northeast: Nineteenth Century Edition.*

"I've been holding on to this for far too long," Mrs. Delvaux says, showing the first hint of embarrassment I've seen on her face. "Hazel checked it out from the library for a report and left it here. When I saw what it was, I just couldn't bring myself to part with it."

I take it and spot a bookmark peeking out of the pages. When I open the book, I see a photo of August Honeyfield standing near what appears to be the launch of a new railway station, with a steam train perched in the background. There's a whole page on who he was, and what he did for the town of Rothbury, as it used to be called.

But it's the photo in the bottom corner that takes the breath right out of me.

It's one of the whole family, standing in front of Honeyfield Hall, surrounded by a spectacular display of flowers. Margaret is only a baby, and Charles not much older. But Hazel looks only slightly younger than I've known her. Where everyone else's expression is serious, Hazel is grinning widely.

The spark in her eyes . . . It's an act of rebellion. A hint of the life she might've led, if her story had been written differently.

"I kept it because it reminded me so much of the reason my father loved this house. It was the garden, but also the family." Mrs. Delvaux folds her hands together. "He always admired Uncle August and Aunt Emma. They'd traveled across the ocean to live a life that was full of love, surrounded by flowers that reminded them of home." She smiles at the thought. "Anyway, I thought perhaps you wouldn't mind returning the book for me. After you've had a chance to look at the photo, of course."

"I could make a copy of it for you," I say, shrugging. "They have scanners for that—you don't have to keep the whole library book."

She laughs. "Don't tattle on me, you hear? We buried a lot of secrets today. Maybe we can let that one go with the rest."

I nod, and tuck the book away. Now I have a photo of Hazel—and I'll treasure it always.

I get on my bike, wave goodbye to Mrs. Delvaux, and pedal down the driveway. Even though I know I'll be back, it still feels like the end of something.

Or maybe it's the start of something.

Babung isn't here, but I know wherever she is, Hazel will make sure she's safe. I trust my friend; just like she trusted me.

From now on, all that's left is to keep moving forward. There are some things I'll never have answers to, but I still have time to work out the rest of it, with the people I love who love me back. My parents are here. *I'm* still here. And that counts for a lot.

Hazel didn't get a lifetime to figure herself out. I don't think I'll ever stop thinking how unfair that is, that some people get a hundred years to be awful, and others get the tiniest blip. But I guess death is never fair—it just *is*.

I think I'm making my peace with that.

I cut through the old railway line back toward my house,

and when the trees flutter overhead, I look up, distracted. The sky is a piercing blue.

A blue I've seen before.

I smile, watching the clouds, and take a deep breath. For a moment, it feels like I'm flying.

I bring my eyes back to the path, but something hanging from the trees catches my eye, and I skid to a halt.

It can't be . . . ?

I leave my bike on the ground, and walk through the woodland area on the side of the road. There, hanging from one of the lower branches, is the rabbit Babung crocheted for me.

The one I threw in the Hollow. The same one that I saw tucked away in the fireplace.

I take the toy in my hand, staring at it like I can't believe it's really here.

And then I realize—it's a message. From Hazel.

I can't explain how I know what it means, but I do. Somewhere in the beyond, Hazel found my grandmother. She's not in the Hollow—she's *okay*.

But more than that, I know Hazel left the rabbit because she wants me to know that I don't have to worry anymore— that somewhere beyond the veil, my grandma remembers who I am.

My eyes fill with tears, pouring down my cheeks as I clutch the rabbit close to my heart. A noise bursts out of me, somewhere between a laugh and a sigh, and I shut my eyes tight.

She knows. Babung knows.

She remembers what we were to each other—and what we'll always be.

"I'd like my key back now," a voice says.

Graham is standing between the trees, hands folded neatly in his pockets.

"You—" I blink, and the image of the skeleton key flashes in my mind. "*Your* key?"

"Of course," he says simply, holding out a palm. "It's not like mortals are running around with spare keys to the Hollow. So, if you'll please . . ."

I return the gold key, and take a step back. "But—you said you weren't the one who left it for me. You told me—"

"I told you the truth." Graham tucks the key into his inner coat pocket, and eyes the overhead trees. "It went missing from my care—a mistake that won't happen again."

Wherever it came from, and whoever sent it . . . It doesn't matter. Not anymore.

I can't stop myself from smiling. "Babung is safe. So are the Honeyfields."

He lifts his chin. "Yes. I've heard."

I hold the rabbit in my fist. "Can you tell Hazel I got her message? Can you tell her I said thank you?"

Graham sighs. "I told you—it's against the rules."

"That's only sort-of stopped you before," I point out.

He doesn't react. He just looks at me like he's finalizing something in his head. "You should go home now," he says eventually, and takes a step back into the forest.

"But wait, what will—" I start, but Graham vanishes.

I stare at the trees. At the space where—

I look back down, where the crocheted rabbit is clutched tight in my fist.

An enormous crack tears through the trees, and I don't even manage to turn around before a massive tree collides against the earth. I'm sure the ground shakes. Or maybe it's just me, shaken to the core, with relief most of all.

I blink several times at the fallen tree farther up the railway line, right in the place I was headed. When I emerge from the woodland to get my bike, a few construction workers appear in orange vests, looking horrified. They shout over one another, and I can only hear a little bit of what they're saying.

"Oh my god, there's a kid out here!"

"What were you thinking?"

"Didn't you see the construction signs?"

"Do you have any idea how dangerous it is to be wandering through here?"

"You missed that tree by seconds!"

"You could've been *killed*!"

I mumble several variations of an apology, and after assuring them multiple times that I'm definitely okay, I jump on my bike and take the long way back home.

Even though there's adrenaline coursing through me, I erupt with joy.

I went to the other side of the veil to save my grandma. But maybe I saved a piece of myself in the process.

Nobody knows how long they have left. But right now, I'm *here*. On this side of the veil. With a family I don't want to miss out on getting to know.

I'm going to be brave enough to let them know me, too.

Because the life I have ahead of me?

I'm not going to waste a moment of it.

EPILOGUE

Graham watches the young girl ride her bike down the old railway line, hat tipped low and his hands at his sides. She looks happy. Happier than he'd seen her on the other occasions.

The leaves rustle nearby, and he turns part of his face toward the sound. "Yes, I hear you there, knocking at the veil."

The breeze sweeps through, and he pinches the brim of his hat to keep it in place.

He chuckles lightly. "I delivered your message, just as I promised I would. And she's fine—riding off toward her long and happy life."

The trees calm, and sunlight flickers above with gratitude.

Graham simply nods once. He'd never considered himself sentimental. But Muriel Katayama had gone through so much trouble to steal one of his keys and leave it for her granddaughter to find. And against all the odds, the girl had managed to do what he himself had never been allowed to— she'd helped guide the lost ones through the veil.

So when Muriel and the Honeyfield family stood together and asked this one favor—well, he just couldn't say no.

He'd always been on time before. He could be late just this once.

As if on cue, Graham pulls his pocket watch from his coat, inspecting the time of death for the next soul waiting to cross over.

The mortal girl was an interesting diversion in his day-to-day routine, but all that is done with now.

There's a schedule to keep.

And Graham the Reaper has somewhere else to be.

ACKNOWLEDGMENTS

Thank you to my brilliant editor, Trisha de Guzman, for bringing out the best in this story. I had such a wonderful time brainstorming together, and it was a joy to see this book go from a weird kernel of an idea to the finished story it is today. It's an honor to share this one with you!

Thank you to my superhero agent Penny Moore, for your unwavering support and belief in me and my stories, and for being there from the start. I wouldn't be here today writing the books that I'm writing if it weren't for you. Here's to book seven (!!) and counting.

Buckets of gratitude go to all the amazing people who worked on this book: Sarah Kaufman, Lindsey Whitt, Eleonore Fisher, Helen Seachrist, Allyson Floridia, Celeste Cass, Stacey Sakal, Aurora Parlegreco, and the rest of the Macmillan team. And a special thank-you to Feifei Ruan for the stunning cover art. It's everything I dreamed of and more!

Thank you to Carolina Beltran, Brianna Cedrone, Allison Warren, Shenel Ekici-Moling, and the rest of the WME and Aevitas Creative Management team who helped champion this story!

To all the booksellers, librarians, and teachers who've helped get my books into readers' hands: Thank you forever and ever. I am eternally grateful.

To every single reader who picked up this book and joined Eliot and Hazel on their adventure: I'm so thankful to share these words with you. I hope you enjoyed your time in Roseheart and the Hollow, and I look forward to the next time we meet within the pages of a story.

A very special thank-you to Emma, for letting me name one of the ghosts after you. (Trill is my favorite. Don't tell the others.)

Thank you to my friends and family who put up with my overthinking (and after all this time still ask, "How's the book going?" even when they know my response will always, always be way too long). Thank you in particular to Lyla Lee and Katie Zhao, who read this book early and gave two of the most beautiful blurbs I've ever read.

And finally, to my incredible kids, Shaine and Oliver. I think you sometimes wish I worked less and played Lego and *Animal Crossing* more, but I also think it's good to show you the reality of what following a dream looks like. Sometimes finding the balance in all of that is challenging, but one thing I *do* know is that being your mom is the best part of my existence. Thank you for your goofy jokes and seventy trillion cuddles. I love you both times infinity.

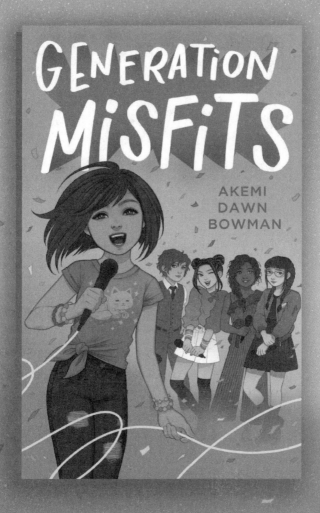